A Reverie of Brothers

By
R.D. SHANKS

I sometimes think about old tombs and weeds

That interwreathe among the bones of Kings

With cold and poisonous berry and black flower:

Or ruminate upon the skulls of steeds

Frailer than shells and on those luminous wings -

The shoulders blades of Princes of fled power.

Mervyn Peake, *A Reverie of Bone*

I compare fortune to one of those dangerous rivers that, when they become enraged, flood the plains, destroy trees and buildings, move earth from one place and deposit it in another. Everyone flees before it, everyone gives way to its thrust, without being able to halt it in any way.

Machiavelli, *The Prince*

Chapter One

Since its sudden birth the city had expanded, swallowing up acre upon acre of the surrounding grasslands and drawing thousands into its domain. Hardly built on the most advantageous ground, miles from the open waters, decades from the mines at the mountain summits, it yet remained the only settlement of note on the isle. This sprawling mass of a city, once a compact kingdom, was now the keystone of the Castilian Empire. The Empire was in itself a formidable territory that encompassed every scrap of hospitable earth within its shores, yet remained unheard of among much of the civilised world.

To walk within the city was to be lost in a maze of stone tenements, narrow closes and courtyards overlooked by houses of sparking white. To pass from one street to another was to be awestruck, for it was uncanny to find a world of wealth so near to a pit of poverty. To observe it from above was to see that it was not a maze, impulsive and nonsensical, but rather that it was arranged in a spiral of differing colour. In the centre stood the turrets and grounds of Delzean, the castle, and a string of other noble dwellings. Around this was a privileged circle of white. Then there came the smaller red and brown buildings. In between all of these were the squares, closes and courtyards. The slum district was discounted as a separate entity from the 'original'. There were two breaks in this spiral, the first a great spread of green, the Zodiac Gardens, and the second a river, if it could be permitted to claim that title. It skulked just a few metres above the ground at its lowest point, a slow trickle between the crumbling banks.

By night soldiers patrolled the streets, distrustful of those they were charged to protect. As the autumnal sun rose in the sky half a dozen soldiers could be spied chancing a premature return to the barracks. They wore their fatigues with a varying degree of diligence. Most had kept the pale blue and grey uniform spotless whilst others went about their duties barefoot, their cuffs torn, their shirts sun-bleached and blood-stained. Those trying to abandon their patrols early were met on the wrong side of the barracks' entrance by Lieutenant Vikernes and bid a hasty, if not especially disheartened, retreat. He gave a booming laugh and led his three fresh-faced followers along the cobbled road.

The strength of the morning light was such that even the white scar above Vikernes' eyebrow was illuminated with cruel precision. He was a bald, bulky figure with a strong face gone to seed. His own uniform was ill-fitted, but the overall appearance was redeemed by the badges he had earned during his years of service that were pinned onto his collar and polished daily. It was his task to present the three new recruits to the Emperor for his congratulations, and after that brief meeting he had a matter considerably less official to attend to with one of his highness' Advisors.

These four men made steady progress towards the heart of the city, passing children in pursuit of stray chickens, women in pursuit of stray children, hearing cries of hunger and protests as one queue for bread wound down the street and halfway back round again, and complaints as the weavers' workhouses shut their doors against those appealing for employment. Scores of people had begun to emerge from the limestone buildings. In the square housing the busiest market families were sitting to eat at tables too large to fit inside their apartments. To the four soldiers none of these events were out of the ordinary and they made their journey in silence, each preoccupied with private thoughts. They would arrive shortly for their audience with the Emperor. For the moment he was seated in a chamber on the first floor of his home, illustrious in reputation if not in size, where his ancestors had lived for seventy-five years since they claimed Horizon for their own.

Every day Eli would oversee the gathering of his five esteemed Advisors, namely Cyrus, Arden, Rous, Milias and Delarus, often with limited patience. An insight into his nature could be ascertained from a mere glance at his imposing stature and keen eyes – he was well suited to the role of leader. His increasing years had caused his legs to bow, his high forehead to crease, his temper to shorten, but his was still an intimidating presence. Only on one point could his judgement be called into question.

Rapping his knuckles on the table, Eli stopped the half-deaf Arden in mid-sentence and began to vent his frustration at having not being informed of the escape of two minor prisoners. In point of fact he had been petitioned by the Advisor seated opposite his son, Chiron, and had authorised the release himself. The pair were but petty criminals and had their uses outwith the prison, if not to him directly then certainly in the long run. Who could argue that spies were more use out among their degenerate brethren than rotting in a cell? At least that was how he would justify it later in a moment of reflection.

The Breakfast Hall was smaller than its name would suggest and plain by Delzean's standards of decadence. There was neither glass nor shutters covering the window, allowing a steady breeze to flow unmitigated, bringing with it the smell of the streets below, of smoke from kindling fires and dirt. The walls had not been panelled and the uncovered bricks were worn. Despite the attempts of the servants to scrub away seasons of grime from its surface the natural colour of the long table headed by Eli was indistinguishable among the stains. Fortunately for the servants the table was covered by a cloth. This immaculate length of material was itself hidden beneath a groaning weight of plates. The diet of the royals was almost as restricted as that of their subjects, the main difference being that theirs was served in abundant quantities.

The plates stacked with flatbreads and the dish of honeyed oil for soaking had been pushed aside in favour of the pastries, cakes and offcuts from the animals gutted for the evening meal, these ranging from pigs' ears to ox heart, and the kitchen speciality of smoked fish, which made an invariable appearance at every meal. Even the combined appetites of seven could not diminish the spread and now that their hunger was satisfied every face was turned towards the speaker. Every face, that is, besides those belonging to the pair at the far side of the table.

Sawney, known only by his fellow Advisors as Delarus (he was well-known throughout Horizon and such was his reputation that it rendered his surname redundant. By those two syllables alone he could be identified, a privilege enjoyed by no other public figure), was alone in the knowledge that Eli's anger was artificial and therefore thought it pointless to trouble himself to listen.

He was smirking at the vacant expression of the Prince Chiron, whose mouth had fallen open as he daydreamed. Sawney was the youngest Advisor, perhaps a year older than the middle-aged Eli. His russet curls, which hung in matted ringlets like a sheep's coat at the base of his sallow neck, were the envy of his colleagues. Advisor Milias had been proud of the patch of white, tufted hair upon his crown until the day of Sawney's appointment, after the previous Advisor Delarus' demise. He was thin but broad-shouldered and his barrel-shaped chest preceded him through doorways. As a youth his looks had been admired. An element of this predatory charm had been retained but he had never married. If he had the time he would still not possess the inclination. His scorning of a normal household, in the accepted sense of a wife and legitimate son, was viewed by his contemporaries as representative of his distaste for their values and for that reason alone the Advisors mistrusted him. They were removed from the rumours of the streets – had it been otherwise, they would soon have found other reasons to revile him.

Chiron was not fond of any of those he was required to join for the so-called Advisory Breakfasts save for his father, for whom he held a grudging respect, but he loathed the man opposite him with all the passion of his seventeen years.

The prince had his father's height; his bright eyes, coloured the sharpest blue; his prominent widow's peak; the same dark hair, only longer; and a similar level of intelligence. The differences between them pleased Eli less. Chiron was headstrong to the point of idiocy. He showed scant interest in affairs crucial to the survival of the Empire, preferring to waste his energy annoying servants and subjects alike. His faintheartedness was a further point of contention. His fear of blood had been revealed on a hunting trip when he shoot an arrow with such horrifically bad aim that it struck his cousin Leon's forearm, and had fallen in a dead faint at the sight of the wound.

For the past year it had been the wish of his father than he was instructed in the governance of the empire. This preparation involved attending the morning meetings to observe the business of the land until deemed mature enough to make a contribution to the proceedings, and then to be tutored by the ancient Silas in every matter related to his kingdom. Hours had been spent trying to decide which practice bored him more.

As his father at last curtailed his monologue and addressed Cyrus about the business of the court, Chiron sank lower in his chair, oblivious of the proximity of his hair to the bowl of water for hand-washing at the side of his empty plate. It had been placed there as an afterthought by the kitchen-porters as compensation for the absence of cutlery. His chin was inches from the table when Rous sneezed and woke him from his reverie. Across from the offending Advisor, Milias wiped a spray of phlegm from his robes.

"If there are no other matters I will call our meeting to an end," Eli informed his Advisors, his tone and manner brisk. "I will see all of you in court. In the meantime, Milias, I require that you seek the counsel of -"

Here the Advisory Breakfast met its first disturbance. Previous to the entrance of a titian-haired maid, none of the servants would even have dared to tread outside in the corridor while the meeting was underway. The maid had evidently not been informed of this habit. In truth, it might be suspected that another servant, wary of the new addition to the servants' dormitories, where the forty resident members of staff slept and squabbled nightly, had watched her progress towards the hall from the foot of the staircase and neglected to intervene.

Ignorant of the effect of her appearance on the hall's occupants the maid began to sweep imaginary dust from the floorboards. She continued to work unperturbed by the lull in conversation for a moment or two, then stiffened, and turned around to find she was being stared at by seven pairs of indignant eyes. She dropped her gaze swiftly to the floor. It was an offence to look royalty in the face.

This token gesture was not appreciated by Eli, who said in a low voice deadlier than a shout: "What cause have you for trespassing here? Leave us!"

"Yes, sire," said the maid to the floor. She fell in a stiff curtsy and sped towards the door before she was rebuked any further.

After Eli's abrupt dismissal the Advisors had taken a second to scowl, tut or snicker as their natures dictated, and then, acting as though there had been no break in the normal course of events, waited for Eli to resume their instruction. Chiron, however, wanted to hold on to the unexpected source of entertainment and forgot that he was forbidden to speak.

"Are you not the one that interrupted Silas yesterday?"

The maid had indeed strayed into the study. She had been perplexed by Silas' request that she would desist and return when they had finished. Chiron did not know that she had come only out of curiosity and thought her instead to be impudent, which amused him. The servants in general tended to be meek creatures but occasionally there would appear a footman with a mind of his own. None of them had ever lasted very long in Delzean. He imagined the rounded girl - her red hair untamed and unwashed, the exposed skin on her hands sunburnt, an emblem of a childhood spent teasing a living from the land – to be one of their kind.

His interest in the servant led only to another outburst from Eli and the cause of the disruption scarpered into the hallway beyond.

"You were told to keep quiet. Why should I permit you to stay if you cannot respect our duty? Answer me, then, if you are so keen to be heard." Eli's anger was mirrored across the table in the puckered faces of the Advisors.

The act of speaking out of turn itself was trivial but Eli refused to be undermined in front of his Advisors. In defence of the tempestuous Emperor, Chiron had been warned thrice before. He was conscious that his inattention at the Breakfasts concerned his father but still allowed himself to doze.

Chiron wondered if he was allowed to answer aloud and settled instead for a shrug of his wiry shoulders.

"Insisting that you remain and bear the scorn of the table would be a fiercer punishment but as it stands I will settle for your removal. If you are not remorseful, pretend to be. Wait outside."

Sawney winced as Chiron scraped his chair along the floor in towards the table with an expression that suggested he revelled in the effect of this action on the eardrums of those present. The Advisor resented how troublesome the first-in-line was proving to be. It was apparent that the boy (for his conduct belied his years) was beginning to present a problem. Not because he was concerned with decorum, no – but because he, Sawney, needed to be held in high esteem by the Emperor. While Eli's approval was not always vital, it was far easier than acting underhand. If some accident were to befall Eli and his son came to power it was clear that Sawney's foothold would be lost.

Eli sighed at his son's insolence. He waited until he was gone from sight and had begun to pace the width of the corridor to start his instruction from where it had first been interrupted. The Advisors followed his example and listened appreciatively.

The corridor reeked with the scent of flowers cut that morning to be placed fresh in the vases which filled every second alcove in the palace walls. Every other one held a candle. These were surplus to requirements as the window on the floor below, which looked directly onto the largest of the two courtyards, provided ample light to free the furthest corners from the shadows. Chiron spied a footman loping the stems of some red flowers at the other extreme of the corridor.

With his eyes shielded against the reflecting sun he heard the approach of Acario before he saw him. He let his arm fall away while his pallid features burst into a smile.

Eli's youngest son was a fifteen-year-old boy bearing an immense difference in temperament from the elder. His lacklustre hair was light brown and wound its way down past his bony shoulders to his waist. He was of a shorter stock than Chiron, but gave the impression of being stretched out due to his narrow frame, which the copious amounts of food he consumed could not alter. The mind encased in this scrawny body was a bright but childish one. He was no simpleton, but his shyness, hesitant nature and slow speech betrayed his potential.

The heavy blazer of imperial blue worn by Chiron had been presented to him on his sixteenth birthday. As Acario had yet to receive his, he was dressed in black school robes. He should have arrived for lessons an hour earlier but had overslept. This was an achievement considering that little in the city ever ran on time. Even the bells in the temples could be counted on to sound the hour with five minute intervals between them. Having ranked breakfast as a higher priority than education upon waking to a very vocal stomach he had gone to pilfer leftovers from the kitchens. After satisfying his hunger he had sauntered back up the servants' staircase in search of an attendant to escort him out of the palace. He was relieved to realise that he had avoided having to eat with the Princess Ava, the daughter of Adema, his uncle Caius' widow. With his overlong robes, half-running gait and hair swinging to and fro he bounded across to his brother and came to a halt.

"Are you hiding from Silas?" he asked.

There no trace of condescension in this question. Acario refused to judge his brother's behaviour; he feared that Chiron would judge him in return. It was his irrefutable belief that the conclusion reached would be less than favourable. The guilt that sullied his dreams was not the fruit of an overactive imagination but the result of tangible horror.

Of the effort behind his sibling's smile Chiron was witless. He shook his head and replied, "Not now. The Breakfast is yet to finish."

As eager as he was to berate Acario for his unpunctuality, he paused for the boy to absorb his meaning. Acario was alone in Delzean for pampering to his brother's vanity (which explained why quarrels between them were rare) and he wanted to share his version of the morning's events with one able to appreciate them properly.

True to form, Acario took the bait. "Then why are you not in there? Is it because of Sawney?"

He was itching to leave but Chiron's stories were always entertaining, if occasionally biased or irrational, and more often than not completely false.

"No, I was told to leave for breaking my silence. But I *did* go three months without saying a word to any of those old bores; they should be impressed."

Acario only succeeded in laughing in reply. He was cut short by the emergence of the Advisors from the Breakfast Hall and sprinted hastily downstairs before his father caught sight of him.

The Advisors trundled out into the hallway in a slow procession. Clothed in white robes which draped their withered bodies like additional folds of wrinkled skin, they resembled a choir of octogenarian angels. In title alone did they command authority.

Chiron straightened his posture and lowered his head at Arden, Cyrus, Milias and Rous as they passed. They recoiled from his gesture and made their departure as though he did not exist.

The shuffling of these four muffled the exchange between Sawney and his father. Until the last had reached the stairs he could hear only murmurs and by then Eli was in the doorway, his head close upon the height of the frame, facing backwards into the room.

"Bring your sons along, if they are free. I - "

He turned and started to find Chiron there. "Hmmph," he admonished before reverting his interest to the comparatively placid Advisor. "Yes, bring them. My son is acquainted with the families of all the nobles. Perhaps yours can be the first to exert an influence."

The last was said only as a matter of course. He had extended the hand of familiarity to Lorian and Mathias (it was a mark of respect that he even acknowledged them) in order to better understand the role they played in their father's dealings. The idea that he wanted Chiron to be influenced by their sort was laughable. The invitation was unlikely to be repeated. He dismissed Sawney with a wave, similar to the motion used to swat a fly, and waited until the recipient was out of earshot before addressing the prince.

"I presume you have not troubled to invent an excuse for yourself?"

A touch of amusement had strayed into his voice. It was hard to take Chiron seriously when he stood with his forehead pursed in a frown, as if he was the victim of some underhand scheme.

"Father, any excuse I could invent would never equal the truth!" But he had no plans to be forthcoming with the truth and asked instead, "*Where* is Sawney to bring them?"

He had met those in question once before - neither party had been concerned with making friends. Eli believed that as he was in ignorance of the arrangement between Delzean and Sawney's enterprise, it was due to the stubbornness of youth that Chiron's dislike for the Delarus name endured. For this reason he was quick to answer: they would be dining at the palace and he must act the courteous host, lest his mistake at the Breakfast be recalled and further dealt with.

"And remember that your anger is directed at myself, not your unfortunate tutor."

With that closing remark Eli nudged him aside and walked across the floor to descend into Delzean's lower reaches.

Chiron begged to disagree but held his tongue and resolved to do as he ought to and report to the study. Although this choice was commendable, he was far from reformed. He skirted around the corner to take the longest route to a room that was already the least accessible in the palace, as its only entrance was not to be found in the main stretch of corridor connecting the entire floor. It was reached by means of navigating an old servant's staircase by doorway of the Red Room. It was an awkward arrangement but it was of small importance. No one had ever suggested it be altered: what did one blemish matter when the remainder of the palace was infallible?

He turned to the right and slowed his pace as much as it was possible to without coming to a standstill. Most of the windows facing out towards the city were fitted with shutters, but those surveying the palace courtyards were empty, and at each of these Chiron paused to lean out as if he was devoted to the inspection of the quadrangle below. He assumed that every member of the family was occupied (although it was always a stretch to consider Ava to be occupied) but that failed to account for the complete stillness of the hallway.

When he glimpsed the vase in the nearest alcove he decided that he may as well *attempt* to coax the interrupting maid from her hiding place. Nothing was lost if someone else materialised in her place: the wreckage would be swept up in silence.

As soon as he was close enough he bent one bony elbow and with a swipe, knocked it to the ground. The sound on impact was terrific in that deathly hallway but it prompted no response, no flurry of movement. Chiron waited by the debris for a long while until his pride admitted defeat. He set off for the study and Silas a quarter of an hour after the conclusion of the Breakfast. Behind his departing form fragments of china and roses were left to swim in the spreading water.

Chapter Two

The school attended by the Princes was held in high regard among the peasants who could only dream of enrolling their offspring there. Although its reputation was founded upon the wealth and status of its pupils it was sustained by the strength of its education, which unwittingly deepened the divisions between the sons of noblemen and the brethren of common labourers. The bulk of the city was taught either in hedge-schools or left to learn through experience.

The schoolyard was protected on every side by lichen-scarred walls. The four classrooms were large and airy enough to ensure the scholars were unaffected by the lethargy oft caused by the sultry heat.

Acario's class, the eldest, sat in the loft under the watchful eye of Master Ricci. The young prince was instructed in the kingdom's trade connections, its history and politics (he was fortunate in knowing these stories from infancy, and was prepared for the interest of his fellows when they heard of his uncle Caius' downfall), and its founding myths. An awareness was growing amongst their number that the Empire had for too long been isolated from the wider world.

The school was a kind of haven for Acario. It was a safe retreat from Delzean, somewhere of his own. Within its confines he was beyond Ava's grasp. Yet it was unable to always provide such a shelter. He had been entreated to end the friendships he had nurtured and to abscond for periods approaching a fortnight at a time when Ava cried for company. If she thought he looked too happy or too free, the school would be robbed of his presence for a while.

After speaking with his brother in the hallway, Acario had been escorted to school for a duller day than usual. His classmates focused fully on the elocution lesson for once and were therefore much less interesting. During the hour's interlude in the afternoon he was accompanied to the refectory by his old, scorned friends but did no more than smile at them in response to their apparent forgiveness. A more embittered soul might have taken their advances to be fake, their forgiveness a ruse to safeguard their family's position. Of this possibility he was conscious, but he chose to favour an agreeable interpretation.

As the last note of the temple bells faded in the late afternoon, he filed out of the loft with his classmates and found a carriage waiting for him by the front gate. Upon his arrival at the palace he was met with a troupe of servants offering refreshments. From them he received his father's message that there was company for the evening. He had to accept a goblet of water before they were assured of his wellbeing. This he poured into a plant-pot as he hopped up the stairs towards his bedchamber.

Until hearing of Sawney's impending visit he had planned to track down his eldest cousin to remind him of the promise he had made to instruct the young prince in fencing. Bearing in mind Chiron's animosity towards the Advisor he conceded that his energy would be better spent warning and calming his brother. At the very least his appearance would prevent Chiron from fostering a temper. With this effort ahead of him he elected to retire to his room for an hour or so beforehand. For all that he revered his elder brother, even his patience had its limits.

The private areas of Delzean were cleaned the most diligently. 'Private' here meant those used primarily by their direct owners alone, rather than the chambers used for recreation and the Reception Room, where Eli held an audience with members of the public. Acario's belongings had been dusted to the verge of erosion and replaced in the exact positions from which they had been taken. Even the spare set of robes draped over the partition, a small, wooden furnishing, had been returned to its original place and looked just as inconspicuous. The stone basin protruding from the wall had been replenished with fresh water, the curtain had been drawn across the open window and there was a bowl of potpourri upon the bedside table.

His personal possessions consisted largely of gifts presented by doting citizens and except for a set of neat golden candlesticks these were hidden variously in the trunk at the foot of the four-poster bed, beneath the bed itself and in scattered crannies throughout the palace. As a result there was little of his personality imposed upon the room. But tucked away underneath the mattress was an object that had been entrusted with a burden of knowledge about the prince.

He retrieved his quill from beneath the counterpane and lifted the mattress to ease out this sacrosanct object and sprawled across the bed with it open in his hands.

It was a book of perhaps half a century old that contained pages and pages of handwritten poetry. The charactery was unlike any known in Horizon and the years had done their part in making the lines on the yellow leaves almost indistinguishable. Not much of a reader (but a fanatic by the empire's dismal standards, where three out of five citizens struggled to spell their own name), it was not the words themselves that had attracted him but the blank spaces around the margins of the worthless verses. These he took advantage of for an exercise as melancholic as it was cathartic. When he felt the need he would scrawl notes addressed to his mother, the deceased Empress. He understood the futility of this, and had long since realised that if anyone were to discover the practice they would think him disturbed, but it did succeed in lightening the weight of his guilt and for that it was worthwhile.

As he tried to organise his fast-paced thoughts there was a faint sound on the other side of the door. Acario was too absorbed in his task to notice and only after he had scribbled *"Mother -"* and paused to reach for the inkpot did he notice the now louder beating against the door.

Hoping it was Chiron come to seek him out for a game of checkers or to take their horses out into the garden, or for one of their more childish activities, such as sneaking into the kitchen pantry to create strange concoctions with the foodstuffs left to rot on the back shelves, he buried the book hurriedly and called for the visitor to enter.

He was answered by an attendant of Lady Adema's, who said as she curtsied, "Princess Ava requests your company, sire."

Nearly a week had gone by without Ava asking to meet in private. Nearly seven days without his arm being twisted while his confidence was trampled under her miniscule feet. He had expected this period of peace to end eventually and accepted this unwelcome development with only a sigh of complaint.

Ava preferred to send an attendant of her mother's rather than make the short journey in person. It was improper for her to have to state her purpose at someone else's door. The attendant thought Ava's command unusual but she had Adema's blessing to follow it through. The Lady was clueless of the twisted, temperamental relationship betwixt the two young royals and was pleased that her introverted daughter often wanted to see her cousin. They had much in common, she believed, for both had lost a parent at a young age and seemed to suffer a harder loss than their elder siblings.

When he was still a considerable distance from Ava's room he was hit with the stench of the overpowering incense she burned in censers and felt the same sense of suffocation that always blighted his approach.

In hierarchal terms, Ava was the most inferior of the royals, as a girl and not of direct relation to the Emperor, but the provisions for her comfort were nonetheless generous. She lived under the joint rule of her mother and governess. The latter was loathe to refuse any indulgence. She likened her ward to an infant, dependent and inherently sympathetic.

Due to this somewhat patronising perception Ava was permitted to take her lessons in her bedroom. When she had turned sixteen in the late summer she had claimed to be too grown for instruction and the governess duly complied. In place of studying the subjects Adema had hand-picked, which were a simplified equivalent of those on the curriculum at the boys' academy, she was supervised in sewing, asked to demonstrate the proper manners appropriate for hypothetical occurrences, and if there was time before the governess took her leave of the twice-weekly encounters they would discuss arrangements for Ava's future, of which they were few, as of yet. It was a touchy topic with the girl and one best suited to the occasional reference or passing remark. The bedroom in which these lessons were held was detested by Acario for a reason besides the obvious.

Brought up in the splendour of Delzean, disorder of the aesthetic type appalled him, and such was Ava's room.

If the incense fumes served a function it was that they masked and partially subdued the frantic range of colours, shapes and contours found between the four walls, three of which were covered with heavy tapestries large enough to carpet the average house. These curiosities dated back to the foundling years of the Castilian dynasty. They had been presented to their owner by her father. Caius had provided only a vague summary of the mythical battles and conquests they portrayed and she saw no value in them beyond the quality of their craftsmanship. She found deeper meanings in the decorations on the remaining wall.

Five paintings were hanging there, around the window. The majority showed the profile of a lone individual and were suitably compact. Two held the likenesses of entire families and were the height of Ava herself. Had the subjects of these paintings, the families of noblemen, been forewarned of the intense examination they would be exposed to it is likely that they would have refused to sit for their pictures. For Ava could squander an afternoon fixating upon an image, deliberating on one minute detail, speculating on the habits of those staring heartlessly back from the security of their gilded frames.

The window at the centre of this scrutiny was deserving of its own description. The original emerald curtains had begun to fade and to remedy this colour-deficit it had been supplemented with various slivers of violet, ruby red and sapphire cloth. The sunbeams piercing through this mesh of material shone on the floor in every hue of the rainbow.

The ceiling was spared any embellishment whatsoever but the floorboards were gifted with a rug of coarse fur, a tangled, ugly thing. An armchair had been custom designed for the princess' use but it was overshadowed by the dressing table. This was the length of the bed pressed against the wall opposite. The tallest of its three mirrors was the height of the bed's canopy.

These mirrors reflected back the features of the girl slouched on a stool before them. She was pale in the sickly way that was fashionable in the city, slender, and her hair, albeit lank, was long enough to sit on. It swaddled her like a light, blonde cloak. There was naught amiss in any singular component of her appearance, other than the skin being a touch too white, the lips bloodless. These minor, natural flaws did not explain why hers was but the deceptive beauty of the poisoned apple. It was not merely that she was shallow, a creature of simple malice: within her tiny skull a storm raged, hectic, vicious and vengeful. The depths of her character were murky and she herself, had she made the attempt, would struggle to rationalise her behaviour. In morals she was well-versed, for they had been imparted to her through fables as a young child, yet she could find no trace of villainy in her own actions. In her skewed world-view she was set apart.

Acario addressed Ava's reflection when he entered while she continued to comb her hair, fixating upon her progress in the mirror. "You sent for me?"

"*Yes*...Of *course* I did, otherwise I would be telling you to go away. You have to do an errand for me, dear Acario."

She bared her twisted teeth in what was meant as a compelling grin.

"...I shan't be able to stay for long, Father should have sent you a message but guests are coming to dine tonight. Sawney Delarus and..." He trailed off as he received an icy glare from the mirrored princess.

"He sent me a message, believe it or not, so you *shan't* be staying here for any length of time," said Ava with disdain. "In the room next to your father's there is a wardrobe with a green dress in it. That is what I want to wear this evening. Fetch it, please."

"That is my mother's dress."

He told her this calmly, as she sometimes needed reminding that there were certain artefacts in Delzean she could not claim ownership of. But he underestimated her obstinacy.

"She has no need for it now, does she?"

He was unable to respond although a refusal was fighting to be heard and a small part of him longed to smash her blank, uncaring face in that intrusive mirror. How she would have protested if he had refused to leave until she withdrew that awful request! To hand over his mother's garment, an article that had once clothed her when there was life in her limbs, to a creature that had schemed to benefit from her demise was unthinkable. And yet what alternative was there? Her involvement was damnable, of that he had no doubt, despite his initial gratitude for their pact, but his implication in Adrienne's final moments was worthy of a far fiercer brand of contempt.

Because of the events of an ill-fated journey, Acario was compelled to retreat from that noxious chamber of Ava's. His face burned with shame as he walked away, remembering the woman he had betrayed.

*

It had been five years since Acario had lived free of Ava's intervention. Then he had been a boy of ten, brimming with energy, eager, curious, and she a languid girl of eleven.

In the last month of a dying year Eli bid farewell to his wife, youngest son, sister-in-law, nephew and niece. He had arranged for them to honour a newly-acquired stretch of land that was sheltered on the far side of the Oslen Mountains, beyond the quarries. The terrain was changed enough for winter to alter the temperate climate there – it was the only place in the Empire where snow fell. He had convinced Adrienne that it was a purposeful undertaking, for they could make the day's trip to the coast to watch the arrival of the merchant ships from foreign shores. The advice of a medic had been sought (Sawney had introduced him to the ever-helpful Doctor Fernandez) to reassure her of the children's safety. It would in fact do them harm, he had said, to spend their youth enclosed in the metropolis.

These arrangements were made because of an unfortunate necessity. Adrienne's concern over Sawney's appointment was still insistent. Eli was planning to pardon a condemned traitor on Sawney's vow that he would prove useful and the resultant uproar would be aggravating enough without her admonishments. It was beyond the Emperor's power to foresee that the criminal would collapse in his prison cell within four hours of the Empress' departure.

Adrienne and the widowed Adema spent a month organising the excursion and their enthusiasm was contagious. It rampaged through the palace and ensnared Leon, Ava and Acario in its feverish grasp. Only Chiron was afraid of leaving the city. Eli took pity on him and equipped the prince with a legitimate excuse: his presence was required in the winter solstice celebration. To compensate for his brother's absence Acario was gifted with a flag boasting the Castilian coat of arms to plant as high as he could manage on the mountain slopes.

The royals and their attendants filled two carriages, circled by guards on horseback while an additional sixteen soldiers travelled in a further three carriages. They faced a thirteen-day journey along the uneven dirt road cut for merchants, for whom comfort was an afterthought. Thirteen trying nights were spent sleeping, or at least attempting to sleep, in the carriages after they had been moved out of sight of the road. The fear of attack by roaming bandits was a relentless worry to the women but for the children, even the fourteen-year old Leon, the excitement was too great to be affected by such earthly trials.

Settlements had been scattered pell-mell across the countryside but became sparser and increasingly remote as the spectre of Horizon dwindled. As the mountains loomed ever closer the villages of the labourers crept into view. It was an unsettling sensation to ride through an environment that was utterly alien in comparison to their home. The same language was spoken but with a disconcerting lilt; the cottages was carved of a wood sturdier than the stones of the city buildings, and as the humidity had lessened the air had grown thinner. A cutting breeze rattled the carriage windows as they skirted around the mountains towards the new territory.

The largest farmhouse that could be found had been prepared by the soldiers on permanent station there. It stood halfway up a steep hill attached to the forest that rose in slow degrees to the mountain peak.

As for their neighbours, they were fascinated by the visitors, if not as humbled as Eli would have liked. They flocked to stare when the fleet of royal horses slowed to a final standstill. These strangely-dressed mountain dwellers had possessed little of what could be called a culture for the invading army to stamp out and in return Horizon had scant culture to impose, but there lingered a sense that they had been wronged, that their ancestors had been betrayed. The old clan-chiefs had either been appeased or imprisoned and their influence was only recalled among the number of peasants that were reminiscent of the halcyon days of tribal rule. They neglected to pay homage to the guests when they paraded through the farmlands to visit the coast.

The duration of their residence had not been fixed. It went unspoken, but Adema and Adrienne both inspected their home with long-term needs in mind. For the still grieving Adema, the change of scenery was deeply appreciated as it opened her eyes to the world outside her private suffering. Adrienne, who knew her husband to be harbouring an ulterior motive, thought he was planning to appoint an ambassador to the territory to tighten his control of the farflung place. If the Empress herself were to assume the post and her family lived among the peasants on a permanent basis, it would strengthen Eli's message that the land and its residents were valued by the Empire, and soon thaw the conviction of the dissidents.

Without knowledge of their children's futures Adema and Adrienne could only recognise the immediate benefits of the relocation, which were numerous. They were able to move freely outwith the borders of their estate and after the first week it became evident that rather than simplifying their lives, the palace servants had created further complications. They had to be consulted, informed and considered when arranging *anything*. Had Eli decided to mirror their movements back in Delzean and take a walk each morning through the surrounding district, the preparations would have been extensive – the routine of the household would have been suitably altered, guards recruited, his attendants roused from their beds hours in advance to secure the route.

Acario adapted with ease to this change. Never before had he experienced such unparalleled freedom. The gaggle of plump women employed in their draughty kitchen always made a great show of occupation whenever his explorations led him to their domain and it was too easy for him, already tall and thin, his hair shorter but wild, to escape the house and play unattended in the forest. He soon learned that escape was needless, as his mother encouraged him to amuse himself however he wished. Happily for the prince Leon became his companion for a fortnight. Most of his evenings were spent practising the card games Leon had been taught by his father.

Only Ava sulked and balked at the notion of abandoning Delzean for good. She excluded herself from her brother's games in silent outrage that he considered her young enough to require a minder. It was a mark of her defensive nature that she refused to entertain the possibility that he could simply have wanted her company. Instead of laughing with the princes in the bedroom the two shared she choose to sit with her mother, bearing a stony countenance and glowering at her aunt, whose low birth (she was related to the Arden family through marriage) meant she had no right to monopolise Adema's attention. Ava resented that such a woman, a retiring creature like her son Acario, could wear the title of Empress.

She could remember, if she ever did cast her mind back, standing before the stained mirror fixed upon the dressing-room wall on the morning her fortunes changed.

Ava's reflection was beautiful in her biased eyes. It was deserving of recognition, reverence, respect – three things she was certain her life lacked. For these things she would do anything, for it was her dearest desire that she should be raised above her contemporaries. She closed her eyes and imagined herself as a queen standing proud on the balcony witnessing the battle between her loyal armies and the invaders seeking to corrupt her kingdom.

When a shout from downstairs brought her back to reality, where no self-respecting soldier would heed an order given in her tremoring lisp, she fled to the darkness of her room. She had a feeble comprehension of the world; her place in it was far from sure.

"Ava! *Ava!*" Leon yelled louder as he thundered upstairs.

She emerged into the hallway with due urgency but continue to scowl. The two attendants shouldering her brother were fussing over his shuddering breath as he said between gasps, "Adrienne and Acario have gone! They left to walk before breakfast...that was two hours ago...Ava, I want you to stay with mother. I'm to go talk to the guards..."

"*Where* have they gone?" Ava bleated but found herself in Adema's room before she could be answered. Leon entered a moment later, and his plan of assisting the guards was forgotten as Adema asked for news of the vanished Empress.

Ava resented that her mother was the focal point of attention. The princess had vowed to change the way the world perceived her but already her attempt had faltered as Leon stood with his back to her – she may as well have been invisible. Then she realised what she could do. She could be the one to find her aunt and runtish cousin; she would find them and bring them back and they would all gush with gratitude. Acario mattered less to her than the Empire's lowliest denizen. It was the judgement of the Empress she sought to alter.

With her brother distracted she was able to retreat downstairs and through the kitchen, her cape flapping behind her as she burst outside. The soldiers had formed a tight huddle further down the sloping grass and she slipped through the gate into the woods unnoticed.

It was a damp and clouded morning. Ava became disheartened after trampling through the mud and paused to bite her lip and reconsider her hasty departure. She stepped forward and snagged her cape on a branch; she was working it free when she discerned the flailing approach of Acario. He was heading straight for her and screaming all the while.

Ava found herself at a complete loss when he appeared. She had expected to stumble across the Empress and lead her back to familiar ground. This crazed boy did not feature in her plan but her confusion could not make him go away.

He sprinted closer still until his cries were almost deafening.

He had recognised the figure ahead and propelled himself towards her despite the trembling resistance of his petrified limbs; now he collapsed on all fours at her feet, a sodden wreck. Acario had let the tears streaking his face run freely when he had fled from his mother in a blind panic but with urgency at the forefront of his mind he reined his emotions in.

When he was hoisted upright by Ava he breathed deeply to steady his nerves. His voice wavered a touch as he croaked: "My mother has f-fallen. She needs help, she won't wake!"

That he had wasted time on offering an explanation seemed to disturb him yet further. He went to move past his cousin but found himself seized. Her nails stabbed at the bare flesh on his hands. There was a predatory glint in her otherwise unfocused eyes as she held him there.

"Take me to her. No-one else can help you; I'm the only one here."

The anticipation of Adrienne's grateful reception was too much for her to conceal. She could not help but sound exultant to be Acario's last resort. Her reasoning was too limited to consider how she could provide assistance to the injured Empress. To be the one to rescue Adrienne when her own son had fled like a coward (she truly believed he was wrong to have left her unprotected) would equate a tremendous advancement for her. That promise was all she thought of as she released her grip on Acario. "Do you remember where she is? Do you remember where you ran from?"

The implication that he was somehow at fault lurking in the latter question was unintentional. For the moment she was too preoccupied with selfish concerns to make the accusation explicit.

"Yes," he said, flustered, "But we need – where are the guards and –"

"We have to hurry, Acario, she is out there alone! *Take me to her!!*"

Acario stepped back, and noticed as he looked at Ava without fear rendering his senses useless that she was beaming, as if his plight brought her pleasure. For the first time he realised that he hated her. He turned and forced his legs into a sprint.

Even in his drained, depleted state he could outrun Ava. She lagged behind until he began to think of the accident that had befallen his mother. Then he gave in to the turmoil turning his insides to ice and slowed to walk in synchronism with the princess. His every step was echoed by a shuddering sob as they plundered deeper into the dense forest.

They stumbled from the beaten track to struggle through a thicket, where the grass was rife with roots and bushes bearing berries long dead, where nettles scratched at their ankles and clambered to pierce the skin, in the hope that it would shorten their passage. Moving together in silence, the intensity of the situation was evident only in Acario's persistent sobbing.

Acario was remembering how his mother had taken him to search for a place to plant the flag from his father. They had walked along talking of home. When they were quiet it was a companionable silence, with no trace of the tension like that between him and Ava. They had been away for perhaps an hour and Adrienne was starting to tire. He scoured the terrain fiercely when her steps became laboured: he wanted both to make his mark on the slope and please his mother. He spotted a clearing up ahead and streaked over the steep ground with the flag held aloft, ignorant of his mother's request that he take care of his footing. Their route had been treacherous.

When his mother cried out again Acario was stomping down the dirt around the flag's base to ensure that it was logged securely. She had been making uneasy progress over a knoll to catch up with him. She screamed as she lost her footing, and Acario turned to witness her falling forward. There was an indent below and he could not tell how far she had fallen to earth until he had gone, with no recollection of commanding his body to move, to the edge of the decline. There was a descent of twenty feet to where his mother lay on the rocks at the pit's floor.

He felt only a surge of adrenaline as he climbed down towards her, clinging on to clumps of grass to keep from slipping. He was too afraid to brush her hair away from her face and instead took hold of her wrist to feel for a pulse. Beneath his fingers there was a definite throbbing but shaking her by the shoulder merited no response.

"I'll have to leave you to get help – I'll be fast, I swear!" he whispered as he stood. (He pretended that he could not see the blood in her hair.)

But had he been quick enough? He wondered if Ava was even strong enough to bear half of Adrienne's weight when they carried her back. Why had he not insisted that they find the guards, who were trained specially to be of use in unforeseen emergencies?

"You *have* forgotten where she is, haven't you! She cannot have taken you this way; no-one would choose to walk through here," sniffed Ava, "I think you were foolish to have left without knowing how to get back."

She was losing her patience with the snivelling boy. Tearing a haphazard path through the undergrowth had doused her enthusiasm for the plan she had made on an unsettled impulse. Her annoyance mattered nothing to Acario and he shrugged in response: "I know where she is."

He thought he glimpsed the blue flag fluttering in the distant and his tears at last ceased as he scrambled up the mountain slopes faster than he had ever moved before. That he nearly lost his balance when he tripped over a fallen branch was of no concern to him. Neither did he pause when he felt the stirrings of sickness in his belly.

He heard Ava calling for him to wait followed by her screech of frustration when she saw that her dress had torn but he ignored her protestations: he had found the place where Adrienne lay. Beyond it the flag stood proud in the glade.

A long while had transgressed by the time Ava caught up, aching and disgruntled. Feeble as her mind had proved itself to be she was astute enough to walk around the precipitous peak she had watched

Acario descend. From its unseen depths she could hear Acario's careful footfalls on the rocks.

It was to reach the flag that she skirted through the trees. She stroked that emblem of the faraway city she remained attached to despite the apathy it held for her, and wondered whether Acario had planted it against his mother's wishes and the Empress had then been injured in pursuit of the disobedient prince. It would help her case greatly if she played the dutiful child to Acario's careless one.

"Ava...." called Acario once, and then louder: "Ava! She won't wake! Please, help me take her back! I can't move her! She can't wake!"

He had never sounded younger than when he cried: "Please, mother, please!"

His cousin strolled over to him, revealing no sense of unrest at his torment. She glanced down to see a still figure on the ground below and another, smaller one crouching nearby, clawing at his hair. "Did she fall because you had to plant your flag, Acario? Does she have a pulse?"

"No, no – no pulse..."

"But how did she fall?" Ava bared her crooked teeth in triumph and yelled: "*Acario!* Did she fall because of you?"

"I – help me, please, together we can lift her!"

"Do you understand that this is your fault? It's because of you that she is lying there, do you understand?"

"I didn't mean for her to – it wasn't my fault, Ava, please!"

"She is dead because of you. Your mother! *If you want me to help stop crying!* Listen, if your father were to learn of this he would be so angry...Do you want that to happen? For him to punish you?"

Save for the demise of her father, Ava had endured little exposure to death. It was impossible for her to accept the fact of Adrienne's death; she could not understand it to be as real, somehow, as the forest around them. It was almost too gruesome to be believed in. So prevalent was the selfish taint in her nature that she did truly not much care to question the cruelty of fate in bringing the Empress to such an ignoble end. The grief of her cousin, however, interested her. Regardless of the extent to which his guilt would be beneficial, to witness his suffering would give her a twinge of sadistic pleasure.

"No, why would he punish me if I explained to him - "

"Explain that she was killed because of you?" she finished.

Acario could not bear to listen any longer. To stifle the pounding terror in his head he scrambled back up to the surface, willing himself to focus on his progress, not to look back. It seemed he was destined forever to live in the shadow of his mother's broken body. He finished the journey on his stomach, streaking his clothes with dirt as he slithered forward through the grass.

It was unbearable for him to remain in Ava's presence. He retched as he half-ran, half-crawled as swiftly as he could under the consuming weight of his grief out of sight of the gloating princess. The words of his cousin echoed and rebounded within his skull, each one burning like a scar, as he sank to his knees and was violently sick. Every wheezing breath sounded to him to be a confirmation of his guilt: *"Murderer! Murderer!"*

They returned to their frantic relatives together and in unison they lied. The cover story Ava had dreamt up for her fretful cousin was a simple one: the princess had assumed the duty of searching for the missing duo and after a stretch had been successful. Adrienne had walked ahead, eager to return to her waiting relatives, and both of the young royals had borne witness to her accidental death. When they rushed down to her they found no sign of life. They had pounded across the forbidding terrain to seek assistance for the Empress.

Upon hearing of the tragedy Adema became shaken and Acario was free to withdraw to his quarters. No one doubted their story to be true. With this fabrication Ava had Acario convinced of the allegiance owed to her for inventing the alibi that had saved him from ruin. The tale spun by the princess was hardly devastating in its falsity but harsh and plentiful were its repercussions.

Her requests began as small favours, innocent tasks such as ordering Acario to spend a scorching afternoon cooped up indoors reading to her, but had evolved steadily into little less than torture. He was entirely in her power. If she demanded that something be stolen he would seize it on her behalf. When she lisped, "You should make a blood oath never to betray me!" he had gone himself to fetch the knife to slit open his palm. To disobey was to risk everything he knew. He had no choice but to do as Ava commanded.

Chapter Three

The Advisor Sawney, whose fate it was to shoulder the loathing of the Emperor-in-training, had founded a rumour-shrouded organisation known as the Eyes – rhyming slang for spies. This group had been begotten on the premise that it would gather information for the nobles on the illicit activities of the lower orders. It continued to thrive only because Sawney had brokered a deal with Eli. In return for informing against criminals acting alone, Sawney's minions could commit crimes to order.

For the past fortnight the Advisor had met with his inner circle, the masters of those that comprised the city's underbelly, to concoct plans for an ambitious project. It was their intention to stage twelve simultaneous robberies in the mountain settlements. The victims of these robberies were the twelve men that had been appointed by Eli to receive elaborate salaries in return for overseeing the harvest of coal, gold and diamonds, the Empire's mineral riches, from deep trenches underground. With the protection of the Emperor, Sawney could have a portion of their fortunes transferred to Horizon to be shared among his co-conspirators. Every man involved, from the inner circle down to the couriers reporting on the burglars' progress, would be well rewarded for their efforts. It was a good policy, for the result was that a whole class of men were eager to offer their services to the Eyes, or at least would have been, had they been able to discover the identity of the ringleader. Sawney was an obvious candidate but it was unthinkable for a peasant to voice such an accusation against a palace official, notwithstanding the scale of the suspicion tainting his name. The very idea of him being tried as a common criminal was absurd. The security of an elevated position provided a stable platform for his ventures.

In an exchange conducted in whispers in the airless courthouse he had gained Eli's approval for this latest endeavour. Within moments of his leaving the court the news had filtered through the alleys, taverns and hovels frequented by the Eyes. By the time he was halfway home the burglars were already preparing to depart.

Vikernes had recruited a small band of aspiring soldiers to travel alongside the hired brutes and ensure theirs was a swift passage, unhindered by the interruptions that would surely affect them otherwise, and to protect against the unlikely possibility that they would desert their duty. Had they dared to return after disobeying Sawney, their throats would have been slit from ear to ear before they had passed the slums. To be killed in that manner was infinitely preferable to being tortured, tried and thrown in prison, the punishment that last deserters had been subjected to. They languished there still, forgotten, forsaken. The prison cells were littered, the gallows haunted, and the paupers' graves filled, by men such as these.

The change from the restive quiet of Delzean's surrounding quarter to the main body of the city was sudden, and would unnerve a less stoic nature than the Advisor's. In the late afternoon the noise of the commons was tremendous as they bustled homeward on foot or horseback. Their shouts mingled with the cries of the flagging market-folk.

Rickshaw drivers skidded to a halt on the red roads when Sawney strode by; giggling children refrained from their jostling races to let him pass. Several conscientious men bowed but were ignored by the angular-featured official. Another group chose instead to question him about the court proceedings. They were told to wait for a messenger to be deployed to the hustings and meanwhile remove themselves from his path at once, but the reproach had no malice to it. The antics of the largely-impoverished denizens amused him. They were so complacent about their lot in life.

The Delarus family called home a minute street nicknamed 'The End'. It consisted of six houses, three on each side of the dirt road. Strangers rarely trespassed upon it as it led only to a low wall that separated the residences from the yard behind the slaughterhouse. This was precisely why Sawney had opted to live in what his colleagues considered squalor in comparison to the estate that should rightly have been his. Modesty was the defining means of defence in his armoury. It was his steadfast belief that to display wealth was to make oneself vulnerable; it was the only view for which he could be termed irrational. For that reason he bought a property hidden in plain sight.

The road he was now pacing had been ground flat by generations of feet. His was the second house on the left and had an unkempt appearance familiar to its neighbours. Chimney smoke had greyed the white stonework. The wood of the shutters, which were closed against the persistent sun, was infested and crawling with insects. The two that also resided in this bleak-facaded building had returned home only an hour before their father set out for the Advisory Breakfast that morning and he deduced from the lack of noise or signs of movement behind the shuttered windows that they had yet to wake. He withdrew a key from the cord around his wrist, proceeding to unlock the stiff door and force it open with a shove.

He entered the room covering the entirety of the ground floor, save for the cupboard-sized privy under the stairs. It was designed to be the centre of domesticity, just spacious enough to accommodate cooking, eating and socialising before the fireplace in the back wall. Nevertheless, it was neglected by its owners and had a dank odour of decay about it, which no doubt emitted from the pot on the table containing what had once been a stew. Its contents had been left to rot after the disappearance of the last maid in their employment.

There was one stool pushed up against the cabinet, but nothing else to suggest that the room had ever been inhabited. A candle on the banister guided Sawney through the darkness to the stairs. As he thundered upwards he learned that his assumption of a moment earlier had been incorrect – he heard footsteps on the floor above.

This sound was made by Lorian as he crossed the room to rifle through a chest of drawers in pursuit of the comb he used every day, in conjunction with handfuls of grease, to slick back his own russet curls.

His features, stature and even his posture bore a likeness to his father. Curiously for someone of his age (he was two and twenty years), he was developing a paunch. A tumourous tier of lard protruded from his abdomen. As his vanity far outstripped his willpower, his solution to this rather inconvenient problem was to adorn a tight, constrictive vest beneath his clothing. This garment, removed but twice a season at the public baths, was stinking, yellow and corrosive with stains. To his placated mind the onset of this bulge was a thing to laugh about and he wore the vest uncovered in the company of his surrogate brother without the slightest tremble of shame.

Mathias was reclining in an armchair, resting his feet, the soles of which were cracked and discoloured, upon a coffee table procured by Sawney's father during a raid on the estates of treacherous gentry.

The modesty Sawney favoured was less evident in the sitting room, where the spoils of his criminality were stored. If the candles had been aided by natural light the finer details of the numerous furnishings could have been divined. This room slept Lorian and Mathias; the mess of blankets they had mustered somewhat dispelled the formality of the place.

The Advisor was greeted first by Mathias. He acknowledged the arrival of his benefactor by bobbing his drowsy head.

He had called Sawney 'father' for twelve years, since he had been adopted and raised as a companion for Lorian, who was two years his senior. Before his adoption he had belonged to the swarm of orphans, invalids, drunkards and other unwanted peoples that plagued Horizon. It was his misfortune, or his greatest stroke of luck, depending on the leaning of an observer, to have been foiled in an attempt to pick the pockets of Vikernes. The Lieutenant had brought the boy to Sawney to be punished; he revelled in disposing creatures none would miss. Instead Sawney had treated the opportunistic, flea-ridden little thief to a life of comfort and luxury.

He and Lorian had attended the academy favoured by the royal household. They had both been withdrawn after Lorian's thirteenth birthday to embark upon an existence nothing like that of the other noble sons. They belonged not to *their* world of pageantry and polite society; neither did they struggle alongside those they drank with nightly in the dim taverns. Sawney had liberated them from the orthodox trials of adulthood. They laboured only in service of the Eyes.

Lorian regarded their lifestyle an entitlement, but Mathias was troubled by a certain degree of indebtedness that caused him, after all the years he had spent cocooned in the Delarus home, to feel uneasy around the Advisor, as though he feared he would be recognised as a fraud. The movements he made in his tailored clothes were awkward. With such a distinct lack of grace he resembled an inexperienced actor playing the part of a lord. His childhood tribulations had left his face pinched, his thinning hair lank, and complexion pockmarked, but an adolescence of contented indulgence had plumped his cheeks and brightened his countenance. His smile surfaced as easily as Sawney's sarcasm. There was a sort of earthy appeal to him, contested by the hideous circles around his eyes.

"Hullo," bellowed Lorian from the corner, as his father paused at the foot of the spiral staircase leading to his private room, "Are we needed to take a message to Vikernes?"

This hypothetical message referred of course to the burglary, the progress of which was enthralling to Lorian. He would have only protested a little at delivering news to the Lieutenant, for he idolised Vikernes, preferring his exuberance to Sawney's sardonic exterior.

Sawney's only child, and therefore the rightful inheritor of his seat as Advisor to the Emperor, had never contemplated life without his father's support to the same extent as Mathias, but he was vaguely aware, in an uninterested sort of way, that he himself had experienced humble beginnings. His mother had been a wench, unfortunate enough to become infatuated with his father, who had made no secret of his ill treatment of her. Her swollen belly was shameful to her family and the only solution was to abandon her. As Sawney did not want the responsibility of a mewling infant, he permitted his offspring to undergo five years of deprivation before forcibly removing him from his mother's arms to rear properly. It was perhaps for the best, in a way, as the consumption killed her a few months afterwards.

"Word will have reached him by now. You have more present concerns, I'm afraid: we three are dining at the palace."

"Another chance to upset Princess Ava!" laughed Lorian to Mathias, who searched for an object to throw full-pelt at his gloating sibling before deciding it involved too much effort. Instead he sank lower into his chair and yawned.

"Curtail your teasing until you have gotten yourself ready; we leave in an hour." Sawney began to snake his way up the stairs, treading carefully on the weak boards.

When Lorian's laughter subsided he lapsed back into silence, save for emptying the drawers' contents onto the floor. Mathias had rested his head on the arm of the chair and had begun to doze when he chuckled: "Do you think the harpy would die of shock if you tried to kiss her?"

"Or..." said Mathias in a half-hearted mumble, "...or perhaps I'll get marry her and appoint *you* court jester. That wit of yours is wasted on me."

Lorian, not listening, replied, "I expect your chances would be better with her mother, the strumpet. Jonas told me that-"

A stomp on the ceiling interrupted him. Unsure whether Sawney had made the noise purposefully, to warn them into action, or not, he stood stock-still, comb in hand, then sighed and replaced the drawer with affected haste as footfalls began to sound on the stairs. Sawney was halfway down when he threw a bundle of clothes, among them the fitted bolero that Mathias believed to have been lost for six months, into the room.

"If you cannot behave impeccably – which you assuredly will not – you must at least comport yourselves as our company expects. It would be an awful inconvenience for me to have to excuse the pair of you."

Sawney smirked as he scolded them, remembering the occasion when Lorian had dined with the grandson of the Advisor Rous. The other boy had disappeared for days afterwards, too ashamed to face his family after succumbing to Lorian's pressure. They had stolen several irreplaceable heirlooms from his home to sell on the black market and frittered away the earnings in a brothel, whereupon Lorian had left the boy to contend with the wrath of his relatives.

"You won't have to excuse me. I look forward to reintroducing Mathias to them. They were so impressed by the state of him last time!"

Lorian had begun to root through the clothes scattered across the place and threw all but his chosen garments over the oblivious Mathias.

His last remark was ignored by Sawney. He drawled, "I want *both* of you ready," and gave Mathias, who continued to lie limp like a corpse in the armchair, a pointed stare and vanished back upstairs.

Their chattering grew quieter as Mathias dressed, adorning his evening clothes with as much enthusiasm as an arthritic centenarian. Lorian wetted a cloth to wipe his face, a token to demonstrate that his father's wish that he should be presentable had been heeded.

Sawney had questioned the ease with which he had scorned the idea of raising his sons in accordance with the norms of their status when he realised that the repercussions, if they were introduced to a member of the Castile family and caused offence, could be severe.

He had managed to avoid their meeting for a remarkable length of time after confiding in Eli that he had chosen for them to be socialised amongst the peasantry. It was beneficial for them to have knowledge of those likely to be involved with the Eyes.

The Emperor was conscious of their absence at court functions but preferred not to press the matter. They were less than welcome in the upper strata of society. Sawney himself was hardly popular, and he had been brought up to understand the manners of Horizon's elite.

His concern proved itself in due course to be misplaced, when the inevitable collision occurred. His sons were invited to accompany him to the ball in celebration of a nobleman's engagement. The Emperor only attended briefly, for it was the anniversary of his wife's death, and his family followed his example, but there remained ample time for introductions and Sawney had never been one to shrink from duty. His vagabond sons had been called forth to exchange pleasantries under Eli's penetrative glare. To the amazement of the spectators it was not them that acted out of course, but one of the royals. Ava refused to extend her arm for Mathias to kiss her hand. Instead she had stared, her disgust overpowering the desire to subvert the attention of the gathered party.

She had heard tales of Sawney's bastard sons (she was unaware that Mathias had been coaxed off the streets like a stray, and thought the men to be brothers), and viewed them both with disgust. Her sense of propriety had left her completely when Mathias was introduced. His deficient appearance suggested that he was unfit to frequent the same ball as her. It was spoiled because of him.

Mathias had suffered Lorian's ensuing taunts, returning the favour whenever he had suitable ammunition, the way they had always done to each other. There had been little point in protesting. The embarrassment had only smarted for a day or so afterwards and was of no consequence to him now.

But here, regardless, was an opportunity to make amends. He would get the better of both of them. Charming the sullen Princess would be enough to soothe his wounded pride, and it would anger Lorian into the bargain, which was always amusing. He finished dressing with renewed interest, and sat back to watch Lorian demolish the living room in search of his shoes.

Chapter Four

Silas, the palace tutor, had learned to anticipate the fluctuating moods of his ward. He supposed, when Chiron arrived late, that he had lapsed into a sullen fit.

The prince was usually able to sit upright at his desk and, if he possessed no interest in Silas' instruction, would either feign concentration while snatching sidelong glances around the study to find a keener source of amusement or try to distract his tutor, who was as elderly as the Advisors and twice as stubborn. The battles that ensued between the prince and his tutor were ridiculous, but those involved failed to realise the comedy in their didactic exchanges. For his part, Chiron had an uncanny ability to make light of most situations yet never appreciate a joke at his own expense.

His thoughts as he sat in the humid study, Silas pacing to and fro across the floor as he lectured, were centred on Sawney. When that old subject grew tiresome he thought instead about the men that had escaped from the city prison, and wondered how they had managed it.

He brightened when he was excused for the third of his fencing lessons with Leon. That Silas followed him to the gardens to supervise only slightly lessened his enthusiasm. Leon was a master swordsman but their fight was not as intense as usual with the presence of a fussing audience. It drew to a close when Leon elected to return to the barracks, and Chiron was instructed to accompany Silas back to the study to gather his notes.

In a low grumble he was admonished for his behaviour before the tutor bid him adieu until the following morning. Chiron was too restless to wander in the gardens by himself, but with Ava discounted, his father engaged in the courthouse and Acario occupied with school, he had only his aunt for company. He was unsure whether to approach her, unsure whether he would derive any pleasure from an hour spent drinking tea in the sitting room, sidling around any provocative subjects, replying to her dull questions about his lessons with a polite smile. He had forgotten that when they had last spoken together Adema had made him laugh until his eyes watered. He had yet to alter the opinion formed in boyhood that age was equal to lifelessness.

When he was clambering up the stairs he paused to peer backwards over his shoulder to double check that neither of the servants bickering in the hall were the one he sought to see. As he squinted he remembered of a sudden that Adema was entertaining a select group elsewhere in the palace. This included her suitor of two years, a man named Javier Rana. Chiron's distrust of Sawney was at least rational, but his suspicion of Javier had little basis in fact. It was because of this foreboding that he resolved to stave off his hunger until dinner, and prepare himself to face four of his enemies at once in the quiet of his bedchambers.

As a boy he had clamoured for a room nearer his brother's but he had come to value his eyrie upon Delzean's topmost floor. The anteroom was a cavern of red and gold. The walls and ceiling were buried beneath thick drapes that had the double effect of multiplying its dimensions whilst creating a claustrophobic air.

The bedroom proper was etiolated in comparison but was brightened by its three windows. The one positioned in the centre was sizeable, and offered a panoramic view of Horizon. Those on either side were stained glass depictions of the House of Castile's coat of arms. A scroll across the centre of the shields read: *'Maior sum quam cui posit fortuna nocere.'*

It was to the central window that Chiron raced. He threw himself down on the seat and pressed his face right up against the glass to obtain the best sight possible of the districts below. He could see figures the size of match-heads scurrying about on the uneven roads. The city was humming: it seemed that hundreds still had business to attend to during the sweltering lull of the afternoon. The unseasonal rain escaped his notice until it began to patter with a violent force against the panes.

There was an illusion of order around him. In actuality an array of assorted objects had been stowed away under his bed and hidden in the cupboard. He was afraid to open it in case the tower of school books and parchment stuffed therein collapsed and spilled out.

Silas' lecture had centred on military tactics. An annotated drawing of the conquest of the mountain settlements had been jotted for his charge to study but it had fallen from Chiron's hand when he had broached his room and had yet to be rescued.

With no profitable activity to immerse himself in, Chiron moved from the window to craft an assailant out of pillows and, using a scabbard in lieu of a rapier, turned to strike it. The purpose of this was to improve his footwork but it appeared more like a game to him and soon he felt foolish and stopped.

He thought again of Sawney and risking an avalanche he eased the cupboard ajar and, taking care not to open it any further, he stuck his arm in to rifle blindly for the record book the Advisor had unwittingly forgotten after a session in the courthouse. Eli had brought it to Delzean for safekeeping, to be returned during the Breakfast, and he had not been tempted to even glance at its contents for he himself oftentimes scribbled notes when he wanted to bear a point in mind for meetings with his Advisors. To him it was a harmless object, but to his son it represented the hope of proving

Sawney to be an evil influence and having him expelled from the Empire. In the face of such suspicion he couldn't help but steal it.

After a moment of scrambling through layers of parchment he felt the spine of a book. He withdrew it to find that it was the one his tutor had had bound specially for him. It had been handwritten by a philosopher who had been, Silas assured, renowned in his lifetime. His work was now reduced to a damp, displeasing volume and Chiron threw it aside. He replaced his arm to rummage more thoroughly.

Four more of his schoolbooks and a text of moral instruction were unearthed and stacked up in the alcove beside the model ships his uncle Caius had collected, now coated in dust an inch thick. At last he held Sawney's property in a sweating palm. He smiled at the prospect of it being responsible for the Advisor's downfall.

Sawney had noted the date, charge and verdict of every case he had attended, enough to suggest that there were numerous record books of his somewhere, although it was likely that if he had no use for them they would have been destroyed. There were several cases that he had devoted more attention to, where he had written beside his customary records in sloping capitals the name of the accused or their sentence and a comment, such as 'farcical' or 'lenient'.

Chiron had marked the page that had piqued his interest. It was a note from the sixth month of the previous year, which meant it was from one of the last cases Sawney had attended before misplacing his records. Around that time the courts executed a man for plotting against the crown. Such was the strength of the rumour that he had threatened to betray the Eyes and been incriminated by them that Chiron had heard and believed it: he had dreamt of conspiracy for weeks. For this case Sawney had made the usual points but had added in an intriguing scrawl the names of the accused's parents and siblings and a reminder to himself: 'Tell Jonas!'

The prince wondered for the umpteenth time why an Advisor would have planned to share the identities of a convicted traitor's next of kin unless that man was indeed guilty of trying to outwit the Eyes and Sawney had a connection with his indictment. He liked to imagine that Sawney was a member of the Eyes and that the second he found incontrovertible proof he would reveal the double-crosser to Eli for what he was.

Scrutinising the note again brought him no closer to the truth. He recovered Silas' parchment but when he sank cross-legged to the floor to read he found himself recalling how early he had recognised Sawney's power to manipulate.

He was aware of having being watched as a child when his father allowed him to wander among the nobles at functions. Jousting had been introduced one summer and had been popular for a while, and Chiron could remember that it had been during a tournament in the Zodiac Gardens that he had heard Sawney consult his father about his observations even though he was not, Chiron estimated, yet an Advisor at that time. Sawney feared the prince to be of an unstable temperament, a careless boy. Spirited, bright and thoughtlessly mischievous, he was also given to periods of listlessness as he grew older. Fully aware that these behaviours were hardly extraordinary for a ten year old, it was Sawney's aim to insinuate that Chiron would reach a fate similar to that of Caius, who, after an erratic youth, had become a drunken figure of ridicule. He hoped for the Emperor to keep Chiron distanced from the affairs of the Empire, therefore not privy to details of his arrangement with Delzean. Without this motive he would have struggled to like the boy - he was unpredictable and cowardly.

Chiron resented the consequences of his singling out when he was old enough to understand that because of Sawney he had been resigned to failure from the beginning.

Whilst Acario revisited Ava bearing a green dress that still smelt faintly of perfume Chiron too was thinking of their mother. He was certain that Sawney had smirked at his watery eyes and hectic cheeks when they walked side by side out of the chapel after her burial but had to admit that he could not really remember whether it had *definitely* happened. His whole memory of the funeral had all the vividness of a half-forgotten dream from childhood.

Someone had entered the anteroom; the surprise of the unannounced guest woke him from his reminiscences. When he stretched to his feet, arms outstretched and fingers splayed, he hazarded an acute guess at the identity of the visitor and called out, assured in his assumption, "Show yourself in, then, sirrah!"

Acario had meant to warn his brother of the evening's guests if he had not heard from elsewhere, and he then planned to suggest that they go out to the gardens now that Leon had returned but he had realised as he approached Chiron's room that there was no hope of him raising his brother's spirits when his own were so low. What he desired was to confide and be comforted but he had too strong a sense of self-preservation to risk the punishment that Ava assured him awaited his confession.

"What are you doing?" he asked, curious to learn why Chiron was standing in the middle of the floor holding a crumpled parchment. His brooding appearance was foreboding.

"Boring myself to death with Silas' notes. I thought you were changing for dinner, otherwise I would have gone to see you earlier." He motioned for Acario to look towards the window and added: "Hopefully it will be too wet for them to travel. They live quite far away, you know, not with the other Advisors."

"I know," answered Acario, understanding too well who he was referring to. "I *will* have to go and get changed soon. Are you meeting Adema's guests before they leave?"

"I assume you think we should be friendly. I will be obliging, for your sake. Trust you appreciate it!" Grinning, he perched on the window-seat but kept his back turned against the outside world. "Let us go now and get Leon on the way."

"Wait for me, then. I shan't be long!" promised Acario as he moved to the door, pleased by his brother's complicity in his distraction.

To prove that he did not consider Sawney and his family to be guests worthy of an invitation to Delzean Chiron decided to forgo making any attempt to neaten himself. As he turned his head to face the window he deliberately turned up the collar of his blazer and noted with pride the stains on his cuffs. He waited there unmoving for Acario's return.

After a few moments of his staring transfixed at the sky the storm had calmed and the downpour began to peter out, leaving only a plethora of puddles as proof of its thwarted menace.

Chapter Five

At the northern extreme of the dining hall the Emperor stood at the head of the table, holding his goblet aloft. For the evening he had adorned his crown. The golden piece seemed ill-befitting of the reverence heaped upon it. It was too modest an affair to serve as the embodiment of princely authority.

"For my foremost Advisor I believe a toast is in order. To Sawney, in return for a career of diligent service."

Eli's toast was delivered to the gathering at large. His sentiments echoed in the cavernous dining hall. It was the largest chamber within the palace, along with the ball room which twinned its precise proportions, and its ceiling was lofty enough to make the exposed beams appear as slim as needles.

On either side of the Emperor were stationed Sawney, the guest of honour, and Chiron. The Advisor was seated upright in his hardbacked chair across from the ashen-faced prince. He thanked his host gratuitously for his commendations and led his sons in a short burst of applause. Their efforts sounded forced, insincere.

Chiron, for his part, had no attention to spare for these three. It was with a great and conscious effort that he raised his own goblet to Sawney upon Eli's prompt, preoccupied as he was with the disturbance caused to his temper, sharp enough to rival his father's, by Ava's choice of gown. Acario was similarly agitated and found the appetite cultivated by the long day following his hurried breakfast (in the school's refectory he had eaten little) was fast depleting. The tense expression etched upon his childlike features was observed with interest by Lorian from across the expanse of platters patterning the table.

Lorian had seized the central place between his father and brother in order to be privy to conversations at both the table's poles and ensure he caught as many tantalising titbits as possible. It would have been nigh on impossible for an onlooker to infer whether the greedy cast of his eyes was directed more towards the youngest prince than the steaming dishes. Indeed, he had not failed to recognise a quality in Acario that the boy appeared to exude inadvertently. Acario had the distinct air of one accustomed to playing the role of victim.

Upon his right, and to the delight of both Delarus brothers, next to Ava, Mathias was trying to distract himself from the ache of his sunken stomach by revising in silence his scheme to charm the Princess. He resented that the twist of fate, advantageous as it had proved, which had swept him into Sawney's household and from there to be shepherded into a life of deviance also meant that he was considered to be as villainous as Lorian; not only as villainous, but even more despicable, as he was but a common orphan. Had it not been for Sawney's charity he would not be permitted to walk amongst the gentry in the marketplace, and never would he have found himself the recipient of a cordial invitation to dine with the Castile family themselves. Before experiencing the scorn of the Princess Mathias had been unaware of the how deeply such a slight could affect him. He felt himself to be grossly underestimated, and just as keen was the sense that he had been wronged. It was not that he held his companion in low regard, but rather that he had long since realised that Sawney's influence had sabotaged any inclination Lorian may have possessed to grow a conscience. Despite his compliance with Sawney's wishes, and the exultation his missions occasionally brought, his perception of himself was as an agent of the Eyes whilst Lorian, the more monstrous of the pair, would surely have come to evil had he been born elsewhere. He was determined to coerce the sullen Princess into reconsidering the first impression she had crafted in haste and prejudice.

Mathias took Eli's invitation for the gathering to eat as they fancied from the banquet before them as his cue. He abstained from filling his plate with reeking paella of which the first of the three successive courses largely consisted, and turned to see Ava reaching for a platter of smoked fish. The weight of his gaze caused her to pause, unsure, and although she neglected to look towards him he used this moment of uncertainty to lift the platter and inquire, fork poised, how much would be to her highnesses' liking.

That she responded at all delighted him; that her countenance bore every sign of one who feels the warmth of flattery against their will pleased him still further. This encounter was the only exchange that passed between them but the atmosphere had undeniably altered afterwards. Every movement Ava made seemed to Mathias to have been brought into the most acute focus.

Within seconds of his gesture he was struck by the desire for the evening to draw with haste to its conclusion. There had been an element of the surreal in their brief exchange, as his firm footing in the city's criminal hierarchy was yet too weak to dispel his awareness that Ava, as timid and trivial as she looked, wielded a power that was fathomlessly greater than his own.

In lieu of the freedom to launch upon an open inquisition Lorian had to settle for aiming as discreet a nudge into his sibling's side as his exuberant nature would permit. He was coaxed into the conversation between his father and the Emperor, and as he could no more ignore a direct question from the latter than a blow to the skull from a blunt object he was forced to quiet the urge to commend Mathias on his daring.

The vacant place upon Ava's right was faced by her mother, a fair-haired woman of suitably regal stature. She, too, had observed her daughter's interaction with the younger Delarus son but had considered it simply a display of the diligence it was only fitting for the Princess to be shown by her guest, albeit one whose reputation suggested he was disinclined to adhere to the conventions of polite society.

Adema was sharing a smile with her suitor of two years, a lawyer of impressive standing named Javier Rana. The yellowed teeth she exhibited were a source of disgust to her shallow daughter.

It was her inability to impress upon Eli that she was unhappy to endure the solitude that came with a widow's existence for the remainder of her days that vexed her son. It was clear to Leon that she should remarry. He wondered whether it was respect for her deceased husband that prevented her marriage, for Javier's intentions were far from vague, or whether it was due to concern for her children in case such a marriage resulted in Adema having to seek accommodation with Javier elsewhere in the city, as she would no longer bear the name which entitled her to assume residence in the palace. Leon was not much proud of his father and while he gladly honoured the man's memory when occasion called upon him to do so, in his line of reasoning it was ridiculous to allow one slumbering beneath the earth to restrict the progress of those living and roving above. Furthermore he was certain that Eli would not cast them from Delzean, not least because Leon was a general of note in the Emperor's armed forces.

The magnanimity of Javier's features, his neat, almost lipless mouth set in a fixed half-smile, was negated to a degree by his twisted nose, broken in an encounter he refrained from discussing. When he offered his flute of wine in salute to Sawney he had sheltered a bemused grin behind his sleeve as he ostentatiously scratched at the bridge of his crooked nose. The importance Eli placed upon Sawney's contribution to the Empire's governance perplexed him. He suspected Sawney more than most.

The presence of the sceptical Javier would have unsettled Sawney if he had reason to doubt the security of his place in the Emperor's esteem. He had been unaware that Javier was attending the palace until the moment of their arrival in the reception room, and his sons required no instruction to keep watch upon their foe. This suspicion was sensible: a relative of Javier's happened to be a close acquaintance of theirs. From that man they had learned that the lawyer sought to uncover as many shreds of information about the Eyes that the convicts he represented were willing to divulge, and that he had taken firm steps to ensure his loyalties were firmly asserted against their order.

Ava likewise felt only contempt for the man in pursuit of her mother's affections. Hers, on the other hand, was not based on solid reason and was rather the mindless hatred of a child for those seen as competitors for a parent's attention.

The tension surrounding Javier was nevertheless dwarfed by that concerning the appearance of Adrienne's gown. In wearing the gown Ava had intended not only to upset Acario, whose inattention of late had become irksome, but to impress upon her mother that she was nearing womanhood herself. At sixteen she believed herself to be ripe for marriage and the glory that came, she was sure, with taking charge of a household. Instead she succeeded in emphasizing the slightness of her frame. The sagging neckline exposed the bones protruding from her milk-white shoulders, and her eyes seemed too large in such a narrow face. Clad in swathes of green material, an unflattering resemblance could be found to a praying mantis.

Chiron and Eli had recognised the dress as Adrienne's immediately had Ava taken her seat at the table. The young prince was prevented from confronting her by the presence of Sawney, in front of whom he had no wish to display any sign of weakness. He also knew it would be unwise to embarrass his father, on whose mind the morning's incident was perhaps still preying. He elected instead to whisper mutinously to Acario in a ceaseless fury.

When Ava had entered the reception room at the heels of her brother, Eli had looked from the Princess to her mother. Seeing no sign of alarm cross Adema's face he concluded that she was in ignorance of the identity of the gown's rightful owner. With curious guests in earshot he resumed his conversation (at her entrance his pleasantries had frozen mid-word) and reminded himself to have a servant oversee the return of the garment. To berate the Princess for pilfering the possessions of his late wife was an undertaking best suited to Adema.

As Chiron hissed into his ear, cursing the nerve of their cousin, Acario concentrated upon willing himself to adopt a similar expression of startled horror in place of the guarded resignation in which he tended to regard Ava's exploits. There was a painful throbbing in his temples; beneath the table he was alternating between wringing his hands and clenching them into tight fists. His shame grew deeper as he listened to his brother, a guilt that fired shockwaves through his limbs.

The cause of the disturbance was beyond Leon's reckoning but he was more than perceptive enough to recognise the tremendous effect that some matter related to Ava had brought upon his neighbours. He could not distinguish specific phrases in Chiron's mutterings but the general tone was obvious.

Few would dispute that Leon was worshipped throughout the city. His popularity was even superior to that bestowed upon Eli, as it was his character that was considered to be worthy of the citizenry's admiration, and consequently their affection for him was not the mere compulsive respect for one with a royal title. He was well suited to the complexities and trials of military life. This selfsame dexterity was demonstrated by the speed in which he observed the looming confrontation and moved to dissolve the building momentum.

"Acario," he said in a voice that carried across the hall, and halted the flow of Chiron's malice, "I believe you wanted to ask for me to instruct you in fencing?"

His words had their desired effect: Chiron, whose anger would have soon attracted the notice of others, had been silenced. Such resourcefulness came naturally to the eldest of the three princes, and had assisted him a great deal when he had first set upon his military career. Indeed, it had taken but twenty-seven months, to be precise, from the time of leaving school for him to achieve the rank of general. He seemed to live almost independent of Delzean, as though it was out of deference for the ties of blood alone that it was to the palace he returned every evening, smiling and wiping his brow with a calloused hand. He was dressed in a blazer the double of Chiron's, but the military uniform he wore beneath was plain to see.

When contrasted to Chiron his patience was all the more pronounced. In appearance each displayed the traits typical of the family, yet to each other they held very little in common. Although the heir to the throne was taller than average, Leon stood a full head above him. His hair was the same jet-black shade, but it was chopped in a neat cut just below the level of his chin while Chiron's fell past his shoulders. Both had the same jaw line and rather full lips but while Chiron's skin was pale with an almost unearthly glow, Leon's skin had been darkened by the harsh rays of the sun and was patterned with freckles. Neither did he share the same distinctive hairline.

As the meal progressed, the initial tension conquered, the conversation died only to be born again in turns, reincarnated in low whispers and heated debates. The light from without began to dull until the table alone was illuminated by the aid of dripping candles. The plates were emptied, cleared and replaced with platters of crystallized fruit, arranged with care into the pattern of a bird, absinthe jelly and the full carcass of a pig roasted to a crisp.

The walls of the dining hall were bare, save for the shield encrusted with the Castilian coat of arms mounted above the barren fireplace. In wait of clearing the last of the courses the servants retreated from their stations to linger in the far corners of the hall. Twelve steps led up from the flagstones to the set of double doors closed against the pillared corridor.

Even the single-minded Chiron was able to bury his grievances for the evening, although he could not address Mathias without a trace of sarcasm betraying his instinctive dislike of anyone related to Sawney. It was his wish to share with Leon and Acario the small observations he had made of their guests – that Ava blushed at the laughter of Mathias, that Lorian had forgotten his manners and seized food with an animal hunger, and most curious of all, the cool dismissal with which Sawney and Javier had greeted each other's remarks. He was far too impatient to endure the wait for much longer, and as the Emperor sipped his fourth glass of wine, and the rest of the gathering leaned back in their chairs with heavy stomachs, he flitted his gaze across the length of the hall, counting the seconds.

Contrary to what Chiron may have believed, it was not for the purpose of his personal aggravation that his father had proffered an invitation to Sawney. Eli was willing to grant Chiron's grudge some consideration and in place of indicating that the entire party should retreat to a sitting room and therein lull the evening to a comfortable, albeit stuporous, conclusion, he announced that an amble in the gardens would be to the group's benefit.

The palace gardens were reached by passing through a gate, rusted and strewn with branches of jagged ivy, located in the largest courtyard.

As the gathering massed towards this gate the tread of their feet on the cobbled stone reverberated between the pale walls. This disturbance went unheeded by the only other living creatures in the yard. Perched on the edge of a stone basin, which protruded from an ornate, miniature fountain embedded into the wall, were two cats. Thin coilings of ivy had crept around the fountain. Water spurted from the fountainhead, carved into a striking imitation of a fish. These blue-eyed felines were content to explore Delzean as they pleased, without submitting to the wishes of a bumbling, human master.

Acario walked at the heels of Leon and Chiron, and as he passed, the last of the group, he cried out to the cats. They ignored his beckoning, and continued to play, lazily, in the strengthening darkness. He replaced his attention, with reluctance, upon the progress of those in front.

From Chiron Leon had gleaned the tale of the feud now emerging betwixt his cousins and Ava. He sympathised with their cause, and accustomed as he was to the indignation of the elder, he found the silence of Acario the most troubling response to Ava's folly. It would be incorrect to suppose that his loyalties were torn, for, while he would defend his sister, of whose nature he had but a faint understanding, against the harshest of accusations, it had been untoward of her to adorn such a gown. He was compelled, however, to counter Chiron's charge: he would not hear that Ava had purposefully contrived to flaunt a garment of Adrienne's before them. At once both a deep flaw and a favourable quality was his eagerness to give his family the benefit of any doubt. He had as little idea of his sister's torment of Acario as he did of her motives for desiring the gown.

It had been her intention to make an impression upon the others, an impression that was at once indelible and distinct. To her mother, she wished to appear older, and sought to adopt an air of sophistication that could be achieved, she thought, through the simple act of taking on the clothes of the Empress. She had not considered this attempt to channel, in a sense, the deceased woman's command, in a great deal of depth.

"Never mind whether she *intended* to cause an upset, which she must have done -"

"What makes you certain she must have wanted to upset the family? She could have discovered the dress in innocence. She may have not considered that the room and its contents belonged to your mother."

"Is that what you believe?" replied Chiron. The question was posed in a voice unwavering; he made no secret of his opinion that Leon was a fool to believe such a thing.

"Once I have spoken to her myself you can hear what I believe. For the moment, just accept that there may be an alternative to the scenario you propose. Ava's explanation may surprise you."

Chiron, somewhat placated by Leon's patient reasoning, offered a final argument with a touch less conviction. "It seems impossible to me to suppose that she has no idea whose gown she wears. To search the cupboards of my mother's room..."

Leon answered in a whisper: "Already we must contend with Sawney tonight. Let us not create another enemy." He called back to the straggler of the group, who, as though in front reached the gate, had fallen several paces behind as though wary of the debate behind brother and cousin. "Come, Acario, walk beside us."

Those accompanying the princes through the courtyard had been occupied with business of their own, for their most part, and Chiron's accusations faded into the darkness without notice.

One by one each member of the gathering stepped through the gate, and entered into the first of the gardens. The path dividing the lawns was lit on either side by a sequence of red lanterns. These illuminations allowed them to wander with confidence amidst the shrouded landscape, whilst casting a devilish blush over every face. As they threaded down the path they could have been mistaken for a procession of demons.

Eli led his guests to desert the path as it veered towards an adjacent, self-contained garden of exotic plants, proceeding instead towards wilder grounds.

The grass here was long and moist. It was strewn with trees of varying species and patches of feral flowers that bequeathed to a night air a scent both sweet and intoxicating in equal measure. Lanterns were hanging from the tallest branches of the trees but the most the garden was in shadow.

The gulf between the three princes and the larger proportion of the party had widened to such an extent that Chiron had lost sight of his father. The nearest form he could distinguish was that of Adema. There was little need for him to linger in the vicinity of Sawney and Ava.

Leon and Acario joined him in a curt abandoning of their fellows to roam at their own leisure. A blistering rage had taken possession of Chiron, rendering him deaf to the light-hearted converse of the others.

The remainder of the gathering had splintered into three factions as they followed in the wake of their leader. Of the seven, only Sawney and Lorian walked alongside the Emperor. The preparations for the early stages of the robberies Sawney had arranged were under deep scrutiny. Eli was interested to hear Lorian remark about Vikernes' role in the proceedings; he had suspected the Lieutenant to occupy a position of greater power within the Eyes than that which Sawney credited him. They navigated the gardens without any of the world beyond their talks.

In a futile attempt to postpone the unavoidable moment when Lorain would, at the first chance, berate him about Ava (he was willing himself to revert to the apathy in which he had regarded the princess' opinion previously), Mathias had fallen back on the pretext of admiring a willow tree, the likes of which, in honesty, he had never perceived before.

He was less successful in evading Ava, for she approached as he paused in thought. A stretch behind came her mother in the company of a man whose name, despite being blackened by Sawney on many an occasion, had inexplicably leapt straight out of his head. He began again to walk as Ava passed, her movement parallel to his. There was a considerable, perhaps deliberate, distance between them, but neither could deny an awareness of the presence of the other, for reasons ill or otherwise.

Through the thick, humid air a faint breeze blew, and at its touch Mathias seemed to reawaken, and regain the self-assurance that had prompted his engagement with Ava. He cleared his throat, his choice made, and called across: "Do you walk here often, Princess?"

With a start she turned her head. There was no doubt: he was addressing her. A few seconds of pregnant silence elapsed before she replied, directing her words towards the sky.

"No, not as often as I would like."

Mathias grinned. Now he had this conversation (exaggerated, of course, out of all proportion) to hold over Lorian when he embarked upon his inevitable inquisition. It would be a harsh blow to the bloated ego of his brother to learn that he, the younger, the *inferior*, Mathias was able to charm not only a princess but one who, until he believed her ripe for enlightenment, had thought him hideous. Serious as the brawls between the brothers may have appeared, these goads were merely a natural element of their relationship, as essential as any other.

Ava sought to demonstrate her maturity to Adema and gained courage from the strength of the desire she felt to impress her readiness upon her mother. To entertain one whose interests ran contrary to her own was an undertaking her governess stressed the necessity of. It was her reckoning that her mother would similarly applaud such a feat. For the first time she dared to meet the gaze of Sawney's son. "I think I prefer the Zodiac Gardens. I like the zoo."

Brief as her contribution to the conversation was, it was nevertheless appreciated. Mathias was now beginning to wish that Lorian had elected to leave Sawney and Eli to their business in order for him to bear witness to this triumph.

"My father brought us to the opening ceremony," he replied, "As far as I remember, my brother was afraid of the bears."

He was certain that he heard a laugh, albeit a feeble one. Later he imagined that the sound may have been just the wind.

It was not long afterwards that the seven came together in a semi-circle and exchanged pleasantries in anticipation of Eli bidding each guest goodnight. The faces of the gathering were luminescent with the glow of a nearby lantern. Above them a solitary star blazed in response. From there Eli escorted the entirety of the party, with the exception of the princes, through the palace towards the entrance hall where, hours earlier, the visitors had been greeted. Here the servants waited to usher the Emperor's guests to the carriages prepared for their homeward journeys.

The princes, meanwhile, lingered in the gardens as the wind gathered and cold grew bitter, an occurrence uncanny in the city.

Their desertion had led them to the furthest corner of the gardens. Leon had heaved himself onto an ancient tree at the boundary of the grounds reserved for the use of the palace horses. The branch onto which he had manoeuvred was thick enough to support a man of twice his weight and he perched there, several feet above the ground, in relative comfort. Through eyes half-closed he watched as Chiron wrenched up clump after clump of grass. He was squatting beneath the branch cradling Leon, with Acario seated, his legs crossed, at his side.

Their positions seemed to indicate that they had found the time in each other's company to be tiresome, and had grown morose, but Chiron, for one, had been infinitely happier in isolation. Their chatter had subsided as each turned away to contend with private thoughts.

"Will they have left yet?" asked Acario in a yawn, eager for sleep and oblivion. His limbs had become weary in compliance with the wishes of his overwrought mind.

With a smile Chiron answered: "Perhaps. But tell me, are you suggesting that I would be so heinous to take you here in order to avoid our guests?"

Acario was yet alert enough to appreciate the remark and tittered, but he would have preferred to learn that it was safe to scurry indoors.

"If your sense of humour has waned that much I rather feel some rest is called for," said Leon from his eyrie, his eyes now closed fully against the scene below, "Sawney and the rest will be long gone; we should race back to the palace and at least make the return interesting."

Before this contest had been agreed to Leon had landed on his feet, shakily, but nonetheless impressively, at the back of Chiron. He aimed a playful nudge into the prince's head and then sprinted onwards, to be pursued by his cousins through the grass.

In places the gardens proved themselves treacherous, as the princes tripped over mounds and tree stumps invisible in the darkness. Such was their exhaustion upon reaching the courtyard that not one feared to enter in case Eli waited beyond, primed to reprimand them for their neglect. They had forgotten, or failed to care, that their rapid progress towards the palace had been in the spirit of competition, and each anticipated instead the welcome of sleep, and indeed, of oblivion.

Chapter Six

Two days had elapsed since Chiron's eviction from the Breakfast Hall. On both mornings he had received a glance of warning from his father upon entering the hall and this threat, subtle as it was, appeared to have registered with the prince, for he exercised restraint against any further inkling to disturb the morning's tepid processes.

In spite of the perfect silence he maintained, and the attention he placed on keeping an upright posture (he was tired of discovering remnants of breakfast in his hair after too close an encounter with the table), it was clear to the Advisors that he had not absorbed one word of the negotiations around him. How could he be listening, with such a mischievous glint in his eye? Eli interpreted his grin as an indication that he was with them in body alone. He decided that a harsher punishment would have been more prudent.

Sawney recalled the warnings he had once given to Eli, that Chiron was too volatile to be trusted with the responsibilities of an Empire, and as he observed this demonstration of apathy he felt the stirrings of an emotion resembling pleasure. He appeared no less stoic than usual, though if his fellow Advisors had believed this exterior to be the result of a conscious effort they were somewhat misguided.

It was on the second morning that Chiron encountered Erin, the maid.

The Advisory Breakfast went without incident, other than the minor upset caused by Rous' bouts of unremitting coughing. Silas had been the recipient of the attention of which the Advisors were deprived. He was encouraged by Chiron's mood but knew the prince well enough to remain dubious of his interest, and cut short his attempts to halt the lecture with questions. While the evidence of previous mornings suggested that his concern was not without foundation, Chiron's interest in the details of a military campaign of particular horror was at least genuine. His curiosity was unaffected by the stubborn resistance of his tutor. When he descended the old, warped staircase from the study at the close of the lesson his thoughts were occupied with dreams of conquest.

The remainder of the day was his to indulge in such fantasies, of the wars fought for the city's throne by competitors both native and foreign, and of the blood shed in his family's name. Other than the structured morning he was obligated to endure, there were no other demands clamouring for his time, not even a meal with his family in the evening. Without the guidance of Eli, who was dining with the Advisor Milias, the family tended to draw apart. It was left to Adema to extend an invitation to the others to dine with her. On this occasion she had decided instead to ask only her children. At their refusal (Leon's excuse was sincere, as his expertise was required in the training of an ungainly batch of recruits, whilst Ava was just brooding), she opted to dine alongside Javier. Had it been Chiron's desire to be served in the hall he could be certain it would not be refused to him, but Adema was correct to surmise that he would prefer to have a basket of food brought to him in his own rooms. It was his plan, at the moment in its fledging stages, to ensnare Acario on his return from school with the offer of dinner and an overdue rematch on the chessboard.

The sounds and smells of Delzean, which played upon his senses as he moved down the corridor at the pace expected of one with no place to be, were so familiar to him as to be almost beneath notice. Much of the palace was haunted by the pervasive fumes of incense, jasmine-scented and sharp. From the courtyard below came the voices of the guards as they embarked on their daily circuit of the grounds. This patrol was scheduled for midday but it was typical of the city people to keep time as they pleased, and it suited them better to complete this task before the burgeoning heat made such an exertion impossible. Afterwards they would report to their stations by the palace entrance. Delzean had not been built as a fortress and its security was reliant on the protection of these men. Chiron wondered for a brief moment whether the guards, recruited from the ranks of common soldiers, had ever seen a battle on the scale of those Silas described, or whether their military lives had been void of scenes of carnage. It then struck him that one with a fear of blood would perhaps fare poorly in battle.

He increased his pace when his thoughts turned to centre upon Ava. It was his intention to ensure that the princess had been convinced to return his mother's dress. He was prepared for a confrontation if she had failed to do so, and with his father, too, if he had not pressed the matter.

It was as he rounded the corner, passing the door to the stairwell which hid from sight the servants lurking there but fell short of subduing their laughter, that he spied the maid. Since her intrusion into the breakfast hall she had become a minor feature in his daydreams, as he considered whether her impertinence could be harnessed for his amusement, though these musings were unable to upstage his imaginings of the enemies he had faced in the meantime.

He only had a second in which to recognise her, the colour of her hair marking her out immediately from the serving masses, for she shot a glance at up and down the length the corridor, and then, having missed the approaching prince, slipped into the nearest room. Her movements suggested that avoiding detection was her utmost concern. It was the promise of this secrecy that prompted him to tip toe across the corridor in her wake.

The sound of his feet as he crept forward was masked by the laughter from the stairwell.

Her seemingly nefarious business had taken her into what was known as the Scroll Room, although Chiron referred to it by the disparate term 'the armoury'.

The scene was a space of average proportion. As its given name would suggest, here mouldered the written records of the city. Proclamations written on official orders to be read to the crowds gathered around the huskings were housed in this room. Those of earlier origin were the more fortunate, for they had secured a place upon the alcove for their final resting place, while the notices from later dates had been piled up by the servants against the wall in four forgotten heaps. The court records were stacked in a neater fashion, as they were frequently requested by one lawyer or another in order to be used either in checking some fact or to be employed as a precedent in another prosecution. On each side of the low table, which rested beneath the window, were the cabinets which sheltered these documents from the elements.

Although Chiron's interest was limited to items of one particular breed, in truth there were a number of objects stored therein that assisted in alleviating the tedium of the formal writings. The low table displayed artefacts that had been deemed too precious to be displayed to the public (or at least for the limited section of the public that would seek, and be granted, admittance to the palace) in the reception room. Scattered amongst these relics were those that held Chiron's fascination. Eli had preserved the weapons that his own grandfather had used in combat, even the rapier he had trained with in his youth. One of the prince's earliest memories was Leon leading him to see his great-grandfather's helmet, and the bronze crossbow that, according to legend, was the first weapon to ever spill blood in the city.

The girl, her plump flesh emphasized, rather than disguised, in the threadbare robes of the maidservants, was edging towards this table when Chiron crept into sight of the door. He stared as she approached the window, and extracted a shaking hand from the folds of her apron.

The object she then reached out to grasp was small enough to disappear in the palm of her hand. It was worth a great deal more than its stature would indicate. The distance between them and the dexterity with which she had grasped the object meant that he could not recognise it by sight, but he could see in his mind's eye what had lain upon the table, and knew what was now missing. It was an idol of a holy figure, delivered to the Emperor from the ruler of a kingdom on the Empire's trade route. The identity of the figure was unknown to those in Horizon; the only sign that it was a gift of momentous proportion was the discovery that the eyes of the idol were made of emerald.

From the swiftness of her actions he could divine that this was a premeditated theft, one which had perhaps been planned since the maid was first brought to work in Delzean. Suddenly this proof of the independent streak he had spied within her was no longer pleasing. He found himself riled by this disrespect, this atrocity, this attack upon his home. On the heels of this anger came another sensation, that of pity. It was her misfortune to be destined to a life of such poverty that she must resort to stealing from her betters. Fate should be condemned, he thought, not her.

Already he had begun to step back as she buried the idol in her apron, and he had crossed the corridor and turned to peer out into the courtyard beneath when she emerged from the Scroll Room, her face flushed.

From the window he heard her leave, sensing, for a second, a heavy gaze on the back of his head, as the servants from the stairwell entered into the corridor. Their chattering ceased when they noticed the prince, and they skirted past him with their eyes to the floor, in the direction of the other maid.

As he stood by the window, Chiron was having visions of himself as a hero, a prince just enough to release a red-handed maid from the bonds of servitude. He would arrange for her to steal away from Delzean; here was no life for an independent mind. He would play the role of instigator, and reveal to her the importance of finding her own way in the world, for doubtless it was to support a set of forceful parents and siblings that she had come to work. It could be that she had taken the idol to sell on the black market, in order to fund her escape.

He was compelled by this false belief in himself, and his ability to champion the benefits of self-determination (the motto of his family passed unbidden across his mind, '*Maior sum quam cui posit fortuna nocere*'), to stalk the maid through the palace and speak to her until she bent to his will; not that he anticipated any resistance, for he had faith in his assumption that she desired freedom, but lacked the courage to leave of her own voilition.

To ring for a servant, and then ask for the red-haired maid to be brought before him, for of course, he was witless of her name, would attract, if not direct questions, then at least a certain level of suspicion, which, considering that the girl had proved herself to be undoubtedly deserving of scrutiny, would be unwise to raise against her. Instead, he would have to seek her out. With that realisation, his idea of pursuing her through Delzean became less than an idealistic mission and more like a game.

He stepped back from the window and began to tread along the corridor, imagining as he did so himself in the maid's shoes. If it was him, he would not dare to linger in the area surrounding the robbed chamber, but would instead hasten to find a reprieve on another floor. It was likely that she now harboured reservations after sighting him in the hallway, and would fear another encounter. In that case, if she possessed a healthy instinct for her own preservation, she would opt for either a place of solitude, where none were apt to linger, or hide in plain sight, amidst the bustle of the servants. Perhaps she was destined for the kitchens, or if she failed to make use of herself there, then the dormitories could suffice. As to be discovered lurking in a lonely corner, which, admittedly, were rare in the palace, would draw attention, he decided that it would be the hub of the servant's activity that she would search for cover.

Her trail led him downstairs. Each room he passed was investigated with a quick glance, despite knowing the majority to be empty. He was distracted for a moment from his quest by the Breakfast Hall, the closed door of which he could not help but ease open. Inside, the room lay much as the Advisors had left it, although the table had attracted a number of flies in the intervening period.

On the ground floor, the commotion of the kitchens as two separate menus were prepared shattered the erstwhile lull of the afternoon. The chefs had received orders on the behalf of Ava (three courses had been requested for her to turn her nose up at). Having devoted the afternoon to the preparation of a banquet sizeable enough to feed each member of the family, a number of tempers had been provoked upon the receipt of this late call for further dishes. Chiron came close to being knocked aside when a gaggle of kitchen boys ran past bearing, between the four of them, the corpse of a pig freshly slaughtered in the courtyard.

He ascertained from this activity that the dinner preparations were underway with perceptible haste. The hour would then indicate that the dining hall would be playing host to the servant's attentions, for before Adema and her guest made the journey from the reception room, the table first had to be primed for the addition of the kitchen's offerings, and the candles brought to life, and the cutlery set for two.

There, he realised with a surge of enthusiasm, the maid would be working alongside her companions, attempting to appear as burdenless as those who were unencumbered with golden idols. She must be conscious of the weight in her apron, he thought; she must be afraid that her movements, as she sought camouflage in occupation, would dislodge the trinket. Equally, if it was held it in place with a steady arm, she would arouse the interest of those busying themselves around her. He felt a pang of sympathy for her plight, and increased his pace as he sped towards the dining hall.

The kitchen boys could be excused in their dismissal of the prince. While it had been due to the fear of their masters' wrath that they had raced passed the prince in ignorance, they could have claimed not to have recognised him. The heat had called for him to shun his blazer, and in the same vein he had left his hair unwashed. There was, as yet, no need for him to be shaved (he was secretly glad of this, as the beards of the Advisors reinforced his notion that age was a blight). His smooth face aside, he still appeared dishevelled without his formal attire. The servants distinguished him by his blazer and lofty stature, and even the latter was easy to overlook, for he was inadvertently walking the corridors with his shoulders stooped. It seemed his thoughts of stalking were reflected in the set of his posture.

When he skirted the last corner, and saw the corridor stretched out before him, with only a slender portion of the dining hall revealed beyond the doors, he found the centre of the servants' activity. He counted seven maids before he discerned the one he was pursuing,

The women were attacking the floor with buckets of water and brooms, striving through their labours to soak up the dirt stubborn enough to have achieved a foothold despite their previous efforts.

It was not long before his approach disturbed them, and they parted to cater for his passage. They stood with their backs against the wall and their eyes to the floor, like sleeping sentinels. He was accustomed to having his presence acknowledged with a bow; the silence, however respectful, that greeted him here was somewhat disconcerting. He supposed they were fretful that he had decided to join his aunt at short notice, but part of him was nevertheless resentful that he should be made to feel like a trespasser when it was they who came from outwith the palace.

The maid, the slightest bulge visible in the pouch of her apron, was third in line against the left-hand wall. As it was not his intention, of course, to force his company upon Adema, the path cleared for him was unnecessary, but he progressed as if he had planned, whilst standing at the other extreme of the corridor and gawking at the maidservants, to tread towards the dining hall. It was his wish to take a closer look at her, to see whether she would betray her guilt.

His steps on the sodden floor were hesitant. The maids did not stir, did not even tremble, as he passed through their ranks. With the eyes of the rest cast elsewhere, he saw no danger in peering directly into the face of the third-in-line.

She met his eyes, and would have divined from this glance alone that he had observed the theft had he not then chanced a knowing look to the bundle in her apron.

Chiron saw her eyes flit down to follow his. He smirked as the slightest tinge of pink blossomed on her cheeks. He began to whistle, and looked towards the dining hall, into which he made swift progress.

He paced down the stone steps and stood long enough behind the half-closed door to observe that the table was ready for his aunt's entrance before turning on his heel. In that interval he heard the distinct sound of footsteps moving in the opposite direction amidst the general clamouring of the maids as they resumed their task. As he emerged into the corridor he strode through the maids without a care for their confusion. The thief had already fled the corner but he was not afraid of losing her trail. If she ran she would incriminate herself. Her only option was to walk on until he tired of the pursuit. Had she been better acquainted with the prince she would have recognised the impossibility of this hope. Chiron could never tire of playing such a game.

The corridor which linked the entrance hall to the main rooms of the palace, the reception room and the ballroom serving as illustrations, was livid with candle light. The high ceiling was unable to dilute the thickness of the trapped air, for the walls were enclosed until the point where the corridor ran adjacent to the courtyard. Chiron wrinkled his nose: the scent of the decorative flowers along the corridor's length was pungent. On this white background the red-hair of the maid in front was almost implausibly bright.

Chiron was correct in his guess that she was bound for the courtyard. From there she could attempt to lose herself in the expanse of the gardens, though to hide from her pursuer would only serve as a solution momentarily. If he had indeed witnessed her theft, an evening spent hidden beneath a hedgerow would hardly be sufficient to thwart his prosecution. The uncertainty driving her flight was reflected in her fluctuating pace. Her steps would be swift for several paces then sharply slow, as if she had forgotten the purpose that propelled her onward.

The prince strolled through the corridor at an even pace. He commended the maid on her self-control, for if he had been likewise stalked he would have been unable to restrain himself from sneaking a glance at the one in pursuit. For her to turn around would be akin to openly voicing annoyance at his presence. It would suggest that she wished him to walk elsewhere, a thought too bold to be tolerated. Etiquette must be obeyed even whilst fleeing with a priceless heirloom. These musings had taken him close to hysterics by the time he stepped into the courtyard, the gap between them lessening with every stride.

In defiance of the approaching winter, the heat outside was intense. As the afternoon waned, the clouds had gathered to form a dense, iridescent screen across the sun, leaving shadows to grow against the palace walls.

After pausing to appreciate the evening's warmth, Chiron removed his gaze from the maid and without a word began again to meander in her direction. He soon altered his course, however, to stand by the fountain where Acario had called to the playing cats. Chiron was not in search of the creatures, who were in any case nowhere nearby, but halted there only to tease the maid by creating the impression that he had no intention of following her but had tread the same path out of coincidence. He believed this small cruelty to be easily forgiven in light of the kindness he planned to grant her.

The water encased in the stone basin was cool to the touch. He swept his hand through its swallow depths before ducking to splash a quantity onto his face. His pretence of occupation was flawless. When the maid opened the latch of the gate leading onto the gardens, she did so with a perceptible release of tension from her shoulders.

Impatience compelled Chiron to resume the pursuit. He counted to three before he dried his hand and face with his shirt sleeve and moved towards the gate. He was very much looking forward to meeting, at long last, the ill-mannered maid.

Once through the gate he experienced the slightest touch of fear upon seeing that she had strayed from the beaten path. To lose her at this juncture would pain him. Although the search could have been postponed until the next day, to delay the experience he anticipated (the two days since she interrupted the Advisory Breakfast had been an intolerable wait for the prince) was unthinkable. He had another reason to support his impatience: if she was to disappear, the proof of her theft would no doubt disappear with her. If she was to keep the idol, he wanted it to be on his blessing.

The lanterns were as yet unlit; several hours could be expected to pass before the sky darkened. With such clarity of vision, he was able to determine that she had doubled her speed once free from his scrutiny as she had evidently moved beyond the lawns. As he hurried along, further stretches of the path became revealed to him – it was clear that, unless she had concealed herself as to be invisible from the perspective of the path, she had taken her own way. He had not equipped her with enough time to secrete herself, and so he renounced the path. His route was that of his father's following the banquet. This realisation led him to a briefly-entertained recollection of Ava's folly but he dismissed the thought as an irrelevance.

Within a moment of leaving the path he spotted her. She was still walking forward with her back to him but there the distance between them was less than slight. It appeared she had considered her safety to be absolute and had found a place to pause and regain her composure. To hear him approach after a peaceful interlude meant her fear was renewed. It was a matter of stubborn resolve that there was no hesitation in her movements.

They were now placed in an odd position: that she had fled from him was indisputable, as was the fact of his pursuit. It remained only for one to confront the other.

"Servant!" shouted Chiron across the grass, "I insist that you stop. These gardens cannot hide you forever."

He stood in the long shadow of a sycamore tree. Had the maid committed a second offence and looked into his face when she turned in surrender, the smile he wore would likely have been missed. He had the advantage of being able to study her without reserve. The conclusion of his swift observation was that she was older in truth than in memory. Although not unattractive for a peasant, she bore a closer resemblance to the rather stout figures of the older maids than the slender frames of the young.

Her conduct pleased him better than her appearance. She did not fall to her knees and beg for forgiveness. Neither did she express any intention to feign innocence – for that he commended her. Her expression suggested a tranquillity that was amiss even in his own.

"What do you call yourself?"

After a pause in which she undoubtedly contemplated the benefits of posing as another, she answered the prince with her true name: "Erin."

A curtsy was added as an afterthought. It amused the prince that she adhered to polite conventions in such a situation. That she complied to perform these little acts of respect after grossly violating the Emperor's trust struck him as witty on her part, as though she half-expected him to be placated by her manners.

"Erin," said Chiron, savouring the impropriety of the address, "I have a plan for you. But *first*, tell me of your plan for that statue tucked inside your apron."

Erin's supposition that the prince had tracked her for the purpose of this inquisition meant that her reaction was not one of utmost surprise. Her stay in Delzean had been long enough to convince her that Chiron was oftentimes difficult. He was, by nature, unpredictable, and as such it was well within the realms of possibility that the plan he spoke of was not her arrest, but perhaps some other erratic scheme of his own invention. In any case, she risked nothing by answering in honesty. She replied without raising her eyes higher than the level of his feet.

"....I planned to send it to my family, your highness."

"And through what means were you intending to do so?"

Had the lack of shame conveyed by her response not been mollified by its quality of interest, their exchange would be in danger of becoming irksome.

"I was going to engage one of the palace guards to make the journey, and offer a bribe for their efforts." Erin wondered whether

her situation and irredeemable and finished, "I will return the idol without a struggle."

Chiron's laughter rang clear across the gardens: "You imply that my guards, the soldiers of this city, are at once dishonest enough to accept a bribe and dim enough not to realise the value of the item they have been hired to smuggle. I assure you, its worth exceeds the value of any bribe you could procure.

"Had you been successful, what use would your family have for such a token?"

For his actions to be heroic she needed to demonstrate a desire to be rescued; her reasons for resorting to theft needed to be grave. Her awkward tendencies appealed to him but it remained to be determined whether he could derive more than mere amusement from the encounter. The course of their adventure together was already fixed in his mind. He had a part to play, a role to fulfil, as did she. If she had then admitted to simply acting out of wanton greed, he would have found a way for her punishment to entertain him, perhaps by insisting on her attending him in the company of his family in order to drop hints at her misdeed subtle enough to escape the others whilst making her suitably uncomfortable, but it would suit him more for her to plead poverty as an excuse.

"To sell it, sire," came her hesitant answer. To her mind it was obvious that the idol would be exchanged for gold, but such was the deficiency of her understanding, limited by his princely rank, that she was unable to decipher from his words whether he had asked in order to fully expose her plans and thus more thoroughly deride them, or if he was instead bemused by such a seemingly reckless theft and thought her aim to be higher.

Her response, concise and candid as it was, he interpreted as an admission that certain circumstances had led her to deviate from the path she would have otherwise chosen to tread. It served to assure Chiron that he ought to rescue her, that he could exult in the pleasure of taking action that would be the venture's result without acknowledging the taint of doubt.

But he was in no rush to liberate her. Here was one he could meet with, talk to, assist. Her company would be frequented until it failed anymore to amuse him, and then he would put his energies to her plight. The possibility that he would no longer wish to 'help' her once he found distraction elsewhere was too far removed from the present moment to be considered. Entertainment sufficient to occupy his thoughts for the day's remainder had already been derived from their encounter; it was a wish to now seek the company of his brother that prompted him to curtail their exchange, rather than the fear that their pursuit through Delzean had been observed.

The estate of the Advisor Arden stretched adjacent to Delzean's gardens. This proximity was, of course, perceived by every sighted citizen with cause to pass the palace, but less known, indeed, hardly known to exist at all, was the gate which adjoined the grounds of Arden to those of Eli. It had been constructed in a distant year to fortify the bond between an ancestor of Arden's, whose advice had been held in the highest regard by Eli's father, and the house of Castile, but had fallen into the ranks of the unnecessary; had it been remembered, it would likely have been torn down, the gap filled with stone. As it stood still in obscurity it remained, recognised only by the prince. To uncover the gate was to battle through the encroaching trees, but the struggle was rewarded by its illicit end. He had yet to wander beyond the shadow of the wall, but Chiron had mentioned the gate to no one.

Rather than share the secret first with his brother, as he had contemplated, he decided to confide in the maid. Or at least, he planned to reveal the passage to her at some future juncture, when her departure became a reality. For the moment he would withhold this gem; he would instead entice her towards the place where it slumbered.

"It seems to me you would be happier to accompany that statue and return to your family. To endure such misery here does not become you," Chiron delivered his proposal with the necessary caution, "I would have you released from palace servitude. I would lead you back to your home, if you so choose it. Or would you accept that you belong here?"

"If I am ordered to go, I will go."

"And what if I ordered you to decide for yourself? If I gave you such power? What would you say then?"

"I am loyal to the palace, your highness." Her theft seemed to argue the contrary, however, and the discontentment evident in her expression served to acknowledge this.

"How far from the city do you live?"

Chiron began to shift his weight from foot to foot, a characteristic sign of restless agitation. Standing stockstill in the grass, the leaves of the bushes untroubled by wind, the twitching prince appeared incongruous, too alive for such a placid canvas.

"A night's journey." Erin was too stupefied by the prince's reaction to ask whether such a inquiry was to be taken as a dismissal.

Reassured that his plan would not be hampered by a concern as trifling as geography, Chiron nodded, and requested that she accompany him deeper into the gardens.

The gate being disguised by a close thicket, he procured a branch from a lantern-clad tree as they progressed towards it, and when their journey reached its end he worked the branch into the grass. This, he said to the maid resolute in her resolve only to listen and accept and refrain from second guessing his intention until alone in the sleeping dormitory, marked the place where they were next to meet.

"You could pretend to have forgotten to close a shutter, say, or clean a table," (the table he held in his mind's eye was the one found in the Breakfast Hall), "and report here for midnight, two nights from today."

Chiron had already turned back towards the palace. "If I cannot find you in the darkness, I will surely find you in the morning. I can only ask for your trust."

He perhaps realised that she was powerless to disobey for his face was relaxed in a grin. In contrast to the freshly incurred encounter, his form as he strode from the maid was as orthodox as it had ever been, in the sense that his appearance conveyed that which was lacking in his conduct: the quality of a prince. He was the image of his father as he swept purposelessly through the grounds.

Erin remained, unknowingly but a matter of steps away from a path which could have then led her to a freedom unencumbered by the fancies of a prince. Her hand cupped the bundle cradled inside her apron.

Chapter Seven

Save for the laughter of the group gathered by Lorian and Mathias, and the muttering of an incapacitated individual slumped across the otherwise deserted bar, the tavern was silent. Heavy shutters guarded the patronage of the tavern, select as it was, from the worst of the afternoon sun. The tavern would remain lifeless until the evening, when leagues of labourers would flock to seek a reprieve from the heat. In the meantime, there was life only in one corner, and even this group were concealed in shadow, for the singular source of light, the lantern above the door, had begun to flicker.

A slouched, wiry man of indeterminate age, the landlord himself, inched out from the chamber beyond the bar, armed with a bucket of river-water, to resume cleaning the previous night's beakers. Even with eyesight as poor as his, it was possible to recognise the sons of the Advisor Sawney. When they had entered, less than an hour before, he had willed himself to disregard any remark of theirs he might inadvertently overhear.

One of their acquaintances, who had made such an impression on his neighbours as to be awarded the prefix 'the notorious' Lisandro, was recounting the tale behind his latest spell in the city stocks whilst Lorian dealt a pack of cards amongst the seven seated there.

Sawney imposed few rules upon Lorian and Mathias, the most important of these scant limitations being that they remain at home until his return from the palace following the Advisory Breakfast and any other business which may occupy him afterwards. The result of this rule was that both men spent the largest proportion of the day asleep whilst their father was embroiled in negotiations with his fellow noblemen. On his return they would take to the streets to run amok until the succeeding morning. Logically, the reason behind this was problematic. Surely it was more dangerous for the house to be left empty at night than in the relatively safe daytime? When the security of their belongings was removed from the equation, it would seem that it had been devised simply to spare Sawney the trouble of hunting down his sons to inform them of the latest developments related to the Eyes, such as the meeting that night of the organisation's inner circle. After reassuring Sawney that they would soon report to the meeting place, they had vacated the house, heading first for the usual haunts of their contemporaries. Once a suitably promising bunch had been collected, they led the way to their favourite drinking den. 'Favourite' in this instance was synonymous with rowdiest, although the current atmosphere would belie this fact.

Their evening in the company of the awkward aristocrats of Delzean had already provided a night's worth of stories for Lorian to spin and Mathias to adorn with colourful touches for their bohemian friends, and looked set to provide another. In the exchange between Mathias and Ava Lorian had found much-needed ammunition to tease his brother with, as despite the speed with which he could deliver a mocking jibe Mathias was the wittier of the duo.

It was to Lorian's advantage, then, that Mathias' thoughts lay elsewhere, as he began to consider their situation with Ava in the wider context of the Eyes. In an attempt to shrug off the unsettling feelings Ava had stirred (that of the inferiority inherent within him), he had turned to thinking on the relations between his family and Delzean in general, and how Sawney was certain that for Chiron to assume the throne would be for their operations to crumble. He had come to the realisation that as Sawney's position had granted him access to the royals, to an extent, it would be easy for him to then forge a deeper bond by courting the princess. If he could use this influence to somehow arrange for Vikernes to be promoted upon his recommendation to a higher rank, the Eyes would have even less to fear from the army, the scourge of Horizon's criminals. The ongoing robberies were the furthest afield the Eyes had ever undertaken such a venture; if they could expand their reach to the most remote corners of the Empire, where the force of law was almost nonexistent, they would be free to act without interference. And if the benefits for the Eyes were cast aside, the notion of exercising more power than Lorian made him grin with the innocence of a child.

He had been chided by Sawney before for the fervour with which he seized upon ideas only to lose interest in focusing his energies onto a specific task, but the course he was traversing with Ava would be one, whether it was to his liking or not, that would been seen through to the long haul.

As the rest studied their cards and glowered at the prospects of their less-than-promising hands (it was to little effect, as other than the two seated at either end of the table, whose wealth was shown in their tailored clothes, they could not afford to play for money, but the element of competition was ever present amongst the restless young men), Mathias caught the eye of his brother.

"Make sure to tell Sawney where I am," he said, holding his face taut in spite of the pressing urge he felt to snicker. To the surprise and indignation of the others he threw down his cards and rose to his feet.

"You had better tell me first, then," replied Lorian. "And whatever you intend to do had better not take too long."

Lisandro and several others were smirking; the conclusion that they had sprung to at Mathias' impromptu announcement dawned on him: "Are you meeting someone?"

By now Mathias had stumbled through the darkness to the door, which opened out onto the glare of the street at his back. "....Meeting a *princess*, in fact."

With that closing remark he winked, and the door swung shut on the retorts of his friends.

Prior to being escorted to the reception room by a team of footmen, the rigmarole that greeted Mathias was very different to the welcome he had received when his visit was expected. He was halfway towards the palace entrance when two guards broke from their ranks to meet him. He was subjected to a brief search, a practice he believed to be reserved for guests of a less savoury nature, and he would have bet his life that Eli would be told of his visit.

When he had convinced the guards of his amiable intentions a servant was dispatched to inform Ava of his arrival, and soon he was alone in the reception room. The knowledge that the guards had stationed themselves outside the doors did not cause him any unease, and he settled himself into a stiff chair.

He could infer from his surroundings that this room was designed to impress. The opulence of the Castile family was displayed in the tapestries, shields and curious, which livened the startling whiteness of the hall at large. Through the course his time in Sawney's charge he had visited the estate of each Advisor, and was therefore desensitized to such prestige. His curiosity was piqued only by the tiger-skin rug upon the raised dais where the golden throne of the Emperor sat above the seats of his guests. The beast had been slain in honour of Eli's father when one of his ships had rescued a shipwrecked man on some forsaken island, long ago.

Despite his stalwart refusal to be intimidated by the grandeur of Delzean, epitomised by this room, he appeared uncomfortable no matter how indifferent he acted towards his surroundings.

He was unsure whether Ava would materialise any time soon, but drew a neat box from his pocket in readiness nevertheless. It contained the gift he would present to her, and a thoughtful gift it would seem, too. He had rummaged through the sitting room that morning, where he had found a worthy supply of stolen goods that had failed to sell on the market stalls allied to the Eyes. The sapphire stones in the earrings he had chosen matched her eyes, although he would neglect to tell her that he thought the cold colour to suit her equally in temperament.

Perched upon the chair he awaited Ava's entrance.

When news of the visitor was brought to the princess, she dismissed the messenger lest the nerves that inflicted her became apparent and spread amongst the servants. The brooding she felt to be of greater importance than an evening in the company of her mother seemed to grant her little pleasure. She had reverted to her commonplace position before the mirror, stroking her hair with a soft comb. Mathias had disturbed her meditations; in a panic she raced to the door and rested her head against the cool wood. She wondered if she was right to see this as the beginning of the next stage of her life: if so, there would be no more languishing in her chaotic room for Ava.

At her approach he stood to bend in a bow that was rather clumsier than he had intended. "I hope my visit hasn't disturbed you, your highness?"

Into the opposite chair Ava lowered herself, as daintily as she could manage. With a polite smile she replied: "....Of course not."

Then, her capacity to pry overpowering the advice of her governess that conversation could take other forms than bombarding her guests with questions, she asked why he so little resembled his brother. The tale of Mathias' rescue from the streets was one recounted in the city whenever news concerning the Delarus family came to light; it was indicative of Ava's wilful detachment from the outside world that she was unaware of his true parentage.

Mathias suppressed a smile, partly at her expense for being so ill-formed, but more at the abruptness of the statement itself. "Lorian is not my real brother. Sawney adopted me when I was a boy."

She nodded, but rather than listen to his response she began instead to search for her next line of questioning. The contempt that a number of noblemen felt for Sawney was powerful enough to have penetrated even her walls, and it was her wish to uncover the source of this loathing, although she had no plans to make use of the information as Chiron would have done. Her desire for knowledge was heavily diluted; she lacked the capacity to appreciate the benefits of gleaning such a token. Still, it would please her to learn more of Sawney, a man whose reputation was undeniably tainted. But she lost her chance to seek an answer, for Mathias swooped in to fill the silence.

"I brought a gift to thank you for your hospitality the other evening."

The small case at his side had escaped Ava's notice until he reached for it. Had the guards followed him into the room they would surely have stiffened as he came to his feet, and protested as he approached the princess. It was unusual for her to be left to greet a guest without the presence of an attendant, especially as the servants shared the general view of the Delarus trio evident in the city. It seemed that their attention to the royal's security slackened in Eli's absence.

She remained seated, and kept her arms stiff at her side, forcing him to leave the gift on the table beside her. He was perturbed by her reaction, but recognised it as another example of her character rather than a convoluted insult for when he looked away to his seat she seized the case and opened it.

Unwittingly, Ava had betrayed the extent of her narcissism, for the thought that the hospitality shown to Mathias had been on the part of her entire family, and therefore any gift granted in return belonged to them all in equal share, did not even cross her mind.

Mathias had no wish to sit down again; he felt the need to negate the languid, claustrophobic air surrounding Ava by staying in motion. He stood at the halfway mark between each of their chairs and rocked back and forth on the balls of his feet. This went unheeded by Ava, who had been overwhelmed by the sense of her own self-importance after discovering the sapphire earrings that the

Advisor's son thought her worthy of receiving. She would see to it that they were placed on her dressing table with utmost care by the servants. Once she composed herself, she sought Mathias and thanked him.

The smile provoked by her nervous lisp was one he failed to smother. The change in her countenance encouraged him to pursue her still further. "I recall you mentioning that you would like to visit the Zodiac Gardens more often, your highness. If tomorrow is suitable, I would be glad to escort you."

For all her rash nature, Ava was not labouring under the delusion that Mathias as a suitor would be a serious or even a desirable prospect. She was nevertheless flattered by his attention, and wished to prolong the experience. "Will you arrange to meet me here?"

"Yes," he answered, and he wondered if he had perhaps been too harsh in his judgement of her. She seemed more agreeable now, although he supposed that a thoughtful, and apparently expensive, gift would placate even the most sullen person, and he decided to wait a while longer before rethinking his original estimation.

The task he had set himself for the evening had been carried through successfully; already he itched to share this achievement with Lorian. He would need to discuss the intricacies of the plan with Sawney, too, at some point, but there was scant need for him to seek advice before it was fully-fledged. On a deeper level he contemplated whether it would be possible to keep Sawney out of the matter entirely, but he discarded this troubling notion, for what cause did he have to insinuate himself with the Castile family if it was not to advance his own?

"Should I come in the afternoon, your highness?"

Ava neglected to answer him at the sound of footsteps outwith the door, and when a maid, one of the three whose laughter had enabled Chiron to spy on Erin in the Scroll Room, broke in upon them, she was granted permission to speak before requesting to breach the silence.

From the direction in which the maid tilted her head it was possible to infer she addressed the princess. Had the subject of her gaze been looked to an as indication, one would have supposed that she was directing her instructions to the floor.

"Lady Adema has arranged for you to be served in your bedchamber this evening. The chefs await your requests, your highness."

"Send someone to ask what my mother is having prepared. Report back to my chamber."

Ava made a very good impression of one accustomed to commanding authority. She stood, and aimed a practised curtsy to her guest, then followed the servant through the open doors. She imagined that her brusque exit would humble her guest, and the effect of this would be to further enforce upon him that she was unattainable.

Mathias was left alone in the Reception Room to contend with his elation upon securing Ava's favour. He had only a moment in which to exult in this victory, for the guards now moved in, and he was obliged to vacate with as much haste as he cared to muster. He sniggered out of sheer glee as he departed, and when he remembered the meeting he was likely to be late for, he increased his pace as he passed the columns of guards denoting the path to the road.

Once in the bustling main streets, he heard the distant chiming of a bell; it resonated seven times and signified to him that the various individuals whose company he was bound to join would have begun to arrive, in accordance with their own agendas. The journey to the designated meeting place was considerable, but equipped with an expert knowledge of the city, the joint result of his prowling childhood, and the nocturnal activities after he was uprooted, he was able to wind his way effortlessly through alleys and forlorn courtyards. He found the building in a third of the time it would take any other man.

This place, essentially the headquarters of the Eyes, had been discovered by Sawney whilst leading the search for a commune of revolutionaries. He had found their den, in the basement of a great tenement building. They had ripped apart the floorboards to expose the sewers below, and had propped up a ladder in order to clamber down to hide in the deepest bowels of the city. When the rebels had created the passage, they had anticipated to immediately meet the dank, gross sludge of the churning water flushed from the dwellings above, and were fortunate to discover instead a sizeable chamber separating them from the water's edge.

The air in the chamber was rank with the stench of the fetid waste, which flowed in a path that mirrored the streets on the surface.

When occasion called for every branch of the organisation to meet, they would gather to sit in the basement, but the inner circle, comprised only of nine, always made the descent into the subterranean chamber. It was astounding that it was in such an environment, where the abundant supply of aromatic candles burning for the purpose of masking the terrific odour succeeding only in abetting it, creating heady and oppressive fumes, that the Eyes' meticulous plans were concocted. The floor was strewn with these candles, whose billows caressed the ceiling of the basement high above with a vaporous touch.

The barrel of wine that had been lowered down, with a show of care that was quite unbefitting of an inanimate object, was halfway emptied by the time of Mathias' arrival. The furniture they required had been thrown down years ago with considerably less concern, and it was through the skill of the carpenter alone that the circular table in the chamber's centre had not smashed to pieces on impact. Many of the chairs scattered across the chamber had been less lucky. Of the nine fit for occupation, there was one vacant place, next to Lorian: the seat reserved for Mathias. Of the eight men present, each one was engaged either in the discussion of the ongoing burglaries or in peering at the maps of the region complied by Sawney himself for their usage.

By Mathias' place sat the Lieutenant, Rotti Vikernes; he was alone amongst the group in having a relationship with Sawney that was akin to what others would class a friendship. Unlike the Advisor, whose infamy rendered his surname redundant, Vikernes was known by his surname alone. He was idolised by Lorian; it was his exuberance he found admirable, and in stark contrast to the sardonic exterior of his father.

The much older man beside him, the frail doctor Fernandez, concealed the malevolence of his mind beneath a feeble appearance. The reasons for his admittance to this most selective group were twofold. From his patients, deceased and otherwise, he had pilfered a lifetime's worth of gold, and was willing to endorse projects that would profit him in return for his efforts. His sharp intellect was arguably more valuable. Fernandez could uncover even the minutest flaw in their endeavours and find a means of vanquishing it. Wisps of smoke from the pipe he held in a trembling hand added to the portentous atmosphere.

Between the doctor and Conn were two soldiers deemed trustworthy enough to be put to use by Vikernes, but Conn dwarfed their importance.

It was perhaps lost on the round-shouldered brute in question, whose face was hidden by curtains of coarse, matted hair, that his name was synonymous with the underhand dealings he made his living from. He had made the acquaintance of his neighbour, Jonas Rana, when he was brought before the court on the charge of attempting to forge a will that would swindle his siblings of their inheritance.

It would be sufficient to say of Jonas that for every outward feature in which he resembled his brother, he differed tenfold in nature. It was his role to manipulate the crooks he represented into committing further illicit acts for his benefit.

Lastly, completing the circle, came Sawney and Lorian. The former was sipping from a chalice of wine and shaking his head in disagreement with Conn, though not appearing to be angry.

With such a distance between themselves and anyone who could overhear, there was no need for the group to lower their voices, and the noise had risen to a raucous din when Mathias clambered down the ladder, and was greeted by a punch on the arm from Lorian.

"Were you permitted to see the princess, after all?" barked Lorian to gain the attention of the others. Sawney turned from Conn and gave his faux-son a sidelong glance.

"Haha, of course!" answered Mathias as he took his place by the side of his brother.

This remark was met with a smirk from Sawney. Lorian began to press him for further details but the majority of the men gathered were waging arguments between themselves, rather than listening or even heeding the new arrival. It was characteristic of these meetings for discussion to turn rapidly from one topic to another, until Sawney steered it towards objects of importance.

The peculiar exchange between Lorian and Mathias, which ended with the comment "You are drawing ever closer to becoming court jester!", went unnoticed.

It was a while later, when they had established whose duty it would be to meet the thieves on their return to the city, that Sawney spoke to his son. He had observed Lorian from the corner of his eye, staring at the rat that was sniffing around the wine barrel. "I hope you are not thinking of taking it home as a pet."

Baring his teeth, Lorian grinned at Mathias. "No, I can remember what happened when *you* brought a street rat home."

"That is no way to talk about your mother," interjected Mathias. Those on either side of the small family erupted into laughter, Fernandez revealing a mouthful of brass dentures.

Chapter Eight

On the following afternoon, Lorian woke to find himself alone in the room he shared with Mathias. When he threw open the shuttered window to discover that the city streets were teeming with life, he ascertained that he had, as usual, slept through the morning on his plump-cushioned bed. He willed himself to dress and comb his hair into submission, and applied enough energy to make a futile attempt to unearth the mirror he needed to inspect his burgeoning sideburns. With no food to appease his growling stomach he was too lethargic after these exertions to do anything more strenuous than return to his bed. He was roused a full hour later, when the front door rattled on its hinges behind Sawney.

It was common practice for the leftovers from the Advisory Breakfast to be removed, after a considerable interval, to be shared amongst the servants, but since Sawney's realisation that there was almost no act too improper to expel him from the Emperor's favour, an additional practice had been established. A portion of the leftovers was taken aside by the kitchen staff when he requested it, and he was spared the expense of providing the extensive meals required to satisfy the relentless hunger of two growing men. He carried the sack, partially filled with the breakfast's remnants of breads and pastries, upstairs and poured its contents onto the table.

It would have been a stretch to consider the resultant mess appealing, but Lorian was too ravenous for such concerns and grabbed a handful of broken biscuits before proceeding to fill his face with slices of stale raisin bread. Sawney sat down on the armchair and snatched a slice from the grasp of his son, who had yet to rise from the floor.

"Tell me, has Mathias gone to the palace again?"

"I missed him leaving, but he must have. To escort Ava around the Zodiac Gardens!" answered Lorian with a snort of derision. "Did the Emperor mention his visit yesterday?"

At the sound of a booming laugh outside, both of their heads snapped around to the open window.

"Our ever-jovial neighbours," explained Sawney in a tone as contemptuous as Lorian's snort. "And no, the Emperor has little time for Ava. I suspect he is curious of Mathias' reasons for visiting her. He will most definitely desire to know of his intentions before long, though, as he would prefer to keep a certain distance between us and his family."

"Has he had any more trouble from Chiron?" asked Lorian, swallowing.

"Alas not. I have no tales of insurrection for you to regale Horizon's denizens with."

Lorian tutted in mock-disappointment whilst his father smirked at the memory of Lorian recounting how he had spread the story of Eli once calling Acario 'the fairy prince' in a fit of anger.

As Sawney paused to tear into the bread with his teeth, an infant began to cry through in the next house, the noise thin and wailing. Lorian at last struggled to his feet to lean from the window and scrutinize the scene below. There was a crowd of people waiting to enter the house of their neighbour and celebrate the birth of the bawling child. Once Lorian had determined the cause of the commotion he tugged the shutters closed. He sighed, "Sometimes I detest living here."

He hardly seemed with their living situation as he resumed eating his way through the mound deposited on the table, now gnawing a pastry with gusto.

"Understandable, but we have reason to remain. It is true that my salary could buy an estate with grounds to rival the palace, with a bedroom each for you and Mathias." Sawney paused to ensure that he had his son's full attention. "But from my experience, it is when we bask in our riches that we become most vulnerable. We have never been harmed in this house because we are living aside our comrades. In spite of my position, we are not envied or despised."

There was silence for a moment, save for chewing, then Lorian replied, "With brains like yours, father, the Emperor could be overthrown with ease."

The Advisor laughed. This, an action resembling more a snigger than a natural, healthy laugh, was the self-contained Sawney's only means of expressing amusement. "And for remarks like yours, Lorian, the Emperor could snap your neck for treason."

After a glance to ensure that the threat was made in jest – yes, his father was wearing a whimsical smile on those features so similar to his own – Lorian scoffed. He emptied his pockets of the coins he had collected from the unsuspecting drunkards in the tavern. With a scratch of his stubbly chin he began to count them. Fourteen coins were piled up before Sawney purloined his concentration.

"Speaking of Eli, are you aware of Mathias' intentions concerning Ava? I would hate to appear ill-formed if he asks. From your talk last night I would have guessed you two planned to embroil her in some sort of contrived love triangle." This notion raised another chuckle from his throat. "Unless Mathias has serious intentions?"

"He said that he longs for the day when he is fawned over in the palace and I am left to slave away for the Eyes. But he really means to prove that he is charming enough to win over even the princess herself."

It was indicative of Lorian's theatrical tendencies that he likened his employment to slave labour when paraphrasing his brother. He acknowledged readily, even boasted of the fact, that he made his living with minimum strain.

As a rule, Sawney refused to become involved in the games and squabbles of his sons, but there were occasions, such as this, when their fights were ridiculous enough to justify his interference. He was unable to quieten the temptation of encouraging Lorian to retaliate; the idea of the infantile Ava being strung along by his astute sons was far too enticingly peculiar to let pass. "Should you not show him that the girl would prefer you?"

Lorian had indeed been considering a reprisal; he was adamant, as always, that he would not be outdone. With his father's blessing, the doors of Delzean lay open to him. "Whenever he thinks to return, I will go and show him to be second best. And I'll be sure to tell him that she was *enchanted* by me and my dashing good looks."

"Then I much anticipate his return."

Even as father and son sat in scheming converse, Mathias was nearing the building, squat and unkempt, that he called home and reflecting on the afternoon he had spent in the company of the princess Ava.

The menagerie was the source of the Zodiac Gardens' magnificence; save for this the city dwellers may have turned to resent the intrusion of the rural (for all things green were of the country) upon their streets of stone.

A deer poached from the mountain slopes grazed with its companion as a lynx sprawled out on the grass of its barred enclosure, just a matter of feet away. The bears had no need to stir from the confines of their shelter to attract a crowd as their enclosure, the most sizeable of all, was surrounded by curious faces even in the lull of the afternoon. Lorian was not alone in finding them disconcerting. It was common practice for heartless children to be coerced into reform with the promise of being thrown to the bears if they did otherwise. For the enlightenment of those without cause to travel beyond the capital an array of farm livestock had been purloined, and in spring the lambs would be paraded through the gardens for children to stroke.

From the menagerie the path curved towards the aviary. The odd cylindrical building around which the cages were built was the last remnant of the quarter demolished to accommodate the gardens; it had once served as a post for the district's guards before they ascertained that it served them better to prowl the streets rather than watch from afar. Parakeets and lovebirds sang in the surrounding cages.

A nearby flowerbed had been dutifully crafted into the likeness of a peacock, with a plumage of freesias, a neck of hedge and a beak and three tufts made of red iron on its neat head. The living creatures themselves had strutted around the gardens until the temptation had grown too much for Horizon's seedier (and hungrier) inhabitants.

Although she had appeared to listen rapturously whilst they strolled through the public gardens at a pace far slower than Mathias' habitual nimble walk, with guards encircling but failing to shield them from the gawking faces of passers-by, she was neither forthcoming with ideas of her own nor appreciated the names and personalities Mathias invented for each of the enclosure-bound animals. He found it tiresome to attempt to goad someone with no forthright opinions into conversation. For a while they were seated together, the guards hovering within view, on a grassy verge sheltered from those on the main paths. There, Ava had reverted to assailing him with questions. Rather than viewing these as obtrusive, he felt her interest to be a welcome change. Presently, however, with their rendezvous behind him, Mathias was toying with the idea of forsaking his plan in the hope of avoiding another prolonged encounter with the princess. Whether she believed it was a prerequisite of her station to present herself as conceited or she merely happened to be so, he pitied her. It was foolish of him to have allowed Lorian's teasing to provoke him in the first place.

He reached his home to be greeted on the staircase by Lorian, who stretched his arms in a yawn as they converged, heading in opposite directions.

Lorian answered him before he was able to question why his brother was moving with such haste. In a bright voice as biting as a snarl he remarked, "I expect you have had time to do considerable damage to the Delarus name. It seems it falls to me to visit Ava and set this right."

In response Mathias gave only a shrug. It was crucial in these rivalries to appear as though the actions of the other were of no concern. He was left to continue upstairs and have Lorian's agenda clarified by Sawney. That his father was deriving such amusement at their expense served to intensify the black mood that had befallen him. He understood himself to be too entrenched in competition with his brother to abandon the pursuit of Ava. The notion was a comfortless one.

Ava, meanwhile, had retired to her room and was dressing in preparation for dinner. As Lorian's arrival caused an uproar amongst the palace guards, she began to ponder the events of the afternoon, flushed with her first success. At length he was shown to the reception room, where the inspection of the elaborate furnishings distracted him from his purpose: to better, or at the very least match, Mathias' progress and regain an equal footing, an equipoise.

After an interval the princess entered sheepishly and found her guest crouched on the dais, stroking the fur rug beside Eli's throne. From there he bounded towards her without an inkling of embarrassment.

She had reacted initially to the news that another man wished to visit her with elation. This had given way to nerves, and a slight sense of annoyance, as she neared the reception room, for it was more the idea of her company being desired than having to endure the presence of others that appealed. Her trepidation increased when she found herself intimidated by the elder Delarus son, whose virile features and stature were rather more beguiling, and predatory, than those of his gaunt brother. She was filled with a deep resentment when she spied him fondling her property (this was the label she bestowed upon most of Delzean's treasures), and had no wish to show him any kindness.

If she conveyed any of this hesitation to her guest, he chose to ignore it. He bowed in greeting, and said "My Lady," with a discernible effort to mimic the clipped accents of the noblemen.

He was acknowledged with a curtsy, and as he waited for the frowning girl to address him he thought her to be ill at ease, which pleased him in spite of his desire to impress her. It was Ava's wish to both forgo embarking upon an extensive conversation whilst hiding her unease, a task that would have proved difficult even for one more socially adept than she.

"May I ask why you are here, Mister Delarus?"

He laughed and bid her another sweeping bow. "Please, call me Lorian. I came here only to speak with you, your highness. Perhaps I could request a walk through the palace gardens?"

"Oh," began Ava, and extracting her gaze from his sculpted hair she saw that his eyes were of an intriguing colour, a mixture of grey and green. Coupled with the shadows that surrounded them, the overall impression was of one who had too much knowledge of the world for their years. It seemed there was no aspect of his appearance that she did not find disconcerting. "I suppose we could walk together. Come, follow me."

Her lisp had cruelly resurfaced as she uttered the word 'suppose', but Lorian, who would have lapsed into hysterics had it occurred under any other circumstances, obliged to disregard both it and her reddening cheeks, and followed her, a flock of guards on their heels, out into the courtyard.

An amoral creature, Lorian was inclined to act entirely inappropriately and had little consideration for the consequences of his reckless decisions. He was reliant on the presence of Sawney, whose imperturbable temperament was the polar opposite, or even Mathias, to anchor him, in a sense. Of this dependence on others to control his excessive tendencies he was unaware. Raised to be cunning, shrewd, and above all deceptive, his father had neglected to instil onto him the importance of self-control. It was fortunate, then, that he was keenly aware of the severity of the consequences facing his family if he were to aggravate the royals and made an admirable effort to be civil.

The gardens themselves, when they entered, were occupied only by one gardener, who hacked away at the clump of weeds that had strayed onto the footpath where Ava and her guest paced. In the light of day the grounds could be appreciated in their full splendour, but Lorian's interests lay elsewhere than in the scenery.

He asked, in an attempt to capitalize on the mutual interests they had been granted through sharing the same status of birth, whether she liked the theatre. He himself adored the spectacle of the playwrights' melodramatic offerings, although it was his preference to stand amongst the struggling, heckling crowd before the stage, rather than sit in the gallery, where three seats were kept on permanent reserve for Sawney. It was usual for him and Mathias to go alone. When Sawney accompanied them, he insisted that they enjoy the proceedings in quiet reverence, for the Advisors seated around them were ever-eager to witness his sons' indiscretions. If they were equipped with an adequate reason, it was within their power to lobby the Emperor for his discharge. He was becoming less watchful of their behaviour as the years wore on, however, for Eli was hardly likely to expel him from the palace unless the city itself threatened revolt.

"Yes, I do. We frequent the theatre in Vorcello. I have seen your father there before, in the gallery."

To her, this seemed a highly personal revelation. He was clever, in spite of his reputation, and she wanted to keep her own nature secret from him. She understood that his motives for visiting Delzean were less simple than he claimed. Her intelligence was not acute enough to make a similar accusation of Mathias; she had no suspicion of the connection between their visits.

"Oh, yes," he replied.

Lorian was growing bored of their conversation. He neglected to lead it any further along the route he had introduced, as he was occupied instead with comparing her to the few women he fraternised with. When considered next to them, she was dull to a ridiculous degree. In the company of these wenches, he would be recounting the incident that had lately befallen Lisandro. Had they been in the place of Ava, in such an illustrious garden, they would tear out the roses from the bushes by the path and take them elsewhere to sell to romantically-inclined men, and with the profits they would drink. He could see the scene in his mind's eye, a more pleasing notion that the sight of Ava and her scowl. If he moved to hold her by the waist as he did with those women, she would not hesitate to call for the guards.

On emerging from this daydream, it took him a while to recollect their previous discussion. In the meantime, together they had made slow progress through the gardens. The gateway back into the palace grounds was yet close behind them. Upon remembering his boredom, he elected to draw the meeting to its close. He firstly had to achieve some guarantee of her preference for him over Mathias, and in the hope of gaining this he asked, "Do you play cards, your highness? You would be welcome to join myself and my friends for a game one evening, if you so desired. I would protect you from any swindling."

In an defensive gesture against his familiarity, Ava had her arms folded around herself, their embrace tight.

"No, Mister Delarus," she answered, although her meaning was unclear: she could equally have been admitting to having no knowledge of card games as refusing his invitation. She was scared of him, or, to be precise, she was unsettled by the emotions that beset her in his presence. A small part of her believed that to suffer this was better than facing a sensation only of numbness. Even the power she felt in tormenting Acario cheered her little. Because of this, her current fear was a welcome contrast.

It was this desire to feel something other than a distant sense of vindictive pleasure that prompted her to agree to be instructed in the rules of his favourite games, although no specific date for their rendezvous was given, and neither, for that matter, was it requested.

She then led him in their retreat back towards the palace. He was satisfied with the outcome of their meagre encounter, so much so that he was unperturbed by the haste with which she bid him goodbye. In delight at his success, for it was without doubt a success – the efforts of Mathias had been matched, the princess' attention had been purloined, and for an hour at least, she had been his - he plucked up her hand in response, and gave a kiss to her limp, white skin.

***

On returning to her room, Ava found herself waylaid by Adema. Her mother beckoned for the princess to follow her into Ava's own bedchamber. Had any person besides her mother entered the chamber without her permission she would have fallen into one of her customary tantrums; as an alternative, the frown she answered Adema's actions with was an almost gracious greeting.

Once they were both seated, Adema began to question her daughter of the two visitors. That Ava had consented to wander the Zodiac Gardens with a son of Sawney Delarus disturbed her: she was aware of her daughter's capacity to be swayed by the words of the others, though more often than not it was to those who would do her harm that she listened. Eli's contempt for the Advisor's sons was known to Adema (she was, however, in complete ignorance of his arrangement with their father) and she wished to convince Ava to shelter herself from their influence. Her company was better deserved by the nobles, her hand in marriage even more so.

To this remonstration Ava replied: "But I would not wish to marry either of them, mother. I wish to make a noble match."

Her cheeks were flushed as she spoke. The subject of her marriage had never been broached with her mother before. The prospect of a triumphant future had at last began to draw near.

"It pleases me to hear that, Ava," Adema's relief was visible as she said, "I would have you wait for a sound proposal."

"How long would you have me wait?" Her mother's concern for her wellbeing seemed to cause only anger; Ava was sitting on the bed, her fists clenched at her side.

"Perhaps the difference of a year or two. Trust me, you will be thankful for it."

"Is Chiron engaged, mother?"

"No, and he is a year older than you. There is no reason for you to resent that you are unwed. Come now to dinner, dear."

"Mother! Would Chiron not be a sound proposal? Would you not have me become Empress?"

Ava had risen to her feet as her voice trembled. Until that day it had not occurred to her that she could marry Chiron; now it appeared that this had always been her goal, and Adema had forever moved to thwart her. It was easy to struggle against an outward enemy than contend with the limitations of her own mind.

"Since when have you wished to marry Chiron? You are not especially close."

"But mother!" Here she stamped her foot in protest, "There is no other marriage to match it. We know each other's characters already, too."

Adema paused before she replied. Her lips tightened as her face furrowed in a frown. "I see no harm in presenting this to Eli. If I do so before we dine, will you promise to calm yourself? He may have other plans for his son. I would be most surprised if he has none."

With Ava's promise secured, Adema moved to embrace her daughter before they parted ways. Ava stood immobile, cold in her arms. She was left to speculate on the Emperor's response, and called for a servant to resume her toilette before dinner.

Previous to Adema's proposition, Eli had considered the notion of marriage for Chiron. He had considered the subject on three occasions and on each occasion his speculation had led him along the selfsame trajectories of thought. No certain conclusion had been reached, other than there being no great harm in delaying such plans for the moment. Chiron had not been betrothed in his infancy because his father understood that the fortunes of the noble families were likely to surge and wane over the intervening period, as was the favour bestowed upon particular families. For his son, his successor, Eli wished a wise match. Over the past year, he had received through his Advisors the expressed wishes of noblemen for their daughters to be arranged in marriage to the prince. The promise of these offers had enticed the Emperor to grant deeper consideration to his son's case. Marriage would provide an occupation for Chiron until he assumed the throne. Yet Eli believed his son too headstrong to provide companionship to another, and too entrenched in his own amusements to divert any interest to another's happiness.

All of this was explained to Adema when she questioned whether Chiron had a waiting bride. Certain as she had been that an agreement was in place, the reasoning behind Eli's oversight was understandable. When she related to him Ava's suggestion, his reaction met her expectations. As a possible Empress she had not been considered, and Eli first asked for Adema's opinion on the matter. At her admittance that she was unsure, he apologised for his refusal to entertain the idea and remarked that the prospect of a union with Ava was far from ideal. Chiron tolerated her as a cousin but would find her unbearable as a wife. While such a passive character would be convenient at times, it was perhaps wiser to look for one with a stronger nature to match Chiron's own. In spite of these objections, out of respect for his sister-in-law Eli agreed to present the suggestion to Chiron himself. He would report to her after they dined, although Adema imagined that she would be able to guess at the outcome of their discussions from the expression on Chiron's face at the table.

After the conclusion of his fencing lesson with Leon, Chiron had begun to search through his bedchamber for the toy soldiers he had been reminded of by a remark of his cousin. Years had passed since they were thought of last. Spoon-fed all manner of exquisite ornaments, he had concerned himself little with the care of his possessions. Their sheer volume stripped them of meaning.

The prospect of their discovery amidst the general debris hidden around his bedchamber was bleak until he recalled the chest in which they were stored. The figures themselves were carved from dark wood. They were shorter than the height of his thumb, and thin, but crafted with an intricate hand. The anteroom harboured no lost childhood toys; neither did the chest linger beneath his bed. Only the cupboard remained to be searched by the time there came a knock on the door, and his father entered. His attendants were dispatched to wait in the corridor.

Eli said curtly, "I will only disturb you for a moment. Your aunt has forwarded a notion of Ava's, and for her sake I agreed to pass it along to you. Grant it as much thought as you want, but treat Ava no less well should you refuse. Is this understood?"

"Tell me what she said, father."

Chiron had been distracted somewhat from his loathing of Ava by his plans for Erin to such an extent that he had yet to ensure that his mother's gown rested in its rightful place. In spite of this omission, he was hungry for proof that his loathing was justly made. The contempt with which he viewed her behaviour had developed and strengthened over the years they had lived shoulder to shoulder in the palace.

"Neither of you are betrothed; it was her idea that a betrothal could be contracted between you."

"Father," began Chiron, before he spluttered into laughter. "You are telling me this in jest?"

He stood close in front of his father. Of the discrepancies in their appearances, the slight difference in height was the most easily perceived, followed in this instance by the expression on their faces. Both were equally rigid, for father and son alike were stubborn, but whilst Eli's countenance conveyed irritation, a vivid frustration, Chiron's eyes twinkled in his laughter. But upon hearing the next words of his father, Chiron's expression hardened, and their resemblance was near complete.

"I assure you I speak in earnest," sighed the Emperor. "Whether you wish to mock your cousin is your own concern. Adema requires an answer and a reason to comfort her daughter with. You can appreciate that to share *this* reaction with the princess would be cruel."

Eli was mistaken in assuming that as the prince was intelligent, he possessed the capacity to empathize with one he otherwise resented. His faith in Chiron's sensitivity was ill-placed, for his son had no sympathy to waste on his cousin's cause.

Although Chiron was himself unaware of this peculiar fact, as he believed the loathing with which he regarded his enemies was almost, if not precisely, even, his hatred of Ava was more malicious than that bestowed upon Sawney. The Advisor was abhorred, but unconsciously respected as an enemy, a man against whom one had to scheme carefully. Ava, on the other hand, was viewed as somehow sub-human, as though her feelings were less acute than normal in line with her intellect. In his treatment of her, he expressed no more respect than was due an animal. He endured her presence in Delzean because of an innate admittance that she was entitled to be housed there, but he believed her to be a creature beneath the rest of the family. It was this dismissal of her as a lower, unthinking entity which rankled. Such disregard for her feelings was evident in Chiron's response:

"She needs no reason other than common sense. Adema was wrong to have indulged this fantasy. As are you."

With a sigh of resignation, Eli instructed his son: "You are not to speak of Ava this evening. If this matter is mentioned, state only that you are unsure."

"But you know my answer."

"I knew before I asked - this exchange is out of courtesy, as I explained. You have angered yourself pointlessly."

It seemed the Emperor's patience had been exhausted. He sensed his son's growing temper and chided himself for misjudging his maturity.

"Not pointlessly! You are treating this idea with too much deference, father, as if you support it."

"You are being ridiculous! Stay here if you plan to continue. The dining hall will be no worse for your absence."

"Leave me, then." Chiron turned his back on Eli, and when the other man moved for the door he dropped down to his knees to scour again beneath the bed for the lost trunk.

Voices in the corridor signalled his father's departure. He sighed as he rested upon the floorboards, then sat heavily on his bed. He had indeed angered himself, but in his mind the blame lay at his father's feet for pampering to Ava's idiocy. He saw Adema as feeble in her obedience to her daughter, although such behaviour was uncharacteristic of his aunt.

The encounter had triggered something within him, or rather, it had played the role of catalyst and unleashed some feeling he had long since recognised within himself: he desired to be released from the hold of his family. He was burning with the urge for action. The need for movement made him restless and he lurched upwards from the bed.

Tomorrow he would meet Erin. He decided, as he paced across the floor to gaze from his window, the blood thundering in his ears, that he would take her from Delzean that very night. What sense was there in delaying his plan to liberate her?

Hungry, unsettled, and consumed with a preternatural agitation, he was in no condition for sleep, but with his mind set on an early rise tomorrow, for it was crucial than an alibi be provided, and if he worked quickly one could be arranged, he returned to his bed. He passed an hour lying underneath the suffocating weight of the sheets before sleep, at last, found him.

Chapter Nine

Though the night was unsettled Chiron felt himself well enough rested to leap from the bed when he first stirred, his eyelids heavy. In his haste to pass the hours before he could begin his rescue, he had neglected to change from his day clothes. This choice had served a dual purpose he had not anticipated, as in addition to sparing the need to dress, the heavy material of his coat prevented him sleeping in comfort until the usual hour when a servant would arrive to rouse him. With these precautions taken, he was free to embark upon the task he had set for himself at the crack of dawn.

The dull light of the early morning was sufficient to strain his eyes. It was with some relief that the ante-room plunged him into total darkness but the reprieve was fleeting, for the third-floor hallway was glowing with candle flames. Chiron stopped outside his door, not to take stock of any possible activity along the corridor or to listen for his father's vociferous snores, but to yawn and crack his knuckles. On a regular morning, Chiron would approach the staircase leading to the level below with every intention of sliding down the banister only to be foiled by the emergence of Eli from his own bedchamber. On this irregular morning, he was able to sit astride the banister and collide into the ornate post at the bottom unhindered. The fulfilment of his long-prevented yearning caused him to grin in spite of his fatigue and added a bounce to his step as he proceeded towards Leon's room.

It was rare that he wandered so close to the place where Ava secreted herself. The knowledge that she slept nearby reinforced the necessity of his task. He was careful to tiptoe past Adema's apartments, although he had little fear of her intervening with his plans. Her understanding of his nature was sharper than his reckoning of hers. Had Adema discovered his plan, she would have recognised the futility of impeding his progress, for it was not the maid herself which mattered but the act of wielding an influence. Chiron believed she would consider her son incapable of deception and therefore would think nothing of their arrangements. He was wary of waking her simply in case she asked whether Eli had related to him Ava's proposal – he did not trust his temper at this early hour.

When Leon's door was reached, Chiron was forced to rap upon the panels with such force he fretted the entire floor would be disturbed. His knuckles ached before he heard the merest sound of movement within the chamber. A further unresponsive stretch followed. He then started when Leon yanked the door open. His cousin motioned for him to enter with a bob of his head as his limbs preoccupied themselves with stretching.

The most striking feature of Leon's bedchamber was its very plainness. It had an air of neglect more akin to Sawney's rancid kitchen than to Delzean. His interest lay outwith the palace, and as such he was unconcerned with the upkeep of his room. The servants were diligent in their efforts but their exertions brought scant merit, for the chamber was more often than not unoccupied.

The hard backed chair by the window was cleared for Chiron. The bemused Leon settled himself on the edge of the bed and waited for an explanation to unfold.

Chiron perched on the chair and offered an apology for waking his cousin. The rapidity with which he turned to his request undermined its sincerity. He was fortunate that Leon cared more to learn of the cause for his abrupt awakening than to listen to pleasantries.

"I came to ask for a favour. Would you permit me to join you at the barracks today? You recommended that I should train there."

"....Yes, I did. The invitation still stands. But unless the notion of a military career has suddenly become thrilling to you, I fail to see why you are so eager to ask that you burst in here in the middle of the night." Leon was taken aback by Chiron's request. He seemed to be livening up; at least he was alert enough to grin at the agitated form of the younger prince.

"My other request will explain that. My father must be informed that I am sleeping tonight at the barracks. It would be even better if he is told not to expect my return too early tomorrow, either."

"But this would be a lie?"

"An alibi, yes. I will have to leave for the eleventh hour. But until then I will be yours to command with the other soldiers!"

"Am I correct in saying that you ask to visit the barracks only for the purpose of this nocturnal venture?"

The prince was hesitant in his answer but a further second of scrutiny could find no outward sign that he had riled Leon. "I would not ask to go with such urgency, no, but I imagine it will be as enjoyable and boisterous as our fencing lessons."

"I was close to taking offence when you implied that the army was important only as means of camouflaging your misdeeds," said Leon, "But if you promise to forget the cause for your visit and commit yourself, there is no reason for me not to oblige you. Where will you be leaving for?"

"I cannot tell you too much. I will call for a carriage to leave me near the palace and will make my way from there."

It had been the sum of the night's feverish mediations that he should keep the matter secret. As staunchly as he believed it was a constructive course of action, the practical-minded Leon would disagree.

"Will you ask my father for permission? We quarrelled yesterday-"

"I expected as much from your absence at dinner. Adema told me of Ava's idea; she was worried it had unsettled you. You will be glad to know that in this case my sympathy lies with you, not my sister."

"I was unsettled more by my father's involvement." Chiron was pleased by Leon's compliance, and when he yawned for the third time he elected to speed their talk along: "He would show my request greater courtesy if you presented it."

"Then I will. You should try to sleep before we leave."

Chiron apprehended the dismissal but refused to stand until he was assured: "Will you speak to him soon?"

"As soon as I can."

No further promises could be gleamed from Leon without trying his patience. Chiron crept back to his chambers, fearing, as he heard the bustle of the servants, that Eli would catch him. Even in the midst of his hunger, attending the Advisory Breakfast was an unappealing notion. As his stomach grumbled, he contemplated visiting the Breakfast Hall in case the servants had already spread the platters there, but as it would be just his misfortune for Sawney to discover him gorging on pastries, the idea was deserted.

To wait, to while away the proceeding minutes until someone, whether Leon or his father appeared to inform him of the day ahead felt to Chiron as torturous as knowing his venture to be a failure. He was anxious for progress. The toy soldiers whose search had consumed him the evening before held no interest but in lieu of a constructive occupation, he began to rummage through the cupboard in their wake. He unearthed parchment decorated with a map of those lands beyond Horizon; the study of this proved an adequate distraction.

Had the sight of the pallid sky not informed him otherwise, he would have guessed the time, after an hour's quiet waiting, to be past noon. When a servant brought the message that Eli wished him to report to the study instead of the Breakfast Hall, his first thought was that Leon's suggestion had been refused. The only cause for Eli to oppose the request was a residing anger at his son's behaviour the day before. But if he was instructed to avoid the Advisory Breakfast because his presence was irksome to the Emperor, it would seem illogical for him to be forbidden to leave the palace grounds. It was not, then, mere optimism which told him that Eli had acted before speaking with Leon. Perhaps the delay was Leon's way of punishing him for the disturbance to his sleep. Such pettiness was hard to equate with the general; the disquiet Chiron suffered was more likely to be inadvertent.

Seldom visited by anyone other than the two forced to congregate there, the study was positioned on a side of the palace largely bereft of the sun's glare. This dullness, which would fade in the late afternoon, abetted the sense of antiquity that the compact chamber exuded. The wood of the desk below the window was scarred and weak with age.

Silas arrived after receiving Eli's messenger to find Chiron already seated by his desk. They greeted each other without warmth, and the tutor began his lesson. He had been instructed to provoke thought in the prince – the Emperor wanted to remove his attention from Ava. He swept back and forth across the room as he recounted to the pupil the history of Horizon. Behind him was a bookcase stacked with calfskin bound tomes, the writings of the city's earliest scholars. The shelves had amassed a prodigious stock of dead insects.

The Emperor's ploy was in part successful. Although Chiron's mind was elsewhere than Silas' instruction (his legs twitched below the desk as he thought of the journey ahead) he had ensured by depriving Chiron of two successive meals that if his attention wavered from Erin it would fall, not to Ava, but to his stomach.

Half an hour of Silas' lecture was endured before Leon entered, unannounced and in full military attire. Silas disguised his surprise with a creaking bow, whilst Chiron beamed and came to his feet.

"Apologies, sir," the intruder addressed Silas, "With the Emperor's permission, I must purloin your pupil."

Leon's claim was too polite to refute. Silas was suspicious of the sudden, convenient reprieve Eli was granting to his son but his trust in Leon, and the lack of enthusiasm with which he had received the early call to Delzean, was such that he permitted Chiron to accompany his cousin without any enquiry.

The arrival of the Emperor's eldest son at the city barracks caused a mass upheaval of soldiers from the dormitories to the quadrangle, a red, featureless yard, where they watched the prince follow Leon onto the balcony of the larger building. Several called out to Leon in familiar terms when he threaded through their ranks and he answered them in kind, referring to people and places Chiron was ignorance of. Two men named as acquaintances of Lorian and Mathias were mentioned but they reached the office of Leon's commanding officer, Morrigan, before he could ask what the pair were reprimanded for.

Morrigan gave a respectful welcome to the prince. His manner seemed cold until Leon came forward with the reassurance that his visit would be no interference to the barracks' routine. It was his aim to present to Chiron a truthful insight into military life, an institution he was eager to share with his indefatigable cousin. He was certain that the fury which had prompted his request would be doused by the day's experience.

The barracks were surrounded by rough stone walls taller than the roofs of the enclosed buildings. Any person demanding entry would be scrutinised by the guards through the peephole chiselled into the stone beside the narrow, and singular, door. Chiron liked that the place was sheltered, a world within the city. A great number of soldiers volunteered to escort him on a tour of the barracks when Morrigan instructed Leon to relieve another officer of drill duties. The bulk of their attention was lavished on the armoury, where the prince fingered lethal-edged swords and the cannons stored therein. They observed from the balcony a troop of perhaps forty soldiers marching around the yard in tight formation.

Chiron was not permitted to be a mere observer for much longer. A sword was chosen for his use, and he was bustled into line with the soldiers, now numbering over sixty. In three lines they stood before Leon and two officers unfamiliar to the prince (one was the Lieutenant Vikernes). They first practised the correct handling of the sword, lunging forward at the command of their superiors to stab the air. Seven soldiers were then called forth and asked to fight. To Chiron's relief they were armed with wooden swords. In order for the soldiers to be victorious, they had to deliver a direct blow to the bodies of their opponents. The fight was accompanied by tremendous noise from the ranks but as the soldiers remained in line no discipline was exercised.

Archery instruction was held in the basement of the largest building. The majority of the soldiers Chiron had glimpsed around the barracks were stationed there until instructed to police the city streets (Vikernes had been delegated the task of selecting areas for the soldiers to pay particular attention to; it was rare that a small band of soldiers ever chanced by the residences of the Eyes). Every third hour, they would report to the quadrangle to march in formation but at the conclusion of the fencing bout most returned to sprawl in the dormitories. Only the younger recruits volunteered for archery practice. The general suspected that it was an interest in the prince rather than a concern for their skills in combat that prompted their compliance but made no complaint, for any enthusiasm, whatever its cause, could be put to use.

Crude, wooden targets were aligned against the wall. The recruits had not been in training long enough for their aim to be much better than Chiron's vagarious strikes. He was as astounded as the rest when he made one lethal hit to the target's centre. Leon permitted him to exult in the praise of the recruits, then proceeded to relate to them the story of his disastrous attempt at hunting. Their laughter was amiable; the prince was embarrassed by the slight but found it impossible to retain his discomfort in such light-hearted company.

From the first Chiron had found the sight of Leon interacting with the soldiers disconcerting. Other than several of the senior officers, the majority of those Leon knew as friends, or at least as trusted comrades, were strangers to palace life. It was peculiar also for the soldiers to meet his eyes: the citizens he encountered most often were of the course the servants. He wondered if he would feel ill at ease when he returned to the palace, brimming with triumph, the following afternoon and the servants diverted their gazes in veneration, or whether the soldier's regard felt more unnatural.

The notes of the city bells were clear even in that underground chamber. By the fourth strike, Leon had ordered the assembled group to replace their bows in the armoury; by the last resounding chime, the twelfth, Chiron emerged into the harsh daylight of the yard at the back of the recruits, whose panicked pace seem reluctant to imitate. They were moving with speed because the naive faith they each possessed in the army's rigorous and unfailing authority, instilled into them by both the scrupulous conduct of the commanding officers and the inflexible routine they were subjected to in their early training days, had yet to be weakened by the inability of their superiors to entirely control the soldiers, a feat made impossible by the lax structure of the institution itself.

Weapons deposited, they re-entered the quadrangle. A transformation had befallen the square in Chiron's brief absence: from the dormitories an outpouring of men had been released. They were now shifting themselves into formation, forming threadbare columns between the central buildings. The Lieutenant Vikernes and his counterparts, and Leon's fellow generals, watched the scene from the lowest balcony, whilst Morrigan and several other men clearly, if ever physical appearance had been considered an apt representation of physical fitness, long retired from practical military manoeuvres, supervised from the platform above. Chiron was accustomed to overt displays of stratification; he would not have thought to contemplate, as others had, whether this positioning was accidental.

Concerned that the presence of the Emperor's son had been overlooked in the turmoil, he lingered by the entrance of the smaller building and waited for his cousin to appear on the balcony opposite, where he was certain to obtain a clear view of the prince's position. Chiron was beginning to feel his recently acquired frustration depleting. As the rage of the previous evening had resulted in his determination to journey from Horizon with the maidservant, this lull was experienced with irritation. Before he could help himself, the blame for this waning ambition was heaped upon his cousin, but he later reflected, as the carriage transported him to the boundaries of the Advisor Arden's estate, that this accusation was highly unfair. In the past Leon had gone to admirable lengths to indulge him; he was able to appreciate that his motivations were sometimes difficult to comprehend.

He was unaware that the progress of the march had been halted until he was removed to the safety of the balcony. Leon shouted for him; he was inspecting the soldiers as he cut through their ranks.

No man under the age of seventeen was ever trusted to patrol the streets but there were a number of younger boys present amongst the soldiers, although it was hard to correctly gauge age when many appeared quite emaciated. To become a soldier was a common aspiration, but with Horizon's limited supply of men both healthy and willing (it was ironic that the healthiest group, the nobles, who had the benefit of the finest living conditions, were the least inclined to enrol for active service), it was customary for every applicant to be given the chance to prove themselves capable. Leon was always watchful of the weaker recruits – three had already collapsed on duty during his time there.

"Come, we watch from the balcony."

They moved between the last two lines of soldiers. Each was poised to march and peering across to where Morrigan stood, waiting for a signal to trigger the mass movement of the two hundred bodies gathered there, but those on either side of the hurrying princes averted their attention to bow to Chiron. It surprised him to learn that having successive columns of his subjects bow their heads in respect made the passage through the silent ranks less unnerving than it would otherwise have been.

He realised for the first time the magnitude of Leon's achievements, to have assimilated himself into a world separate to Delzean. He felt himself, for a sharp moment, inferior and then further encouraged to release Erin as he had intended. Fate had cast his role in the palace but perhaps had greater things in line for him; Erin's rescue could lead him anywhere.

Once settled on the balcony, leaning over the balustrade to study the scene below, the princes fell to the discussion of Ava. Introductions had been made between Chiron and the other watching officers but some sense of distance, of preoccupation, seemed to have been recognised in his bearing; they had grouped themselves at such a distance to allow both parties to speak without fear of being overheard.

A signal unseen by Chiron had been given from above. The soldiers were moving as one rhythmic being in step to the pulsating beat of drums. These instruments were hidden from the view of a casual observer. Chiron searched for them with a diligence true to the wilfulness inherent to his nature, though oft forgotten in his actions, until he discovered their source. The four figures standing directly beneath his own platform were concealed but the sound of their drums convinced him of their existence. The sound came from another corner, too, and he soon spotted faces through a window on the front wall of the opposite building. The distance obscured much of their forms but they appeared, the three drummers revealed by the open shutters, to be as small as children.

He interrupted Leon to inquire after them: they were indeed children, the offspring of an officer killed whilst serving in the region by the Oslen Mountains. Their mother had abandoned them as infants at the barracks' entrance with instructions that they should be cared for in gratitude to her husband's sacrifice. At seven years of age they lived entirely within the confines of the barracks. Compared to the alternatives their situation was enviable, for they were fed, housed, and kept busy with minor tasks, and if parental affection had been denied them they were at least doted upon by the soldiers.

"They reminded me of Mathias, when I first heard their story."

Leon had his cousin's full attention as the marching ceased and the soldiers began to disperse at Morrigan's command. "You cannot have heard that he came to visit my sister, have you? He escorted her to the Zodiac Gardens. Lorian arrived at the palace not half an hour after her return, according to my mother."

"Oh, no," said Chiron with a snigger, "No one had thought to share that with me."

"If they planned to capture her affections they own not the scheming charm of their father."

There was a tremor of pride in Leon's voice that Ava had proved herself immune to their flattery. He had been glad to hear that she rejected them with the wish 'to make a noble match' until Adema revealed her suggestion that she marry Chiron. Unlike the prince in question, he had found the idea as tragic as it was ridiculous. To her family the notion was laughable, but she believed it to be in the very least plausible; in this she was truly deeply misguided.

Before beginning their patrol rounds, each soldier had to sign (or make a mark that could be used to identify them, as illiteracy was common) the parchment nailed to the door of Morrigan's office. It was Leon's task to fetch the previous day's sheet and spend the afternoon checking that every man had attended to his duty. With swift steps the general drew Chiron behind him and moved to collect the parchment.

Although inferior in rank to many officers, his princely status granted him an office on the same scale as Morrigan's. To Chiron, however, who was unappreciative of the density of the barracks' populace, it appeared no larger than a servant's chamber. The room bore the homely touches missing from his palace quarters. The largest proportion of wall space was occupied with a portrait of his father. His ceremonial sword was mounted on the wall opposite. In the middle of the worn floor stood only his desk and two lattice stools, yet the room appeared to be bursting with this burden of furniture.

The window faced out upon the outer wall but there was some interest to be found in the view: a flank of younger men accused of falling asleep whilst stationed at the watchtower were being subjected to the wrath of a superior officer.

On either side of the desk the princes took their seats, speaking with emphasis over the voices of the soldiers below. Chiron would derive little pleasure from observing his cousin's work but by the other officers he would be treated as an honoured guest and permitted to do no more than admire the army's fortitude; it was preferable that he endure an hour of boredom before Leon met the twelve recruits currently entrusted to him and instructed Chiron in line with them. It had been years since the cousins had spent such a length of time together. It was the perfect opportunity to interrogate Chiron of his motives but Leon believed a more general discourse would be adequate as an insight into his state of mind.

The punishment facing any soldier exposed as a deserter was a harsh one, that a first offender could expect to suffer a dock in wages and twenty lashes for their oversight was indicative of its severity. Vikernes, regurgitating an opinion championed by others in his position, had argued that failing to serve the Emperor by preserving the peace of his domain was akin to treason and should be likewise punished. His argument was dismissed with the charge that to inflict the death penalty for such an act was barbaric. Nevertheless, it remained a subject of some contention. Leon was therefore stringent in his comparison of the signed sheet with the comprehensive list. The names of those to be reprimanded would be forwarded to Morrigan - Vikernes could be relied upon to question the effectiveness of his 'meagre' punishments.

Still, Leon was capable of holding a conversation with his guest as he worked: "Has your father told you whether he plans to withdraw Acario from the academy once he turns sixteen?"

"No, and as far as I know Acario has yet to ask. But he *has* only been fifteen for a few months."

"But I imagine he will want to continue. He can be far too passive."

There was a pause as Leon rummaged through the heap of papers on his desk, comprised largely of the patrol registers from previous days, for a spare sheet; unsuccessful in this attempt, he tore a strip from the piece in hand. One name had been found to be missing.

"Do you consider yourself passive?" asked the general.

Chiron faltered as he turned from peering out at the gathering below to answer his cousin. "I would not say that I am. Why, do you think so? If I was passive I would not dare to leave here tonight."

He was not angered by the intimation, though it did seem to have unsettled him, for he sat less comfortably upon his stool, as if tensed for confrontation.

"That is true," said Leon, focusing on his examination of the parchment, "But unless you tell why you must leave I can offer no judgement."

"You would only try to stop me." This exchange returned them to familiar ground; the prince, relaxing, began again to listen to the scene outside. It seemed the reproof was at its end, and he looked back to his cousin for amusement.

"I quite agree."

The general was prevented from replying at length by the need to decipher a particularly horrendous attempt at handwriting.

With no person willing to captivate him, Chiron had to occupy himself for the remainder of his time in the office. The open window was incapable of dispelling the building heat and the air in the cramped chamber grew thick, stale, as the hour progressed. The prince began to fidget; he sifted through the papers on Leon's desk without managing to disturb the work of the officer concerned, though not through want of trying, then navigated himself around the desk to examine the portrait of Caius.

He bore little physical likeness to either of his children, thought Chiron. But in the set of his jaw Chiron could recognise the doggedness he associated with Leon. Caius had met his demise three years before the Empress' accident. His father had explained that the man had grown lethargic of his family, of his home, and had embarked on a career of self-destruction. Chiron's memories of him consisted only of his turbulent rages, his infamous disputes with Horizon's public figures, the eccentric campaigns he presented to the army (these were among the anecdotes taught to Acario by Master Ricci), and the morning he was woken with the news of his death.

In his haste to keep Chiron from reflecting on the quarrel with his father, which would surely strengthen his resolve to depart that night from the barracks, the register was scrutinised with less than Leon's usual assiduity. In exchange for the parchment bearing the name of the lone absentee, Morrigan directed him toward the dormitory where the dozen recruits duty-bound to obey his instruction had been confined since the midday march.

Along with these recruits Chiron was shepherded into line, in the spot behind the building where he had spied upon the disgraced soldiers. Despite the manifold windows which overlooked this training ground, it was pleasantly sheltered in the contrast to the place Leon would have chosen, had such a choice been feasible: the main quadrangle itself.

With no hint of nepotism to aid him, the prince was taught the steps to the marches he had witnessed earlier. As an instructor, Leon was harsh but never strayed to become unfair. He behaved justly when he dismissed their attempts as ineffectual because he believed a mastery of the marching drill to be within the abilities of any man, not least a set of zealous youths. The process was made the more difficult by the effect of Chiron's presence on the twelve others, who had heard of his arrival in the barracks with an uprush of patriotic sentiment but had not once contemplated their being introduced to him, by the

Emperor's own nephew nonetheless, and furthermore, that the prince was expected to train amongst them as an equal. But their trepidation was perhaps diminished by that of the prince himself. His was also the harder to comprehend; while it was understandable that he should feel out of sorts among the common men, it was harder to comprehend that he felt nervous, pressured, even slighted, in their company.

At length Leon coerced their limbs to move in unison. Unfortunate, then, that at this same point, Chiron began to unbend towards his fellow pupils, a change which revealed itself to be to the detriment of their progress. In pleasing his urge to exaggerate his strides, and move with great, clumsy gestures, he proved an unanticipated diversion to the soldiers. They warmed to him considerably, and bore only the necessary concern for Leon's ensuing reprimand.

No less than eighty soldiers had crowded themselves into the hall when the disgruntled general led his wearisome regiment to dine. One meal only was afforded to each soldier (those without business in the barracks at that hour, such as those hurried from their beds by patrol duties before daybreak, were denied these provisions); its portions, though often derided by the sustenance-starved patrols, were generous in the eyes of those who appreciated the precarious state of the army's finances. Its situation was that of every institution Horizon boasted: it persevered through sheer force of will alone. The prince was gifted with a double serving, and three of Leon's underlings volunteered to fetch him water from the barracks' private well. It was a sign of the proliferate regard the citizenry bore for their rulers that eighty clamorous voices hushed to a whisper for the duration of Chiron's presence.

His thoughts had turned full-circle to fixate upon Erin. For the remainder of the evening he was only a partial visitor, as his mind wandered elsewhere, in regions by the city's edge.

The march to mark the sixth hour was delayed as a custom until the chimes rang for the seventh. On the last note the soldiers began again to march to the sound of the drums, among them the dozen youths instructed hastily by Leon. Their deficiencies of movement, well disguised by the crowd, were discussed by the princes on the balcony. Chiron was unabashed by Leon's comment on his behaviour, which, despite its intention only to usher him towards reflection, was delivered in a tone quite contemptuous. The general was not vexed enough for there to be a question of forgiveness. Before he uttered the words he regretted having to chastise his cousin, as he wished the prince's experience to be wholly positive for reasons both numerous and complex, but for the sake of his pride, the reproach had to be made.

The hours before Chiron's departure were dwindling. He followed his cousin to the offices of the high-ranking officials, beginning with that of the Lieutenant Vikernes and concluding in the rather larger domain of Captain Morrigan, in order to pay a respectful farewell to each. These formalities were completed in as brusque a manner as they were able. At the ninth hour another marching drill commenced. The count of both observers and participants had depleted as those conscripted to patrol in the small hours retired to sleep in the dormitories, and the officers without obligation to remain took belated leave of the barracks. Afterwards the twelve soldiers were sought again. Such a number could not be accommodated in the minute office of the general. Instead they were taken to stand in a shaded corner, where Leon detailed to them the conduct they were to suppress whilst patrolling, those stretches where conflict was most likely to be encountered, and the procedures for placing a citizen under arrest. To conduct a lesson in swordplay would have been his preference but the youths were to be escorted through the city that night as apprentices of the patrol headed by Vikernes and needed to be prepared, as the Lieutenant would quiz them tirelessly. While Chiron showed an interest in the workings of the city guards, information he would have otherwise had little cause to know, only fragments of it were retained as he rehearsed his instructions for the carriage-driver. He was assured of the clarity of his instructions to Erin. The uncertainty lay in the journey ahead and the reception of her family.

A carriage was soon called to return him to Delzean. He knew from the anxious glance of his cousin that he was flushed with anticipation; he felt himself alert with nerves in spite of the day's exertions. The driver was persuaded firstly that he was due to attend the Advisor Arden's house, and secondly that it was desirous for the palace to be avoided. The man seemed understandably reluctant to abandon the prince, who was, save for the driver, unattended, to the street as he requested. He was persuaded by his passenger's resolute refusal to alight elsewhere.

It was truly dark by the time of his descent from the carriage. The hours of endless sunlight were becoming a feature of past seasons. Sounds from the district behind could be heard but not distinguished; he guessed the streets would quieten as the night progressed. Although the wind was still, it was bitter, and no one native to Horizon had much tolerance for the cold. The darkness spared him the notice of the palace guards as he walked from the road to the grounds of Arden's estate. From his home he was now shielded by a wall, from the sight of Arden's servants he had only his wits for protection. He walked by the side of the wall, feeling with one hand, after a distance, for the gate, despite remembering it to be further along. Before he passed the Advisor's house he had restrained himself from running in case of his movement attracting detection; with the main obstacle evaded he burst into a sprint, growing warm beneath his coat.

The immediate pursuit prevented his thoughts from leaping to the encounter ahead. When it was found, the gate was eased open without reserve. He had forgotten, since his last venture, the clump of trees that remained to be battled through. At this early stage of the journey he sustained three injuries, his hands cut in retaliation as he forced apart the ensnaring branches.

Already the form of Erin was visible. In her hand she held aloft the branch left as a marker of their meeting place. She wielded it as a weapon, seemingly to ward off the approacher – she feared the offer she had thought whimsical to be a trick, a trap to reveal and exploit her disloyalty. The branch was lowered as he drew closer, and when he at last staggered out onto the grass, dropped entirely. Her attitude to his endeavour had undergone a slight alteration in the ensuing days: keener was her longing to be reunited with the family left behind. Assimilating herself into the palace staff had been a struggle;

perhaps she was unsuited to labour in the city. Indeed she found the Empire's capital foreign, the temperament of its inhabitants strange, including that of its ruling caste, if the prince was trusted as an indication.

"You came," exclaimed the prince, struggling against the urge to whisper instead as the darkness stretched silent and taut around them, "I should have given you warning: we leave tonight for your home."

This change of mind was not altogether unexpected. There had been ample time between this meeting and their last for Erin to ponder the endless possible outcomes; in trying to second guess the prince she had speculated more than once that he would be too impatient to delay what he termed her 'rescue'. She could not help but be thankful for his erratic venture. The idol had been carried on her person every waking hour since the theft, at night slipped carefully beneath the bed; tonight it was tucked inside her apron, ready to be presented to her family in the morning. That the journey with the prince was likely to be awkward was a trivial concern. Even if he became disillusioned with the pursuit and turned back to the palace, she would be determined to press onwards. Her knowledge of Horizon was too limited to fully appreciate the dangers of a solitary passage through the city at an hour when such men as Lorian and Mathias stalked the streets.

In assent she nodded, but admitted to being uncertain of the route to her home. Of her lonely journey to the palace she could recall only the passage to the city boundaries with any clarity. Beyond that the onset of dwellings, prodigious in number, had set to confuse her, envelope her, and the path outwards was forgotten. Erin's family had been no exception to the tradition that every peasant should pay homage to the capital on the solstice days but her mother alone had attended, fearing some tragedy would befall the farm if they absented themselves. This attachment to a settled home was inherent in the land's scattered occupants, and was perhaps symbolic of the search for stability in light of the Empire's relative youth and obscurity.

The prince, for all his ancestral bonds with the city, was no better versed in its roads than she. But he had a sufficient grasp of its topology to know of the duplicate watchtowers stationed near both of the principal roads. This posed the greatest threat to their plans, but if capture was evaded, the maid would be able to direct them from the boundaries onwards. The most apparent difficulty, then, lay in reaching whichever of the roads would project them onto the desired lands. Chiron had to rely on conjecture to ascertain how arduous it would be to negotiate his city without being recognised. The most pressing difficulty, however, was to determine which of the two roads needed to be traversed.

"Are you able to remember whether you crossed the river?" asked the prince, at last succumbing to the call to whisper.

If such small details had been perceptible in the darkness he would have been amused to observe that even as they had embarked on a journey that defied all propriety she avoided his eyes. The habitual gesture was impossible to disregard.

Again she nodded, and taking her silence as his cue, Chiron turned to grapple for the second time with the trees shrouding the gate. Erin walked immediately behind him; he could feel her heavy breaths as she struggled, the jagged branches clawing at her skin.

In his visions of the night's trial, he had envisaged a heated discussion taking place between them as he learned of her history, and sermonized on the reasons for his intervention, his belief that misery should not be willingly endured. In her own artless terms Erin contemplated, as they traced a path by the side of the garden wall, whether he was in fact acting in response to a feeling that the circles in which people moved should be limited, that he sought to expel her because she was not of Horizon. If Chiron had attempted to preach his reckoning of their undertaking he would have found himself challenged.

Neither prince nor servant felt compelled to express their reflections, recognising their differences to be such as to render understanding between them flawed. They shared no common platform of thought.

Their escape from the vicinity of Delzean was conducted in the uttermost quiet. The larger district in which they were still entrapped housed the gentry, and could be relied upon to be void of any hindrance to their advance, other than the possible appearance of a carriage. In contrast to the reassurances Leon offered his father, Chiron had been told that certain streets existed where no soldier ever walked on patrol. He expected that although the estates of the Advisors and their ilk were the grandest, the most valuable, the possessors of objects desirable to any trespassing hand, it would be the districts of the poorest breed that were under the strictest guard. The residents were guarded in the sense that they were protected from the consequences of their own base practices. As within these regions Chiron would be careful not to linger (his urge to escape the infamy of recognition would allow him to do nothing else), Horizon's guards were discounted as potential saboteurs.

A constant source of life, the river was at its deepest when detected by the keen senses of the palace strays. They ran down adjacent pathways until the voices of those lingering still by its edge were lost. Chiron became aware that he trembled in his fear but cursed the failing of his courage rather than the stoking endeavour itself. Erin was yet to earn his trust; he suspected, in the event of their attack, she would desert him and flee with the spoils of her employment.

The estates of the landed families faded into insignificance as together they stole across one of the sturdier bridges linking the water's sunken banks. Notwithstanding the gulf between them in mind, in matter they appeared to draw continuously closer. Enigmatic as the prince seemed, Erin wished to stay beside the only being she saw as familiar, whilst the youth himself felt it his duty to shield her.

The full moon glistened above them in a cloudless sky; beneath it, Horizon shivered.

Inside the decaying kitchen of his modest home, Sawney scolded a messenger for his late report on the convoy expatriated to the mountain slopes. Fernandez oversaw the exchange without interference but scrutinized every stuttered apology from the messenger, alert for any hint of betrayal. His caution had been provoked by the man's flustered entrance into the sanatorium. He had claimed his agitation to be the result of fatigue but to accept this unconditionally would be to ignore the experience of his dealings with like-minded men: obedience would always come second to the interests of the self. In time the messenger was proved to be honest but Sawney's reprimand remained deserved.

Had Sawney been privy then to the enterprise in which his sons were currently entangled, he would have chided their tenacity; when the prize of their labours was presented the following afternoon he commended this same quality. Mathias had clambered onto the balcony of the courthouse in the wake of his brother, where now both crouched in the shadows as the night watchmen prowled. In feigned innocence of the effect such information would reap, Jonas had told them of a blade, lethal in edge, rare in craftsmanship, which adorned the judges' chamber. Unable (or unwilling) to resist the urge to pilfer the weapon, it was merely a matter of them acting with stealth.

Leon slept meanwhile on the floor of his office. Less comfortable even that the stifling dormitories, there he was at least able to lend his energies to considering the subject of his cousin without disturbance, before easing into a sleep untroubled by such concerns. He grew deaf to the tumultuous activity of the barracks, pursued long into the night. His thoughts of Chiron's plans did not extend to the prince leaving the city, unbidden, and in the company of a servant girl.

The youngest prince was denied a sleep as restful as Leon's; his dreams were disturbed by the likeness of his mother. Acario yearned to struggle from his sheets, storm through the palace until he reached Ava's chamber and order her to tell his father of their oath, tell anyone she pleased, and he would shoulder whatever punishment, as long as he could taste freedom, however fleeting. These dreams were the fruit of an insipid evening spent in the reception room with the princess, enduring her reminisces on the visits of Lorian and Mathias.

Whenever a clamouring of men's voices stirred him into agitation Chiron altered their path, recognising the centre of these raucous gatherings to be the taverns. Thrice did silhouetted figures emerge from nearby buildings before they could conceal themselves but if the spectacle of the pair in discrepant attire aroused interest, it was not to the extent that passers-by were inclined to gawp or berate. The prince felt his chest ache with nerves; the sensation was in some sense exhilarating.

Erin walked as Chiron's shadow as they trod down a winding road, the apartments on either side shuttered and blind to their approach. They had advanced without rest for close upon two hours when they were forced to sprint into the shelter of a doorway. A mass of soldiers returning from their patrols passed on oblivious, both to the proximity of the prince and the cajoling of the men behind them.

Their progress was already laboured by the need to skirt around the crowded districts, hence their numerous and swift changes of direction; the wait for the group to move beyond sight was almost unbearable.

Only a scarce word had been shared for the duration of their travels, but in that shrouded corner Chiron began to whisper phrases intended to comfort. He asked how long she could endure without resting. As the prince had risen early in a state of agitation and suffered a day of exertion, he was the more fatigued of the pair, despite Erin's spirits being somewhat dampened by the knowledge that her home lay an exhaustive distance from the city's edge.

By slow, circuitous degrees the boundary came nearer. The watchtower was spied while they were yet far enough distant to be overlooked by the guards. Chiron was able to keep them on the side of buildings removed from notice.

Occupied from the stroke of midnight onwards until the sunrise, the guards' platform stood almost twenty feet above the soil, built atop a construction of stone. It was roofed, and boasted a red flag to signify that the city was on alert, that those caught meandering in the guards' vicinity without apparent reason would be questioned. Had invasion from another power been a viable threat Horizon's defences would have been strengthened; in practice, the tower served merely to intimidate any planning to commit a nefarious act in the area.

Experienced soldiers only were trusted to stand in the towers, and received instructions on the rigid conduct they must obey: to be ever watchful, silent, and to report any fellow guard who dared to sit down, or even to fall asleep. These rules were followed with an obsessive, fervent passion by every freshly-promoted soldier for a period usually extending to a month. Afterwards, a resurgence of their native indolence was experienced, and they guiltlessly allowed their diligence to evaporate to the point of calling out warnings to those wandering at night if they failed to hasten towards their homes but rarely climbing down to make chase. The prince would have taken bolder steps to exit the city if he had been aware of this negligence. His perception of the watchtower was of a barricade against all malevolence, all diversion to the norm.

Tonight the guards posed a particular threat, unique to Chiron. Four of them leaned against the balustrade, and half of that number belonged to the Eyes – the soldiers conscripted by Vikernes. To the wild children scampering between the houses these men were as unimportant as any other adult, and the vagrants likewise ignored them. Indeed, to those sleeping on the balconies (by removing themselves from the ground they became less of a target for thieves) the unanticipated decline in heat was a greater threat. But if these men had devoted their best efforts to the task they could have skilfully cornered and captured the prince. Being learned in Sawney's dislike for the youth, and in their duties as watchmen, they could have interrogated him and without doubt gained a morsel of information, given consciously or otherwise, to use to their advantage.

That the soldiers had no cause to scour for the prince played to his benefit. In their ignorance Chiron was able to pass, and was noticed only by the inattentive soldiers when he and Erin were little more than distant figures on the road. Had they been aware of the prince's flight, a degree of surreptitiousness quite beyond his power would have been called for.

Once they had fled fully from Horizon's borders into what could rightly be termed the wilderness, a sense of triumph possessed them, and had the darkness not been so dense as to make stumbling an inevitability (Chiron held up a hand before his face and had to squint before he could distinguish it), both would have chosen to run in place of their timorous steps.

Chapter Ten

The exertions of the previous day were soon forgotten in their detail, but Chiron was reminded by the ache of his legs of the distance he had travelled, however dreamlike had been his perception of the passage. Although an hour fled without the prince and maid sharing a glance, neither turned their attention to reflection. Their limbs heavy with fatigue, they moved at the pace of sleepwalkers. At last they agreed to rest. Chiron's sole thought was of the dread he feared he would feel upon waking: to not suffer a wrench of regret at having wandered so far from the palace would be miraculous.

Tormented the night's length by the wind, which cut through him as he lay unprotected by flanking walls, Chiron greeted the morning from the knoll he had supposed secluded enough to shelter a prize as worthy as himself from the prowling men of his imagination. The dawn's light revealed it to be a field as open as the road. He was as drowsy as if he had lain awake the night in rumination, and said little to his companion. Erin took the lead when they at length began to walk, recognising the place to be familiar. Her trepidation was overshadowed by the thought of seeing her family and the prince may as well have turned back for all the consideration she granted him. Whatever nerves they both felt were now bolstered by hunger. Their thirst was endured until Chiron stumbled into a stream.

They were in agony of spirits for the final stretch of their journey, until Erin pointed to a cottage, huddled beneath a spreading tree, alone on the edge of an orchard. Her village, such as it was, was divided by family loyalties: for close upon seventeen years she had lived there with her mother and brother, and for twelve years her sister, and of the forty scattered neighbours only eight were closely known to her.

To be surrounded by the residents of Delzean without reprieve was to feel oneself limited, for it brought no advantage to the prince to look solely upon his own likeness. But it did not follow, necessarily, that to stray beyond his circle would counteract this tedium. Chiron already believed his venture to have backfired, for in rescuing Erin he had disturbed himself. He brightened when she described, as they approached the cottage, which seemed the size of a stable, how her mother had been honoured by her employment in the palace, and he wondered how his arrival would be received.

No introductions were made, however, or at least none that he would deem fitting. In a plain chamber he encountered mother, brother and sister all; the eldest a stout woman of middle years, in whose expression he met the twin of Erin's obstinacy, the brother whose name he failed to master, a man both taller and older than he, on whose labours the family depended, and the sister, Emilia. From the first Chiron was compelled to compare her favourably with the others. Her manner and figure were those of an unassuming child. There was a quality of indescribable tenderness in her voice when she remarked on the privilege of his visit, even if she only parroted the phrases of her mother.

The brother bowed to him when his identity was explained (the truth of the story, which he dictated without revealing any uncertainty on his part, was verified by the idol Erin placed upon the altar, where it overshadowed the paltry libations and suffered the family's inspection) but made no other motion, save for staring upon the face of his sister. Had she been unaccompanied by a prince, her return would have been greeted with shame. Their lives were centred upon Horizon. Despite their distance from its border it featured daily in their thoughts, and Erin's expulsion from the great steering city of the Empire would have been viewed as a disgrace to their number.

Her mother was nonplussed, understandably, and felt unable to show affection for her daughter when the circumstances of her return were so odd. She addressed only Chiron but had heard the rumour that servants of Delzean were forbidden to look their masters in the eye, and while she was too poorly practiced to avoid his gaze entirely, her stilting delivery was further retarded by her attempts. There was some confusion regarding the emerald-eyed idol, for if it had not been stolen, and how could it have been, if Erin was not imprisoned in irons, it stood to reason that it was a gift.

Erin's mother asked what endeavour had caused the maid to be deserving of such notice. She almost seemed disappointed to hear that it was given to be sold to support them in lieu of Erin's employment abroad rather than as a reward. Her reaction to the prince was weaker than it would have been had her knowledge of royal conduct been sufficient to appreciate that such an escort was somewhat unusual. The signs of disturbance others would have perceived were overlooked by this peasant, who saw not the heavily-lidded eyes and twitching fingers, but only the title of 'prince'.

"Where are your servants?" was the first question Emilia asked of him.

Unlike her sister's, the boldness she displayed seemed the fruit of a natural innocence, a youthful vigour. Whilst in Erin's peculiarities of character he had sought amusement from his own ends, in Emilia he saw an object to preserve. That the sisters stood but inches apart invited him to compare the two. Chiron's judgement fell in Erin's favour; the tanned skin that aged her sister was healthy on her frame, svelte even for her age. Her feet, bare as the cottage interior, were freckled with mud. Of the impression he gained of her face, the strongest image was of her hair, red, long and curled as her sister's. In her he had uncovered the antithesis of the pampered Ava. He consented to answer her, with patience verging on condescension.

The discovery of Emilia was not quite enough to smother his mounting unease. He stood among strangers, and more than that, had brought himself into their den. It was his own recklessness that had taken him thus far. This thought was borne of fear but was met with an unexpected surge of pride: his voilition alone had made these events possible. His decision to release Erin from Delzean was credited to him alone. The nocturnal course through Horizon's streets was his, as was this reunion. He could make allowances for the coldness in her brother's reception. It was only surprise, and likely abashment, which prevented him showing the proper diligence to the prince's comfort. He welcomed this turn of heart. The success of his adventure was as hard to determine as it founding cause. This, for the present, played to his advantage. He could consider the successful deception of his father to be the objective if he chose, and feel the flush of achievement.

Erin desired that he take his leave; such was her happiness to be home she wanted no reminder of her time elsewhere. The corridors of Delzean were already fading from memory. If the theft of a treasured artefact resulted in her release from all future labours, with the exception of lending strength to the local harvest, she was willing to accept the prince's behaviour as balanced. From the look of her brother she understood him to be alarmed. His concern lay with her role in the proceedings, as opposed to that of the prince. He appreciated that the youth held in his veins the right to order them to hang if they displeased him, but this power could not quite make manifest here. Their home was too far removed from the palace for his importance to be more immediate than Erin's, their daily companion. An interrogation was in order, between brother and sister. Her side of the tale would be heard. It would likely agree with the family's view of the city, while Chiron's story had shaken their estimations.

Her mother ushered the prince outside, and asked Emilia to have the courage to join them, which served better to convince the young girl to leave her elder siblings alone than a strict command, and in their absence Erin spoke freely to her brother.

Accustomed to the stone and cobbles of Horizon, Chiron saw the lands of the country as vividly green and lush, despite the dryness of the grass, parched until it neared the stream. The air as he stepped out into the open was hazy and thick with heat. When they had walked some distance forward Chiron turned to look upon the cottage. It lay in the shade of a swaying willow tree, which at once reminded him sharply of the distance between himself and his home, and for the same reason, that it resembled the flourishing trees of the palace gardens, endeared the place to him.

From his reverie he was wrenched to answer on his wellbeing. As a gesture of politeness he asked the older woman of their lands and neighbours and affected an interest in his surroundings that his companions took as insincere. He understood the offer of a tour to be a ploy to question Erin, but it was simpler to become immersed in their play-acting than to admit that which he had omitted from his version of Erin's rescue, that he first intended to seek her out as an antidote for his boredom, and that his resolve had been propelled, if not ignited, by the wish to spurn Ava's advances.

Emilia studied him without reserve. Clothes as fine as his were new to her experience. When he felt the weight of her curious gaze, he smiled. His voice weak in his longing for water, he allowed the conversation to lull, preferring just to enjoy the company of the girl before making his homeward journey. It was fast becoming apparent that reaching the palace without guidance or sustenance would mean a struggle against not only his own will but against the threat of detection, which was doubled by the morning's light. In point of fact it would be evening by the time he crossed Delzean's threshold, and the chances of escaping notice in the day's liveliest quarter were slender.

The grass around the cottage was enclosed on its eastern side by the orchard, in the depths of which Chiron glimpsed two figures running as if in play, and on the other by a field, which was itself bordered by a knee-height wall of stacked stones. In the hills beyond there lived the bulk of the settlement, but as word of their esteemed visitor would not spread from Erin's home until the evening none ventured forth to meet him. The view of the orchard, field and placid peasants gratified Chiron's romantic opinion of city-less life.

Erin's mother asked after the health of his brother, father and aunt in turn; the dates of their birthdays were known throughout their territories, and to demonstrate this knowledge was believed by the woman to be a show of patriotism. He was glad to answer when she made no mention of Ava. It was curious to hear of the qualities the subjects attributed to his family. He wondered if the inactivity of Ava was widely known. It pleased him that she was perhaps below the notice of the peasantry.

They were interrupted by Emilia's shout of delight as she crouched to pick up some trinket she had spotted in the grass. She rose again with a ring clutched in her palm. It was the likely property of a travelling merchant en route to the city, who often conducted the sales of similar tokens, such as the idol Erin was now obliged to supply for barter, although it would be among the most exquisite treasures ever sighted in Horizon's markets.

The merchant would have hardly lamented the loss of the ring that Emilia now held up in offering to the prince. The band was silver-coloured beneath the dirt which clung to it in swathes, and thin. It was the perfect size to fit with any comfort only upon his smallest finger. She presented it in exchange for the return of her sister and the gift of the idol; it was a mark of her ignorance of that gift's true value that she thought the ring to be a fair tribute.

Chiron was neither annoyed nor perturbed to receive such an inconspicuous return for his efforts. Instead he plucked it from her outstretched hand and wiped it on his blazer. Once clean, though it remained rather dull, he held the band out to admire it and apparently satisfied, bowed to his benefactor in the manner of a doting parent affecting gratitude to a child. The satisfaction he took in the gift was to an extent unwarranted, but Emilia made no protest when he lavished words of thanks upon her, taking comfort in a small pleasure in the midst of uncertainty.

In the cottage behind them brother and sister were exchanged in a discussion of a circumstance quite beyond the comprehension of either. Erin had robbed the palace of its treasure, had been observed in this practice, stalked through the grounds by the prince and then confronted in the gardens. There he had spoken to her as she could choose to abandon the drudgery of servant life. He asked of her plans for the idol but not for the reason which drove her to theft, preferring to make his own assumption. Erin expressed her fear that the prince's temper would turn, and herself and the idol would be hunted by his guards (she imagined that the idol would be treated with utmost care when it was captured, while she would be dragged to Horizon by her hair). Her brother countered that however Chiron twisted events he would yet appear in part responsible.

It seemed that whatever strangeness had led to Erin's homecoming, they were best placed to simply accept that consequences. It remained apparent to both that the continued presence of Chiron on their land was beneficial to no one and they contrived how best to make him scurry homewards. Erin supposed it unlikely for him to linger in a place he found so discomfiting; he would soon desire his native comforts.

Her hopeful estimation was correct: Chiron itched to return to Delzean. He fingered the ring and slipped it inside his pockets, and vowed to seek Emilia out at the earliest opportunity. The girl would not be quickly forgotten. Indeed, as he jogged along the road several embellishments were added to her character until she became at once the very opposite of Ava's indolence, her sister's staunch obstinacy and the infuriating age of the Advisors.

He recalled scant detail of her house, and his understanding of her family was piecemeal; two faults he desired to fix, yet the longing to leave was stronger. Even if he had been offered food he was trained to refuse it (the Emperor required every dish brought to the royal table to be tasted; the kitchen staff seized upon this permission to sample the chef's delicacies with aplomb), and while he could suppress the need to walk on familiar terrain the ache of hunger was harder to ignore. That he had the excuse of physical exhaustion was some relief; it spared him the need to admit to his cowardliness.

An hour had sounded in the temples of Horizon since he had followed the maid in approach to the cottage. He judged the day early enough to occupy a safe passage to Delzean before the streets were fully roused. To Emilia he presented his profuse thanks. Had they not been in the vicinity of her mother an invitation to visit him in Delzean would surely have been issued, an extremely foolish notion, for if she managed to convince the guards of the validity of her claim the fact of her arrival would trickle through the palace. How could he explain their acquaintance without revealing her relation to Erin? He would be fortunate not to be connected with her absence.

To her mother he bowed. Although he wished to know for certain whether she was pleased to receive her daughter, he had not the boldness to break the barrier between them. She was stupefied, at first, but then directed him towards the road. He was a touch perturbed that her countenance lightened when he announced his departure. His annoyance at this discourtesy was not such that he turned against Emilia; if she hadn't been hurried away he would have asked her to walk with him further.

He watched the mother usher her inside without a backward glance and wondered if they thought him mad. For a while he stood there, too warm inside his clothes and too thirsty to be comfortable, and observed the cottage. Through the window thrown open to the heat he could distinguish the form of Erin. To her brother she held up the idol and together they leant towards it. He waited but saw no hint of Emilia.

Summoning the little energy he had left to invigorate his limbs, he began his solitary trek home. He struggled to find the road as he was directed. When at last it was found he sank to his knees in exhaustion. Before him it stretched indeterminately into the distance, a long, straight, endless path. It was a great encouragement when he clambered uphill a league later and the expanse of the city was revealed.

As he walked ('trudged' might have been the more appropriate term for his slow, pointed steps along the road, which ran onwards and onwards as if apathetic to his plight) he remembered the meeting of a few days past. He struggled to acquaint the fatigued Chiron of the present moment with the idealistic prince who had cornered Erin in the gardens.

Erin's family were unlike the set of forceful parents he had envisaged but it seemed strange that they would send her so far away; perhaps he was close in his assumption, for he could at least be certain that she was unhappy in Delzean. It occurred to him that she could have been sent there for the purpose of theft, to profit from the Emperor's trust and to later mock the family's ignorance when she deserted the palace, laden with jewels at their expense. This notion he discarded with a shudder.

His wish to instigate, to influence, had been fulfilled. This small victory was enough to add heart and hasten his progress. He would not dwell any deeper on the matter until his journey met its end. There was no sense being distracted when he attempted to navigate the streets of Horizon.

His spirits failed him when the midday sun rose, and found him still battling with the road. He encountered three groups of travellers: the first, a man alone on horseback, from whom he had hidden, flattening himself behind a tree near the roadside, the second, a carriage heading in the opposite direction, Horizon-bound, drawn by an elderly man, and the third, a merchant caravan. From these two he opted to remove his shoes and blazer, and so pass them as a fellow peasant. His longing for water was palpable.

In his weariness he at last drew close to the city. Now he faced another stretch of the journey that could swiftly prove itself the more dangerous – to repel the attention of three people had been taxing, a trial to his nerve. Once inside the city boundary, he could easily have to fend off the attentions of three hundred. That he was spared the threat of the watchtower was a feeble consolation.

His blazer he carried over his arm still as a safeguard against recognition, not as himself, for although his likeness was widely known he doubted that any citizen could distinguish his face in a crowd, but as one with such an ample stock of wealth that he might provide a fair target for quick-fingered thieves, but he had no qualms about replacing his shoes.

Only because Horizon's furthest reaches were unfamiliar did he find the initial transition into the city daunting. The noise of the streets grew in the slightest, most imperceptible of intervals, so that when he emerged from the first quarters, occupied largely with workhouses, the domain of weavers, carpenters and fletchers alike, the prodigious chorus of voices that accompanied the bodies crossing through the market streets came as little shock to his ears, though his other senses, notably sight and smell, were somewhat offended.

Chiron would have been better aided in his quest if there existed some precedent from which he could learn. If another prince had gone before him to troop unaided through the selfsame streets, he would have gleaned from this example whether it was wiser to quicken his step until the limit of his strength was tested, and to keep his head down, as if to pass unseen by all, or to attempt to move as one of the peasantry, at a calmer pace. The latter was no doubt kinder to his frame, which ached with hunger, thirst and disquiet, but the former was concurrent with his will to curtail the torment. Later he would wonder if it was strange for a prince to view the crossing of his kingdom in this light.

For his present concern, the prince decided upon an admirably astute approach: whenever he felt the number surrounding him sufficient to disguise his hurried flight, he would race as if pursued by Silas. Had his tutor been twice as agile the speed at which Chiron raced forward would perhaps have been better illustrated. But on the narrow roads overlooked by residences, he had to slow his pace lest he aroused the suspicion of those with legitimate care to linger on those streets.

He reached the bridge within a minute of the time it had taken himself and the maid to travel the same distance. Acario was the object of his thoughts as he jogged across the water. His excursion with Erin he opted to keep secret from his brother, while his journey beyond the city and his acquaintance with Emilia would be revealed. Why he elected to share his relations with one sister but not the other was too complex a question to be dwelled upon then.

He crept though the streets on the bank opposite, into the shadow of the palace district. Ahead he spied three men clad in fatigues. The practice of marching drills had rendered these soldiers incapable of walking as individuals; their movements were so closely matched Chiron would have been nonplussed not to hear their footsteps sounding in synchronism on the road. From the fervour evident in the swiftness of their progress (they scanned each window and every face for signs of deviance), he deduced them to be soldiers freshly embarked on a patrol. As the hours bore on they were apt to station themselves somewhere an adequate view could be commanded and converse amongst themselves.

Chiron found himself drawn to them. For the army he felt a new affection – they were an extension of his father's authority, they were compliant with the proper order of things. The minds of the soldiers he could read, so he believed, while those of Erin and her family were as unfathomable as the depths of the river. Yet he had to resist the urge to run towards what he recognised. If he announced himself to them a barrage of questions would follow. The rumour that he had wandered the streets alone would surely reach his father. Until then he had forgotten that Leon had lied on his behalf. He was implicated in any punishment Chiron faced.

The prince was forced to turn on his heel, taking care to move no faster than the others on the street, all of whom seemed intent on barging into him as he sidled past. In his panic he was unable to determine whether those he passed looked into his face, he mistook casual glances for starts of recognition, and when he slipped free from the soldiers into the parallel street, his heart was hammering.

Delzean's forecourt was decorated only by the soldiers fixed in lines descending from the palace doors. No statues to rival the spectacle of the gardens had been installed as the azure dome that crowned the entrance hall harboured all attention. It was the brightest shade of azure imaginable and the only feature of its kind in the Empire.

When Chiron strode between the guarding soldiers, hoping to create by his even pace the illusion that his solo return from the barracks was in no sense abnormal, they each bowed their heads and permitted him to pass unquestioned. He prayed Leon's alibi had held thus far.

The guards stationed to open the doors for those permitted entrance were able to observe the sickly cast of the prince (his feet, inexperienced in such exertions had started to bleed before he even entered the city) but made no remark. As Chiron refused to suffer a troupe of servants as personal attendants, he was at least spared their well-intentioned fussing.

Inside, he found Leon. He resented this call to report on his behaviour; the reality of his departure pleased him less to dwell upon than the result, the meeting with Emilia. His cousin stood across the room, humming under his breath. Chiron would have thought from his silence that he had entered unnoticed but it became apparent when the general met his eyes, nodded and folded his arms behind his back that he was expected to provide the first words.

The stone of the pillars along the length of the entrance hall were eroded further by the touch of every passing guest. When considered in assembly they appeared grand, yet they were too plain to impress upon visitors the grandeur of the palace. For that task the fishpond in the hall's centre was looked to.

Shallow yet just deep enough for the princes, in their younger days, to each have paddled in, the pond boasted two benches on either side for its better viewing. Chiron was glad to sink himself down onto the one facing Leon; even if he protested this delay to his homeward journey, which he would not believe complete until he collapsed upon his bed, his feet were grateful for the reprieve. His pleasure in finally resting his legs was so great, in fact, that he neglected to greet his cousin, who pointedly accepted the seat opposite.

"Your father was under the impression that you should rightly return this morning, Chiron. Had I not intercepted the messenger every soldier in the barracks would be searching for you."

Leon's words were mirthless but in their delivery he conveyed a sort of exasperated amusement. Even this disappeared for a moment when he finished: "And I hear no offer of an apology from you. Not even an explanation, false or otherwise."

"You *did* allow me to go, whether I told you or not," answered the prince. In spite of his defiance, he felt a prickling of shame. "I am grateful for your help."

"That is true," smiled Leon, although not without a sigh, "I did permit you to leave."

He said nothing more. Chiron was about to excuse himself when the general stood, his expression serious once more, and intoned: "Be assured, I will not hurry to lie for you again. It matters nothing, now. Whatever business you have outside the palace is beyond me. But I would advise you to speak with your brother. It's the anniversary of your mother's birthday soon, if you care to turn your attention to Delzean."

Chiron watched the koi carp wriggle through the water as he listened. This reprimand was most unwelcome, yet he had to admit to his guilt.

"Go and dress for dinner, and I will tell Eli of your return."

Leon paused before he passed into the hall to call for his cousin, who remained by the pond in a dream. He thought the prince to be disturbed by his harsh, albeit justified, indictment, and attempted as they walked together to demonstrate the fleeting nature of his annoyance. To Chiron these friendly shows made little difference. He could see what lay plainly before him, a much-needed meal, an inquisition from his father and at last the comfort of his own chamber, but his mind lingered still on the morning past and he was reluctant to coax it forward.

Briefly he wondered whether Erin's disappearance was a cause of much concern but found he did not truly care. The fete was over, and it seemed in helping her he had only unsettled himself. Emilia's life and his were never meant to have crossed paths, their fortunes were independent, but despite this (perhaps because of this, this sense that he was pulling free of invisible shackles) he wished for his destiny to become entangled with hers.

Chapter Eleven

Eli had deserted his rightful place at the head of the table to pace behind his chair. To his right Adema observed his progress, but the dining hall was empty save for these two. Outside the servants waited with their ears to the door for their entrance to clean the chamber to be sanctioned. The meal in honour of Adrienne, for the morning would have brought her thirty-seventh birthday, had lain untouched for close upon two hours, when the family had united in a toast.

"Have you reported to Ava with Chiron's refusal?"

The Emperor had likened the distracted air of his elder son to the obvious grief of the younger; had it been other than Adrienne's anniversary, the abstracted look, the hesitancy to answer the remarks of his neighbours and a posture that suggested a readiness to flee from these familiar faces to think alone on secret objects of which he made an unreserved show would have warned his father that something was amiss. As Eli could not imagine another cause for these behaviours than the natural, the reminder of their household's loss, he viewed them as correct, in the sense that an occasion as bleak could be greeted no other way.

Ava, on the other hand, acted in a fashion most peculiar. It was her norm to be sullen; on this day he expected no deviance from the habit. Yet she appeared to eat with a heartier appetite, and smiled in response to Acario's glances as if sharing a joke. The darkest interpretation of her actions was that she surveyed their grief with indifference, a theory supported by her recent donning of the late Empress' dress. This Eli did not even trouble to consider. Ava was ignorant, he believed, but never purposefully callous. Such audacity was beyond her abilities. There were left two possibilities: either she remained in high spirits from the attentions of Lorian and Mathias, or she had not yet learned that Chiron had dashed her hopes of becoming Empress.

"She has heard," replied Adema, after a pause in which she was occupied with her own reflections, "Admittedly I was kind in presenting his objections, but she bears it well."

"I would guard against offending your daughter but I confess her appearance this evening to have surprised me."

"Surprised you? How has she surprised you?"

The princess had proved to be a dangerous topic in the past, for loath as the adults were to quarrel, Adema for offending the man that permitted her to live in the palace after the death of her husband, while the option existed for her to be quartered elsewhere, and Eli for upsetting the balance, whose precariousness had been illustrated by minor upsets beforehand, between the two families, neither were willing to acknowledge any oversight in their opinion of Ava. She would always know her mother's love, even if her greatest faults were revealed to meet the disapproval of the entire Empire, just as she could lose all faith in his eyes and never be abandoned by her brother. Adema considered her a child still at sixteen years. She believed it best to guide her away from those who would do her harm but refused to indulge the instinct to protect her child from the world completely. Hence Ava was not mollycoddled, a treatment she would have preferred to suffering the effort of occupying herself.

While Eli would agree on the difficulty of understanding her, his affection for the girl was too minute for her trespasses to be quickly forgiven.

Adema's tone suggested they had strayed onto treacherous ground. If not apologetic, Eli was at least swift to relieve the tension: "I mean that she appeared unaffected by the news."

A fire had been lit in the hall for the first time since the previous winter. As the sky darkened the flames caused Eli's shadow to flicker against the wall as he paced.

"Yes," smiled Adema, "Perhaps she saw fit to change her mind."

Eli was closer to the truth where Ava's conduct was concerned: she felt nothing, not a touch of sorrow, to hear the others speak in memory of Adrienne. The smiles she bestowed upon Acario were designed to upset him, as she reacted to Chiron's rebuff with a surge of furious malice. Her frustration was poured straight onto her cousin; she refused to suffer the blight alone. She was glad to have gloated to Acario about the Delarus pair rather than the proposed marriage. If he had been aware of this choice he would have been glad too, for if her rejection had been known by the young prince her wrath would have been the greater. The fear persisted that Chiron had told him, that they had met to snicker at her, and in her anxiety the princess picked at the skin of her thumbnail until it bled.

For the moment the matter seemed settled. It brought Eli no closer to finding a wife for his son but the need was hardly pressing. From this thread of discussion he leapt onto another, that of the maid reported to have vanished the night before last. The subject of his wife had been mulled over at such length in his private ruminations to be quite exhausted.

To find motive for Erin's disappearance he ordered the servants, through the senior footmen, to consider closely the palace treasures, looking not at those objects they were able to wipe down and dust but to search for those that had possibly been removed beyond their reach. In the event, the attempts of the servants, keen as they were to incriminate one who had moved among them as a stranger, proved fruitless. Eli brought the Advisor Cyrus to the Scroll Room to resolve a conflict through the study of a record filed therein and glancing over the table, noticed the idol to be absent. The deserter then became a thief in the eyes of Delzean. It was the prerogative of the palace to recover the item; as for the girl, she would be overturned to the mercy of the city courts. One obstacle existed to obstruct the passage of this justice: she called no district of Horizon home. The length of the Empire was hers to hide in.

It was crucial nevertheless that they acted to find her without hesitation. Anyone that considered themselves cunning enough to steal from the palace would also, if this opinion of their abilities proved correct, appreciate how foolhardy it would be for the item to circulate in the city markets when the effort to recover it was at its zenith. If the peasant Erin had been instructed by those merchants that rode through her village, the idol would remain in her possession for another week yet. Therefore the hunt could be concentrated on finding her.

These talks, which concluded as the tenth hour began, were conducted between Eli and Adema without either appearing particularly enraged by the theft, or especially anxious that the girl be brought to trial. They elected to question the servants in order to retrieve from their memories any remark of the girl's that could suggest an address. This would soon prove itself futile, as no friends of hers were discovered amongst the servants, but even at this early stage there was no mention of the Emperor deploying his army to scour the countryside for her. A more vigorous, and likely effective, search would have followed had this day of mourning not clouded their minds.

***

On the evening previous, Chiron had acted as Leon advised and had forced himself to postpone retiring to his own chamber after dinner until Acario was comforted. He was prevented from following him immediately from the hall by the request of his father that he remain and talk of the barracks. The look of pride he bore as he listened to his son, whose weariness he attributed to the trials of the soldiers, brought a shameful, sinking feeling to Chiron's gut.

Their interview was cut short by his plea of exhaustion. Afterwards he trudged reluctantly to his brother's door, only to be ignored. He entered to find Acario asleep, fully dressed on top of the bed sheets. Acario's sleep was deep and restful, a rarity in which he was relieved of troubled dreams.

Chiron endured an hour of restless thought before his mind succumbed to the will of his body. In the darkness he fumbled to retrieve the chain Adema had gifted him for one occasion or another, and to it he attached the ring. When he finally submitted to his exhaustion he lay the night's length with one hand clasped around the chain. Come morning it was covered beneath his clothes. The touch of the ring's chilled weight against his skin elated him. It was a sensation as private to him as the knowledge of his venture. He had not altered his decision to tell Acario only of Emilia. That he expected his story to be of equal interest to his brother on the day Delzean mourned its Empress was indicative of the extent of his distraction.

In homage to his mother Chiron was suited in his most formal attire; however, as this was the blazer he wore nearly every day, and which had acquired such a quantity of dirt over the course of his travels to warrant being removed by a maid to beat in the courtyard, he seemed no more respectable than usual until his hair was washed and combed. This contributed excessively to neatening his appearance.

He would have felt the day to be languid after his antics (his memory was furnished with several embellishments – he seemed to recall demonstrating commendable bravery in their passage through Horizon, warding off those who would have snatched Erin from his grasp); its dullness was yet enhanced by the fact of the misery inherent in every aspect of the occasion.

The Advisors spoke of business at the Oslen Mountains (some robbery was reported there) for the purpose of indicating to the Emperor that they had remembered the date without broaching the subject candidly. Chiron's meetings with Silas were often morose but that morning tutor surpassed himself: he embarked on a monologue once Chiron had taken his seat, outlining the qualities for which his mother was remembered and describing the ceremonies that would take place throughout the day in the temples. Until then the magnitude of his loss had not quite affected the prince; it came as a surprise that the ramblings of an ill-favoured man who was, in any sense, little acquainted with his mother provoked his grief. He spent the lesson with his head bowed. Silas moved on to inquire after the subjects discussed around the Advisors' Table and Chiron did not even care to laugh at his undisguised attempts to gather news before it spread to the citizenry (or indeed, never reported to them at all, for rarely were unfavourable stories detailed in the proclamations).

Afterwards he declined an invitation from his father to pay his respects at the temple. His avoidance of the gravesite, which he had attended once since the burial, was not an act of cowardice but rather an assertion that he preferred to grieve alone. Leon, Adema, Ava and Acario quitted their respective pursuits to accompany his father, and his reflections in the garden were undisturbed.

Dinner commenced upon their return, a smaller, graver meal than usual, and Chiron apprehended Acario at its close. Together they retreated to the comfort of a chamber entitled the Red Room.

The brothers lounged on opposite wooden benches, the length of the crimson carpet lying between them. Acario sat with his legs curled up beneath him, his eyes wide and pensive.

Beside Chiron there stood a candlestick the height of a man; as this was the sole source of light in the room, the younger prince could scrutinize the face of his brother without fear of similar study. Acario looked, if it were possible, more diminutive than ever inside his school robes as he dwelled upon his mother's death. He was wondering then how Chiron would react if he were to confess it all. Because of Ava the spectre of Adrienne held no happiness for him, only plaintive reminisces. He believed her to be wrong, grossly wrong, to have manipulated him when his grief was at its highest, but he believed too that he was responsible, and he would gain nothing from disobedience. If he hadn't ran from her in his haste to plant the flag she would not have fallen. With that thought he stiffened: he deserved to sit there timid before his brother, unable to voice what he wished to voice, because he had betrayed his mother and brought misery on their home.

"Do you want to talk of her, Acario?"

"...No," came the answer, after an interval, "I would rather not."

Between them, their mother was rarely ever mentioned. It seemed to Acario that his brother was loath to think of their mother at all, but this convinced him further of his guilt, for Chiron would never speak of something that pained him. Yet it was odd that while Acario kept an old book for the purpose of scribbling to his mother, and their father had preserved all of her belongings, although he had not anticipated the avaricious hands of Ava as a threat to their conservation, Chiron had no similar means of expressing his loss. And he had known Adrienne for two years more than Acario, too. It had affected him, of that fact no one would be cruel enough to deny, but unlike his brother he had been able to mourn her death as a tragedy, rather than the fault of an ignorant son, and so he had grown to accept it.

While if Leon had been told the truth of his excursion, he would have suspected that Chiron seized upon Emilia with such fervour because their meeting coincided so closely with the date of his mother's birthday, the revelation that Chiron had thought little of the date until his return would soon have collapsed his theory.

Chiron allowed silence to settle over them. He was reluctant to change the subject because he had only one other subject in mind. Acario could protest at his quickness in moving to a topic that brought him pleasure on a day he should be grieving, or he could call him out to be a fool for leaving the palace, prompting Leon to deceive the Emperor and fraternising with a girl likely younger than himself, which was worse.

He reached for the chain and extracted it from his clothes to twirl the ring between his fingers, forgetting in his reverie, or at least feigning to forget, that every move he made was illuminated fully in its detail to his brother.

Acario stared at the ring for a few seconds before asking where it was from. His relief in finding a distraction from circuitous thoughts was diminished by the encroaching sense that Chiron had been biding his time until he could impart a tale of his own, which related in some way to the ring. This sense was abetted by the apparently deliberate way in which he had brought the chain into view.

"If I am to tell you, I will first have to swear you to secrecy," answered Chiron with a playful smile.

In return Acario affected a grin. He felt his suspicion dwindle but was no less miserable for it. "Secrecy from who, from father?"

"Yes, from father, but from everyone else, too," Chiron leaned forward, revelling in this confession, a hark back to their childhood games, "You recall that I visited the barracks with Leon yesterday?"

"I do," said Acario before remembering aloud: "Leon agreed to take me soon, before his birthday. What did you do there?"

Annoyed by Acario's slight deviation, Chiron waved his hand as if to dismiss the question. "The visit to the barracks is unimportant now, you understand; it was only ever a ruse. Leon knew from the first," he hasten to add, "or otherwise I would never have dared to leave there."

"But you must have visited the barracks then, at least for a while?"

This attempt to guide him toward Acario's question was ignored. "I wanted to travel beyond the city borders," (he very nearly began his story by saying "I accosted the maid that father is hunting for in the gardens...", but his wish to deceive triumphed over the desire to reveal that it was he who had fooled the servants and stolen one of their number away in the night), "And I had to find an alibi to feed father. He believed I slept that night in the barracks, when really I walked alone on the merchants' road."

To each syllable he gave careful emphasis in order to capture and heighten Acario's interest. The sole consisting member of his audience would have been trepidatious at the mention of what was a needless, dangerous and foolhardy pursuit had Chiron not reported his idiocy in the manner of a story. The following phrase struck him, however, as an allusion to some deeper woe:

"I was tired of Delzean, Acario, tired of Silas, Sawney and Ava, the cursed fools," Chiron heard Acario exhale as if to intrude and hurried on, "I met a girl amongst the peasants, and she gave me this ring. Her name was Emilia. She was as delightful and uncorrupted a creature as I have ever seen."

Acario understood his brother well enough to hold back a smile of bemusement at his concluding remark. Even in the partial darkness such a move would be folly. He wanted to prolong this confidence but could not help but ask if his brother had been walking in his sleep, perhaps, and discovered the ring lodged in a cranny in his room as the girl presented it in his dream, to which Chiron laughed long and heartily, and the wild look was shaken from his face.

He was spared, for the moment, further scrutiny of the count of Emilia, but Acario suspected his brother to have concealed something in his story. Indeed, the reason he had given for desiring to leave the barracks did not seem satisfactory. Or if it was true that he was powerless to quell the urge to wander from the confines of the city, Acario feared him to be in the throes of a growing madness.

He was inclined to see his brother in the light of a trickster rather than a figure of despair; it was this perception which prompted him to ask after the maid Erin, who had wandered beyond the city on the selfsame night as he.

But Chiron would not divulge such a secret against the strength of his will. "Our paths did not cross on the road, which I imagine was better for both of us."

His speech was curt. He found himself deflated; his revelation about Emilia was of no one's amazement but his own, and it stung.

"I am unconvinced," Acario should have said but for his pride, which his misery pressed and constrained, *"I believe you left with her."*

There remained a great deal to be puzzled through: why would he volunteer himself to escort a thief from the palace, for example? In the event Acario kept his questions silent. Whatever business Chiron had with these girls, the maid and the peasant, was certainly done with now. In the coming days he would have little cause to leave

Delzean and amidst the celebrations the pair would be forgotten, save as characters in another of Chiron's tales. Yet tonight the prince was unwilling to speak of anything else:

"You cannot understand until you see her," stressed Chiron, "She is the opposite of all those things I grow weary of."

He realised then that he sounded defeated, and sighed, his nostrils flaring.

It would have been very like Chiron for this show of passion to be an act, designed to test the extent of his brother's gullibility and discover whether he was thought capable of such sincere emotion. But for the pained expression straining across his face Acario might have believed it true. Here was his talented, self-righteous brother, reduced to a wretched man.

Acario wondered if his brother was afraid of Delzean, if he yearned to attach himself to something outside of it and pull himself free. This thought came in a flash of understanding and left just as swiftly, leaving only the impression that Chiron had attributed more value to the encounter with Emilia than what it was rightly worth.

"I guess I cannot understand, then," agreed Acario.

For a few minutes more they each endured the company of the other, before rising almost in synchronism to depart to their respective chambers. When Acario called goodnight to the shadow of his brother his words were left unanswered. He had no pity left to heap upon himself; instead his head began to throb with frustration, and his legs clamoured to chase after Chiron, and tell him how ridiculous his venture was, how insular and selfish his concerns were compared to those of his family. His plight had become entangled with his mother's death but as he seethed they separated, and he was angered solely for the sake of his mother. The fury of that moment was fleeting, for he soon remembered that grief was capable of driving some to the distraction shown in his brother, but had Chiron turned to observe it he would have ashamedly abandoned the plan on which he brooded as he trudged towards his room.

The doubts of his relations were thrown aside, trampled upon and forsaken; there existed only him and his wish to see Emilia. He could bribe one of the palace guards to search through the realm as he directed, and to deliver onto the girl the message that she should report to the city boundary, where he would await her on the road –

-No, of course that was impossible. Chiron came to his senses with an undisguised shudder. To find a soldier corrupt enough to carry out the deed and yet deserving of his trust would be a marvel of note; to find a willing guard able to find the girl, and be sure of her identity, would be touching upon the impossible. If he was so fortunate that his messenger was successful, there was the scantest of chances that his command would be obeyed, for the reprieved Erin would be watchful for word from the palace. No intruder on their land would receive a welcome reception. Emilia would not be offered up for Horizon's taking.

He pictured himself waiting alone on the road for her. At the image he almost had to laugh; it was ludicrous. Yet he had convinced himself he desired it more than anything.

Chapter Twelve

The river was burgeoning over the banks, soaking the soil and licking at the heels of the wagons abandoned for the night by the merchants. Come dawn there would be a rush to greet the vessels sailing downriver from the sea, laden with fishes. The journey to the coast was short yet treacherous; the villages along its length were apt to storm any craft unwilling to barter at least a third of their crop. Eli forbade any settlement to form at the mouth of the river to protect the interests of his city-bound peasantry, a portion of which was starving in spite of the trials of the fishing boats. The dawn was an age away yet; nothing stirred without the depths of the water.

No light played upon the river until the approach of three men, whose gender could be determined by the low, harsh voices in which they snickered as they traipsed towards the river's edge. On such a night they would be forgiven overstepping the banks, for the static water was almost indistinguishable from the land. Had they fallen, they would indeed not have been the sole causalities; three others mistook the black mass for the road and sank down, struggling against the stuporous intoxication of their limbs. One succeeded in clambering free and returned home sodden to dampen the rags on which he slept, but the bulk of the nocturnal swimmers were carried downstream, and by morning lay either half-submerged in a shallow stretch, as if the corpse had made a last crawl along the bank, or in the case of the last to take the plunge, were buried at the bottom to suffer the disinterest of the fish.

Of the dangers of the water the three approaching were witless. In their raucous laughter there was the taste of strong spirits but their balance and senses were unimpaired, as if tolerant to this sort of alternation. The last of the trio to reach the banks and pause beside a cart, one crafted seemingly for the employment of a child in purveying the goods of their parents, held limply in his left hand a lantern encasing a tallow candle. This was Aldous, the principal companion of Lorian and Mathias. Tonight as usual he had been singled out to join them when they slipped free from the apartment of Lisandro. The acquaintances gathered in that slum were content to talk of their bleakest deeds and of the city's miseries, but these three desired to stretch their limbs, and left to seek keener amusement.

The game they sought to play was of a simple nature, that it pleased them to commit their strengths to a practice so devoid of meaning was a mark of apathy. 'River-tipping' had been invented on the first night that Sawney had permitted his sons to wander the streets as they pleased, an occasion they each could vividly remember, the strange feeling of invulnerability as they prowled streets that appeared alien without the sun's casting glare. It consisted of as little as its singular title would suggest.

In the beginning they had targeted only the wagons left carelessly by the water, though as they progressed in the space of a week to dismantling the wooden vehicles first, clawing the panels apart with their hands, to destroy utterly any hope of retrieval, even in its rudimentary form the game was destructive. In the instant of the act this simplicity was satisfactory, but with age it was enhanced, and morphed from a stupidly childish pursuit into a show of brutal, considered malice.

They would steal goods of no worth to Conn but which were yet cherished by their owners, a crude toy perhaps, or the final letter from a prisoner to his family, who would report to the courthouse to collect the correspondence only to hear from the guard that their letter had been claimed by another. These tokens they would toss into the water with undisguised glee. If a handkerchief speckled with a lover's perfume failed to sink, for example, they would group to pelt it with stones.

Cherished goods were not their sole target, as in their cruelty there was a pressing need to do mischief, to create difficulty, to obstruct, to somehow impair the normal course of things. Shutters would be torn from downstairs windows to drown in the company of gates. To the extent that a decision had to be reached to embark on a spree of river-tipping, the game was premeditated, but beyond this initial decision no other detail was thought upon beforehand. It was a curious sort of impulse that led them to seize a cart or door-sign as they passed.

Aldous halted behind the brothers as they scrutinized the children's cart. Before their efforts to dismantle it rendered conversation impossible, for although they were near immune to the intimidation of the patrols, to be caught in action would complicate to an inexhaustible degree their pleas of innocence, and in such a situation it seemed senseless to add to the noise with idle chatter, he asked in his gruff, crude speech to be told at last the intelligence they had learned from Sawney.

With his face obscured in shadow, the most distinctive feature to be observed of his person was his odour, the stench of clothes unwashed for months, of a body skinned in sweat. A more thorough knowledge of his character would have strengthened the disinclination to trust him. Yet Lorian understood that the claim of one nefarious youth to have been educated in the Emperor's secrets by the Advisor's sons was only another slight dent in their reputation.

To the dismay of Mathias (he stamped upon his brother's foot each time he hinted at having some titbit of palace gossip, a claim he had made profusely and to anyone who cared to listen, since they were ushered into the apartment), he turned to Aldous: "The prince was taken by Leon to visit the barracks, and there met our friend Vikernes. He was supposed to sleep there, and the prince told his father so, but Vikernes found him missing in the morning."

Lorian imparted this morsel with relish, savouring the feeling of superiority to the prince. Chiron's failings were his to deride.

Aldous hooted, a response Lorian deemed satisfactory. "Where had the prince gone?"

"That we have yet to learn, but Sawney will hear soon enough. He was as worried about Chiron as you might expect," he smirked, "The Emperor sat deluded in the hall and excused his absence until Sawney corrected him."

"Ha, ha! And the Emperor knows he lied then? Where was he?"

A disinterested Mathias bent to spin the wheels of the cart; in his head he was reiterating the discussion that had followed the conclusion of Sawney's news and steeling himself to interrupt should Lorian become overexcited by the daft, deviant notion he had shared with his father and risk their undoing.

"Chiron was never asked to admit to it! In some lapse of judgement Eli ruled that it was wiser to permit this one slip," growled Lorian, "But Chiron will slip again."

Eli's reaction to the revelation had agitated even the stoic Sawney. At the table he credited his son's absence to an interest in the army; Sawney had endured the remainder of the breakfast with a patient, indulgent manner until he was able to approach the Emperor alone and repeat Vikernes' message. He was met with offence, and the matter was abandoned as Eli gathered himself. In the courthouse he asked if it was known for what purpose his son disappeared. With the response to the negative, he reached a similar view to Leon, that he must have intended to frequent the house of a Lord's daughter. He possessed no inclination to have his opinion verified. The proximity of Adrienne's death made the thought of conflict unpalatable. His son's errors were easily dismissed by the looming of this greater grief.

Eli could not be accused of cowardice or foolishness; he realised that Leon must have been aware of the deception, in which case Chiron's plan cannot have been excessively imprudent, although it did disturb him to contemplate how casual the general appeared as he appealed on Chiron's behalf. He much desired to learn of the incentive that pushed Chiron to such lengths. If it was truly to meet a noble daughter that he had requested his cousin's support his father had reason to interfere, but he was willing to accept the indiscretion and dismiss it, a fete he would have found impossible at any other time, yet which came easily to him now, and permit Chiron to go unpunished. If, however, the prince attempted another excursion or seemed to grow bold at his father's ignorance the incident would be swiftly plucked from memory.

In the dank kitchen of the Delarus home, Sawney had divulged his exasperation at the Emperor. He appeared as uncaring as ever, but there was an edge to his voice as he expressed his hatred of Chiron. This loathing was not unreasoned dislike, either, for the prince threatened to prove troublesome as an Emperor. This incident was merely the latest in a chain of improprieties. Sawney's primary concern was the continuity of his position, and that of his enterprise, but even an unbiased man would fear for the Empire if it was governed by such an errant prince. To tackle this eventuality he formed a plan: to turn the Emperor against his son by outlining to him the faults he observed. The support of the other Advisors would be mustered. In spite of their dislike for him, which arose from the infamy that could not fail to pollute even their clouded vision, they would not refute the claim. Various scenes in recent months had illustrated his unsuitability as a leader of men.

Mathias had agreed, and slammed his tankard down on the table as a sign of vicarious fury.

The cool manner in which Sawney iterated the solution to any object threatening his progress impressed him. He wondered whether the Advisor would act with any more reluctance if his own son had looked to become hazardous to *his* empire. After a moment's rumination he decided that Sawney would never have allowed Lorian to dream of becoming other than what he was, a lazier, crueller version of his father. In the eventuality of this divergence, he predicted that Sawney would have disowned him and bequeathed the Eyes' leadership to his surrogate child. With the bond of fatherhood severed, Lorian could be slain if he dared to betray his old friends. The conclusion of this idle speculation was known to him from the first and as such did not excite any panic in his breast. Had the Advisor been capable of another course of action he would not have been worthy of the name Delarus. At least the certainty of his character could comfort his sons.

Lorian had noted Mathias' agreement and gone one further. He suggested wildly that they seek a worthier end than Chiron's destruction and defeat the House of Castile itself.

The idea was welcomed by Sawney, who should have appreciated the danger of entertaining such fancies. Mathias personally believed Lorian to be overreaching himself, and he failed to understand Sawney's indulgence. While not opposed to the thought, he considered too ridiculous to discuss. The heated laughter of Lorian as he described the slaughter of the prince was normal to his experience; he had heard far worse through the years, and spouted scenes of matching carnage. Sawney's inability to quell his son's lust for power was the more unsettling.

Of these treacherous talks Lorian was wise enough to hold his silence. He complained of the prince, and painted for Aldous a caricature of the royal family. The ineffective Emperor, the ignorant, thoughtlessly rebellious son, the effeminate and positively useless Acario. Then with a snort he remembered Ava.

"We are seducing the daft princess. Mathias brought her earrings, and I walked her through the gardens."

He was interrupted by an eruption of gruff laughter from Aldous' quarter.

"You should tell us of Ava's proposal," added Mathias, a rueful, tipsy grin on his face.

"Oh, I will. But business first."

Around the minutely proportioned cart they crowded. Each feared the others would seize the prize first and lunged. Lorian and Mathias gained a wheel apiece, which were rolled into the river in unison moments before Aldous shoved the body of the cart.

The sleepers in the nearby apartments slept on, and the distant whisper of footfalls continued without a break in step. Suddenly this activity seemed too timid. They should strike again with flamboyance; this increase in momentum was mutually apprehended, and to achieve it they hurried across the bridge, jeering as if deaf to the city's slumber.

The three wound a drunken path through the dwellings on the nether side. These buildings were tightly-packed and streaked with dirt around the doors and window. The only reprieve to the neighbourhood's dense poverty was the courtyard into which Aldous, Lorian and Mathias hurtled. The shadowed stones felt cool against the bare soles of Aldous' feet, and mitigated the stupefying effects of the alcohol. He bounded forward, enlivened.

The stillness of the scene added an impression of incongruity to the progress of their nocturnal venture. They had no cause to prowl the streets while their fellows rested; it appeared they exulted in this difference, in the very abnormality of their habits. The decrepitude of the flanking houses was such that when Mathias leaned against the wall to keep himself from reeling he could hear the snores within. Children's games were scrawled in chalk across the stonework but they were already too obscured to be worth defiling.

Rather than being exploited by the residents as a place of seclusion and respite, these courtyards had become continuations of their crowded houses. The apartments too compact to accommodate dining tables were redeemed by the simple manoeuvre of erecting tables outdoors instead. If the trio ever repeated their excursion on a successive occasion, and this time fell prey to a particular symptom of intoxication, and found their senses too removed from their bodies to command their limbs to bend and carry themselves homewards, and could only curl up by the side of that very yard in which they now shrieked and crowed, they would have been jolted awake by the rush of the peasants in the morning as they prepared to eat breakfast, eight persons to a table.

It was their intention to complicate the business of breakfast for these families; it was in celebration of this goal that they screeched. Lorian climbed on to the table they would attempt to remove to a gloomier existence on the river bed, and with a grand, sweeping gesture, silenced the others.

Mathias' coherence had been suggestive of sobriety up until that instance, when he staggered, and asked Aldous if he had heard yet of Ava's proposal. Aldous was posed to answer to the affirmative before he realised he had not, in fact, heard the detail. He turned to Lorian, understanding even with his normally-inadequate brain capacity impaired, that he was the only appropriate narrator.

"She begged her mother to ask for the prince's hand," bellowed Lorian, as if dictating to an avid courtyard-full of listeners, basking in the memory of his own mirth when Sawney announced their stabs at wooing her had proved counter-productive, "Our little princess dreams of being an Empress, Mathias. But the prince refused her. The Emperor commented on how well she was coping. I hold that she's crushed not to gain that eunuch for a husband!"

He continued to ramble on in this fashion, embellishing the proposition with lashes of desperation. He remarked that Chiron was too weak to take a wife, even one as gullible as Ava. Mathias intervened to outline to Aldous his exchange with the princess, but Lorian grew bored of speech, and leapt from the table. He ordered them to cease making such a clamour.

Mathias toyed with the idea of arguing that he had likely disturbed every person in the district with his rant, and then those in the district beyond when he landed awkwardly on the stones and cursed furiously and without reserve, but he was spared the effort of following those thoughts by Aldous' request that they stack the chairs against the wall and begin the second phase of river-tipping.

His companions agreed but were too careless to remove the chairs by any means other than kicking them aside. Lorian grappled with the end of the table closest to the yard's entrance, after an outburst of further cursing, whilst Aldous seized the opposite end with considerable less complaint. They suffered the greatest strain as the table was heaved towards the river; Mathias assumed a position near its centre and pretended to hold it only with one hand as he yawned into the other.

In these stances they jerked the table across the courtyard. Lorian's inability to walk backward proved itself to be more of an impediment to their plan than Mathias' meagre contribution. Onwards they staggered until Aldous tripped and the table was slammed down, causing birds to flutter from the rafters. The disturbance was greater than they anticipated, but they staggered on for several moments more, before Mathias observed the opening of a shutter in the wall directly opposite. In the dark recesses of the house behind his eye met the pair of a stranger, whose next action was to yell out for the patrols.

The observer rushed from the window to apprehend them in the courtyard. He believed the thieves to be a nuisance rather than a contentious threat. He mistook the three dedicated criminals for desolate vagrants. At the appearance of this man the intruders hissed with laughter, and Lorian tore the shoe from his foot to launch at his head.

In the second he was struck the table was abandoned, and they ran wildly onto the road. The trio broke ranks as the bridge drew closer; Aldous, sagging under the weight of his inebriation, loped into an alleyway. He was able to slink back to his lodgings after an interval in which he dashed the alley with the contents of his stomach and brawled with the men sleeping nearby beneath their coats.

His fellows were strong enough to escape the threat of arrest, and for another hour they targeted those vehicles deserted by the river's edge. To the early signs of daylight their flesh responded with the first sensation of fatigue. They hurried towards Lisandro's apartment to make use of the last of the night's pleasures.

Lisandro was graced with the only story they had not exhausted for the purpose of Aldous' entertainment. They had forgotten to tell him of their invitation to the ball Eli planned to host in honour of Leon's birthday, and atoned for this oversight by informing every one of their acquaintances who they had yet to lose to sleep. Sawney had been granted an invitation on the most cordial terms, but he conveyed to his sons the sense that their attendance was perhaps desired less than that of the other Advisors' offspring. He expressed a wish that they understand this to be no hindrance; there was no question in his or his sons' minds that the guests of Delzean could be denied their company.

The promise of their attendance could not dampen the preparations for the approaching celebration. Leon was unperturbed when Eli reported the names of the confirmed guests; perhaps the significance of two names was diminished by the fifty which followed. In the days before the event he pressed his company upon both of his cousins, attempting to comfort Acario in the wake of his mother's anniversary, a fete it seemed Chiron had founded overtly strenuous, and simultaneously to convince Chiron that his attention was better spent focused on the palace. From Adema he learned that Ava was still refusing to show any sign of offence or dismay at Chiron's refusal, but rather than intervene to demand that she talk to him openly, he chose to assume that she was happy in seclusion. Adema adopted a similar practice; she would have been afflicted with guilt for this lapse in motherly concern had Ava not expressed a wish to be left quite alone. Leon likewise felt justified in his behaviour. He wanted to enjoy the event of his birthday without having to pander to his sister's brattish fits.

The only problem with rightful cause to disrupt the impending celebrations was the failure of the soldiers to capture Erin; after seven days Eli ordered them to forsake the search. Her name was mentioned once more in an official proclamation, which read that anyone caught in the possession of the missing idol was to be brought before the court on the harshest charges, before the matter was pushed aside. If Lorian and Mathias were not permitted to upset the Emperor's undertakings, neither was an insignificant thief from the country.

Chapter Thirteen

Delzean's servants were quick to forget of the member missing from their ranks as the event hurried closer. Half of the ground floor was impassable for the week preceding Leon's birthday as the maids queued to join the frenzied activity in the hall. Ladders were erected in order for banners and elaborate threads of bunting to be strung from the rafters of the hall. Identical in proportion, the quality of solemn austerity that the ball room shared with the dining hall had been changed utterly by the addition of these decorations. Leon's birthday was treated as the most important occasion to befall the palace in years; it seemed equally a celebration of his achievements as of his age.

Two tapestries were recovered from the reception room to drape the walls on either side of the fireplace. On the left was detailed the Castile family tree, complete to the birth of Acario, whilst its neighbour bore in gold the family's coat of arms. Their motto was adopted on the evening as a toast. In the absence of natural light, candlesticks were stationed along the walls. Even if their number had been tripled, large stretches of the hall would still have slumbered in half-darkness. It was decided the hall be perfumed with incense. From the droves of censers carried into the chamber it was apparent that the smoke would be prodigious, and the scent pervasive. Indeed, the fumes spread throughout the palace and lingered for months, enduring the fresh winds of the imminent winter.

Chiron learned of these preparations through the instructions of his father to the senior servants, who were asked to attend the Advisory Breakfasts for a spell to save him the trouble of seeking them out. The prince was impressed, and somewhat envious, when Eli confided that he had ordered the throne to be moved into the hall for Leon's private use. For the evening's length he was to be the most honoured man in Delzean.

The ball and the banquet scheduled to preclude it were the Emperor's gifts to his nephew, but Leon made a point of remarking to Eli that his greatest gift was the hospitality shown to Adema and her children following Caius' death. As grateful as he remained for these tokens, both the present celebrations and the years of enduring, though unexpressed, kindness, it was with some relief that he welcomed the present his mother had arranged; he wished to possess a tangible marker of the date. She had commissioned a portrait of him, and for four days Chiron went to watch, in the languid hours after dinner, his likeness develop on the canvas.

Sawney believed that Eli had taken no action at all against his eldest son for deserting the barracks and, what was more, that this negligence was not the fruit of a growing apathy towards the boy's misdemeanours but rather the result of an innate trust that he would have lied for no purpose more sinister than to meet with a girl. On both these counts, however, the habitually astute Advisor was incorrect. Eli's trust in Chiron was not quite explicit; the prince avoided an inquisition only because the Emperor was concerned with matters of deeper resonance. He may have forgone a direct confrontation but it was unfair to accuse Eli of inactivity, for over the course of the ensuing days measures were established to keep Chiron occupied. Eli feared that too much time to dwell on empty thoughts had unsettled the prince and driven him to outlandish endeavours.

To combat the effects of a year's worth of afternoons with only his own mind for company, Eli invited his son to observe the business in the city courts with himself and the Advisors. Chiron had visited on several previous occasions, but now he was granted a voice when cases deemed too complex for a mere citizen's judgement were presented for the Emperor's opinion.

Although Chiron was permitted to leave Delzean for this purpose, when the business of the court called the palace officials forth, and although he not once suspected that he was otherwise forbidden to stray beyond the gardens, Eli was adamant that the need to obtain a present for Leon would not provide an excuse to venture outwith his rightful domain. Instead he requested that the city's most renowned merchants called at the palace to exhibit their wares before the household's children. Acario, Chiron and Ava were hurried from their beds on the morning of the ball to the reception room, where they walked back and forth in front of tables spread with rarities, jewels and the craftwork of the peasantry, while the merchants stood in a silence that came unnaturally to those accustomed to boasting of their goods, their hands clasped nervously behind their backs.

Sifting through the contents of the last table brought to Chiron's attention a ring much resembling that which rested still against his chest, and for the reason of this resemblance he decided it worthy of his cousin. It was in fact of greater value than the ring gifted to Chiron by Emilia; no stains of grass or dirt diminished the glacial beauty of the silver band, and it was crowned with a diamond, small and unimposing but fine enough for Leon's tastes. In spite of the ignorant basis on which it was selected, the ring was among the most expensive of the treasures brought before the family. It belonged to the ranks of the jewels christened 'immortals' by the merchants, as it had been rescued by an undertaker from resting with its owner in the necropolis and appreciatively returned to the clutches of the pedlars. Had the merchant been able to speak, of course, he would have detailed a rather different story of the ring's origin.

Acario's decision proved hesitant, and not until the best part of an hour had been wasted in debate with his brother did he reach for the sword Leon would receive with sincere gratitude when the family convened before the banquet. It was a work of foreign craftsmanship, exchanged by a soldier with a sailor on a trading ship at the port beyond the Oslen Mountains and passed from nobleman to nobleman to gather dust in various collections. In Leon's hands it would at least know the action for which it was crafted. The brothers thanked the merchants and moved to retire before discovering that Ava had slipped from the chamber already, with no gift to show for the morning's viewing. To the merchants her behaviour was excused but they were content to let her face Leon alone.

Already prone to indecisiveness, Acario's hesitancy in choosing a gift for his cousin was worsened by his desire to present an object whose value was expressive of his thanks for the kindness Leon had recently shown him. With his father's permission, Acario had been withdrawn from the academy for three days to be educated instead in the barracks.

There, under the cautious gaze of the general, Acario felt at once young and spritely mature as he moved in step with a hundred others. The pace of life in the barracks was a welcome contrast to the lethargy in which he spent his schooldays. Those soldiers versed in palace lore understood the youngest prince to be the least suited to a career of comradery and defence, but he proved himself equal to his brother in every task he was led to. Vikernes was his only critic; he summoned Acario before the senior officers to reprimand him for sporting such long hair. In doing so the lieutenant strived to humiliate the prince, to goad him perhaps to tears, as he had heard of Lorian's notion and exulted in the thought that his acquaintances could end Eli's dynasty, and as such harboured no respect for the timid Acario. To his severe disappointment, his victim remained stony faced. On the third morning he reported to Vikernes' office with his hair bound in a ribbon-sheathed ponytail and Leon applauded him when he thanked the lieutenant for his suggestion.

That the spell in the barracks was beneficial to Acario in a far greater sense than adding muscle to his narrow limbs was indisputable, but unselfish as the prince was, a shiver of irritation chilled him as he discovered that the three days in which he had known a happiness denied to him for years were the cause of an upset to both Chiron and Acario, the two occupants of Delzean on whom his wellbeing usually depended. If either were wronged in some way, it would be his responsibility to bear the brunt of their frustration. Acario thought it grossly unfair that he should be greeted with Chiron's complaints of boredom when he arrived at the palace after ten hours on his feet. But he was willing to lend his energy to raising his brother's spirits, guessing that his sullen mood was not entirely caused by Acario's occupation but also by the girl Emilia, with whom his infatuation persisted.

If the sympathy he offered his brother was an effort, the patience with which he endured Ava's agitation was excruciating. As his last visit to the barracks coincided with the beginning of the academy's half week holiday in honour of Leon's birthday, Acario spent the eve of the ball in Ava's chamber, crouched on the floor amidst suffocating wreathes of incense. He would have much preferred the company of his school friends to the princess perched atop her dressing table.

From there she frowned down upon him and whined of the inattentive Lorian and Mathias. The former had promised to come fetch her whilst Mathias had showered her with jewellery (Acario knew this to be an exaggeration but saw no point in correcting her; he consoled himself with the thought that Ava would suffer a much deserved bout of shame when they gathered in the reception room to present Leon his gifts). Yet neither had called for her or sent a messenger with wishes for her health since the days following the banquet with their father.

Of the change in Chiron she was oblivious, and as she had nothing to share on the subject of either army life or the guests of the upcoming ball, her words were worthless to him. While she raged at the injustice of the Delarus sons, he examined the years' old scar from the oath she had once had him make, which shone like a fresh burn on the palm of his hand.

That evening Eli detailed the arrangements for the ball and the preceding banquet to his family over a rather more sparse meal than usual, as the kitchen staff were saving their strength, and the pantry's choicest morsels, to feed a livelier hall the following day. Leon received his first toast, and it was fortunate that he was unusually fatigued after the afternoon's training to notice the preoccupied, somewhat sullen expressions of his younger relations. Adema asked her daughter whether she would desire a hand in dressing for the occasion; she meant, of course, in choosing a gown, as Ava already possessed attendants to help don her garments if she ordered it, but the princess heard the remark as a an insult to her capabilities and stormed from the chamber. The Emperor dismissed her behaviour as the result of becoming over-excited by the impending celebrations, and advised his sons, with a wry smile, to retire shortly lest they similarly erupt.

Chiron confined himself to his bedchamber until he was fetched by Adema in the late afternoon; by choosing to squander the morning hours dozing and lingering over half-formed plans to find the girl Emilia, he missed the chance to fence with Leon in the gardens, an opportunity seized upon by Acario in his stead. His brother had been awake to greet Leon when he rose for his customary early breakfast with a drowsy murmur of congratulations.

Eli had instructed them to gather in full formal attire in the reception room for the fifth hour. The gifts from the younger princes were greeted with interest, and Leon demonstrated a commendable lack of irritation at his sister's negligence by dismissing her muttered apology to offer a compliment on her gown. Had Chiron been in a lighter mood he would have struggled to suppress a snicker at this utterance: Ava had strived to imitate the voluminous fashion of the season but had only made herself appear more diminished in the attempt, as her frame, already slender, was drowned beneath its layers, and to the colour her skin bore a sickly contrast.

The flustered face of the princess was deemed unworthy of attention from the Emperor. He waved her aside and shook Leon's hand between both of his own, then inclined his head towards

Adema. She swept from the room to call Javier, whom custom required to wait elsewhere while the family exchanged gifts.

Before the multitude of guests descended upon the entrance hall to be welcomed by Eli and Leon, those prized individuals invited for the banquet arrived to receive the first taste of the festivities. Another table had been lain as an extension of the original to accommodate the party, which consisted of four of Leon's superiors, bedecked in military garb, and a handful of soldiers, whom he trusted as his closest comrades.

The fervent conversation of these men put the princess ill at ease, but Acario had resolved to be neither silenced by Ava's ill looks nor unnerved by the jostles of the soldiers, and in obedience to his wish that the evening be agreeable he found the meal to be the most pleasant to have taken place under Delzean's roof for years. Even Chiron was unable to maintain the doggedly brooding air he had adopted.

The banquet was interrupted after what felt an age to the princess by the message that the family of Advisor Cyrus awaited an audience with Leon. Adema shepherded the hall's occupants across the palace to the ball room; Chiron and Acario paced ahead to admire the chamber before its decoration was lost amidst the coming onslaught.

A stage had been erected at the far end of the hall, upon which a nervous band of musicians had already begun to ply their trade. The music sounded then thunderously loud but Chiron supposed it would become only a murmur beneath the chorus of noblemen's voices. For a moment he wondered if a girl as fine as Emilia could be found among the Advisor's daughters. In the same instance Acario was praying not to be coaxed into dancing with Ava.

They were each called from their reveries by Adema's gesture towards the throne; in its usual place it no longer attracted their stares, but it was undoubtedly an object of merit when viewed alone, isolated on the left side of the stage. The chamber was growing hot with incense and the licking flames of the fire; the ceiling seemed low in spite of its prolonged proportions, an effect perhaps of the candlelight, which shrouded the furthest corners, and the banners of flags and bunting hanging from the rafters, whose colour was sufficient, with the help of the two tapestries, to impress a sense of claustrophobia upon those who strolled within the hall. By the time of Chiron's entrance, the scene was swarming with servants bearing platters of cutlets and wine. Within five minutes these figures were swamped by the soldiers, and by the close of the first hour a dozen pairs danced in step with Adema and Javier.

Sawney prowled somewhere amongst the phalanx of bodies, pursued in search for Vikernes by the nephew of Milias, a stout youth with whom Lorian had quarrelled. Intent on snatching an apology from the Advisor, it was only when Sawney threatened to send for the guards that he yielded. His sons arrived too late to be extended the privilege of a personal greeting; when they at last entered the ball Sawney insisted they make amends with Leon.

The Delarus brothers were in the grip of a reckless fervour, for as they approached the palace on foot, an hour late, they each thought of overthrowing the Emperor and having the spoils of Delzean for themselves. To Mathias this thought came in a moment of indulgence, whilst despite seeming as equally unfeasible to Lorian, he found the idea itself irresistible. Then with a laugh like a bark he asked his brother whether he intended still to seduce the princess Ava.

"You understand I was never serious," replied Mathias in an affectedly curt manner, "She's too cold even for my charms."

"But Aldous knows of our plan now; either compete or call me victor. Just pretend that the future of the Eyes depends upon her. We need to have *some* means of entertaining ourselves this evening."

Against his better will Mathias agreed to toy again with the girl's affections. He decided not to try Lorian's temper when it had been tested already by the rigorous bathing routine their father insisted they were subjected to. The vest Lorian donned every day to disguise his stomach had been set alight and destroyed in the fireplace – a new scent of decay had flourished in the kitchen as it burned. They had visited the public baths a week earlier on the advice of the doctor Fernandez, who prescribed a thorough cleaning to combat the tremors Lorian had begun to experience. Against the effects of alcohol dependency this direction was useless, but against the complaints of their companions it proved effective. Then, on the morning penultimate to the ball, Sawney ordered them to bathe before they encounter the Emperor. He was answered by Lorian's ready protestations that he should not be forced to cleanse again after such a minute interval. In his opinion another bath would not be necessary until long after the winter solstice. Sawney's wish triumphed, but Lorian was no more aggravated than Mathias. Conn had donated a lotion he claimed would alleviate Mathias' pockmarked skin, and a suspiciously-similar looking concoction that would assuredly thicken his fair hair. Neither substance had its desired effect (Conn accredited this to Mathias' lack of vigilance in the products' application) and Mathias resented smothering his face and hair in the foul smelling paste.

They appeared placid when they bowed in reverence to Leon, yet hastened to return to the crowd before their courtesy was exhausted.

Throughout the course of the ensuing hours a prodigious number of remarks were made by noblemen and courtesans alike, and to those who lived in the amber of the moment these remarks undoubtedly seemed worthy of note. To the likely dismay of the guests in question, only three incidents from those six hours, in which the crowd chattered and twirled across the breadth of the hall and the figures on stage were replaced without a perceptible break in the music, emerged as deserving of further relation:

The most exceptional of these occurrences was the change that came over Acario when he was introduced to the third in a queue of beaming guests; he realised that he had not been near enough to the bulk of those eyeing him appraisingly to utter a word since he was a child. Here he was released from the snare of the past. In the company of these strangers he was transformed from Ava's puppet to the prince who had marched to the beat of the barracks. A touch of timidity persisted, yet he longed to remain among the guests far past the hour when the oldest began at last to leave in droves. Tonight he felt more like himself, or to be exact, more like the self circumstances had denied him, than ever before.

When Eli spied him in conversation with Arden's daughter and her husband, Horizon's prized playwright, he interrupted Adema to alert her to the scene. Chiron perceived his brother's nervous mannerisms and moved to rescue him. He drew close to find the playwright laughing with the younger prince; with a swell of jealously he shoved a path through their group.

Even amidst the crush of bodies it was inevitable that Chiron should encounter Lorian and Mathias; it was through luck alone that he avoided treading on the toes of their father, with whom he was less inclined to indulge in affected pleasantries than ever. Somehow it was the fault of these three that he was trapped in his place; these three were the easiest to blame of all that resolutely played their role in the palace. From their earliest introduction Mathias had sensed a distinct, almost palpable, mistrust in the manner of the royal family, and he detected no difference in Chiron's conduct when they spied the prince sipping wine as he turned his back on Adema, who had been asked to dance by the Lieutenant Vikernes, and elbowed several stately older gentlemen to the side to reach him.

At their appearance Chiron rolled his eyes, exasperated, but when they drew familiarly close and dropped into identical, sweeping bows he felt his face relax into a smile. He may have ached with a desire to be elsewhere but in the company of nobles, in formal garments; in short, on occasions such as these, he was comfortable, and understood what was expected.

For the pair before him, he expected that the conventions and sombre conversation of these gatherings was agonising to endure. Accustomed to roaming the city as they pleased, in the trappings of the ball they seemed less certain of themselves than usual. Lorian's resemblance to his father was unmistakable without the usual smattering of wax in his hair; he had growled at two women in the past hour for remarking on this similarity, and kept flattening the curls behind his ears. Mathias fared little better, as he rarely acted with quite as much assurance as his brother. As they rose from their respective bows, Chiron glimpsed something like desperation on their faces. In him they sought some entertainment. He would not pander to their needs, of course, for the thought that they suffered in the company of men he had known since childhood was highly pleasing.

"Good evening, prince," bleated the elder, "How are you enjoying the festivities?"

"Do they seem tedious after visiting the barracks?" finished the younger, before Chiron could answer.

It was their intention to hint that they had learned of his furtive escape from the palace, to see if they could discern in his reaction the cause for which he had lied to his father.

Their quarry was unaware that anyone suspected the truth of his outing and understood them instead to be insulting the pace, arguably tepid, of life in the palace. In this vein he answered: "Only to a tedious person could they appear so. Excuse me, gentlemen."

He had spoken lightly enough, and was not truly much angered, but the suggestion (he found a meaning in their questioning more subtle than that which they intended) that their lives held greater excitement than his own was infuriating. Perhaps he was coddled and enclosed by his family, but that was the fault of fate, not any choice of his own. Had he not defied fortune by finding Emilia? But then it struck him that if their meeting had indeed been the work of coincidence, it was unlikely to ever occur again. He preferred to believe that there was a plan in wait for him. Removing Sawney from Delzean's service seemed an irrefutable component of this plan, but of late he had neglected to tend his loathing of the Advisor. The notebook purloined from the city courts had lain unexamined for weeks.

Acario had begun to approach the group, recognising only the back of his brother's head. In the same moment Chiron swept away to the left, he distinguished the figures of Lorian and Mathias. They had already noticed his advance.

The young prince was dwarfed by the brothers. The esteem the evening had mustered began to leave him but, like his sibling, he would not permit the pair, whom he disliked on their own merits, the relation they bore to Sawney notwithstanding, to gain any satisfaction at his expense.

In place of bowing Lorian offered his hand. Rather than the strict reverence conveyed by the former expression, this gesture suggested the two were equals. Lorian's grip was crushing, as if he knew the prince to be incapable of objecting. His hand was shaken again by Mathias, and Acario vowed to wipe his hand on the back of an unsuspecting guest the moment he was free of the encounter. During these greetings not a word had been spoken. Acario had a faint suspicion they were straining to unsettle him and he broke the spell of the silence first: "Have either of you danced with Princess Ava yet?"

"Not yet, but she has no need to worry: we are sure to spare her the time in a while," replied Mathias. He wondered if Ava had complained of their ebbing interest.

Lorian smirked at the image of a frantic Ava (they had agreed to postpone contact with the princess until the later hours in the hope that she would seek out them, therefore sparing half the effort on their side). "I trust she has been occupied in our absence," he continued, bearing sand-coloured teeth, "But I must compliment you, prince. It must take an effort to participate tonight, so soon after Adrienne's anniversary."

Whether it was the effect of this speech as a whole, or the reference to himself as 'prince' rather than 'your highness', or the mention of his mother by her first name, the three syllables drawn out to excruciating lengths by the mouth of the foul Lorian, Acario felt himself overtaken by a temper he was unaware he possessed. But unlike his father and brother, who often fell victim to a rage credited to the Castile blood, he was able to master it.

"She would not have wished for me to sulk in a corner. Nor to listen to any other that suggested so."

He bowed his head in farewell, and retreated back towards the circle of Advisors around his father, his legs weak. Anyone who looked upon him, his hair loose and long as ever, clad as always in his school robes, would hardly have appreciated that the evening had changed something in Acario.

The devastation that the relationship Mathias and Lorian had fashioned with Ava was capable of was then unfathomable to the prince. The brothers were as oblivious as his family to the power Ava held over him; had there been any chance of their pursuing Ava to obtain the truth and use it for their own ends, he would have pressed to curtail their acquaintance. But the Advisor's sons were as woefully ignorant as everyone else, and he trusted Ava to be too selfish to share her stronghold. In this assumption he was proven to be grossly misguided. Yet he could not be blamed for seeing no threat in Mathias as he bowed to Ava a short time later, and led her to dance in the centre of the hall.

Mathias had rushed to the princess for the purpose of besting Lorian, but as Vikernes had materialised in his place he doubted Lorian cared much for the defeat. He liked to think he had a more considered purpose in appealing to her affections than to merely compete with his brother or mend his pride. By appearing to befriend Ava he schemed to secure a future for his family if Chiron assumed the throne, as Adema would be loath to see the father of her daughter's friend, or indeed his brother, if Lorian had succeeded Sawney by then, dismissed. The reasons Mathias was content to occupy the princess were twofold: namely that he was the least committed to destroying the Castilian line entirely, which stood as the only valid alternative, and that he alone was equal to the task: Lorian could not manipulate in half measures.

It would be a while before he was accustomed to Ava's peculiarities, however. This led him back to the afternoon in the Zodiac Gardens, and it was of this that he spoke.

There was no cause for him to trouble to invent new stories for her delectation. She seemed pleased to lap up the words he had used before. She perceived him as a pitiable youth, eager for her companionship, to whom she need not offer anything in return. Ava behaved as though it should be stimulating enough to move hand in hand with her. It would have humbled her to learn that Mathias resented the feel of her pale, flaccid skin. She was not unpretty, but had her title been removed Mathias would have dropped her for a different partner. When this thought occurred he recognised the same prejudice that had aggravated him into action, that of believing surnames to be worthier than minds. He laughed to himself at the notion, that an orphan could come to inherit the prejudices of the royals.

Yet the thoughts of the pair were hidden from the onlookers, and only to those with knowledge of Mathias would they have appeared as anything other than a modest young princess and her courteous companion. Adema was perturbed to see them together but, remembering Ava's insistence that she had no thoughts of marriage to the Delarus name, permitted them to waltz past.

Their steps were somewhat awkward until a watching noble suggested Ava stand on Mathias' feet and allowed herself to be steered completely. Hoping to move into view of Lorian and tempt him into laughter, Mathias complied. But he was hardly much taller than the princess, and found the close capacity that resulted discomfiting.

Ava took the abrupt ending of their dance to mean that he was overcome with passion for her, although even she was uncertain whether she truly believed this. As Mathias stalked through the now depleting crowd he wondered whether the perfume that had tickled his throat emitted from the princess herself. Regardless of its conclusion, he considered the evening a small success.

In the absence of his brother Lorian committed an act the surrounding guests found abominably offensive: he had seated himself upon the Emperor's throne. The Advisor Rous had threatened to have him removed if he insisted on sullying the chair, and with the reluctance the youth desisted. While Mathias educated Ava on the animals contained in the gardens, Lorian stood but a few paces from the throne with Vikernes and his father. The presence of Sawney prevented Rous from ordering Lorian to slink further away, but still the Advisor lingered nearby. These three discussed nothing more sinister than the progress of the burglaries, from which their men were imminently to return, yet the carrying, raucous laughter of the Lieutenant, always almost joined by Lorian, unsettled those that remained around them, discussing servants' wages and betrothals.

When Mathias resurfaced the Delarus family joined the queue waiting to congratulate Leon and exempt themselves from the festivities by the foot of the steps to the hall.

The queue grew in length, and the actions of those celebrating still became somnolent, the conversation wearisome. It was close upon two o'clock when Eli called for the musicians to depart. The silence seemed to remind the guests of the lateness of the hour, and they hastened en masse to pay their respects to the family. On the unsteady heels of Silas, the last guest to praise Leon on the ball, Eli led his relatives from the chamber.

Acario captured a final glance of the ballroom before the servants slammed and bolted the doors. He expected to see some proof of the confidence he had employed, a sign that it was as he had perceived it. Yet the change in him was not reflected by the ballroom. He turned away, and contented himself with the evidence of his memory.

Chapter Fourteen

Chiron paused outside the Breakfast Hall while the guards appointed to the task reported to Eli their failure to uncover any knowledge of Erin amongst the servants. The Advisors lingered, curious of the outcome of the maid's desertion, the news of which had been suppressed so as not to shame the Emperor, until Sawney coughed and strode downstairs. Their wish to hear firsthand of how a mere peasant was able to evade trained soldiers was trumped by the desire to deprive Sawney the satisfaction of being the sole punctual arrival at the city courts, and within moments the hallway was again quiet and vacuous, save for the stretch where Chiron paced. It was now midwinter, yet the light which glanced upon the walls was as bright as ever, though a draught had succeeded at last in infiltrating the palace, creeping under doorways to spread the still-strong scent of floral incense.

The small fluctuations of the seasons were too timorous to be noted by the prince; he wore his blazer out of habit rather than sense, and seemed unaware of the chill which nipped his fingers and etiolated his skin whenever he stepped out into the gardens. He waited for his father to request to join Acario in the barracks.

His brother had been excused from the academy in order to take lessons in fencing with Leon. The arrangements had been made out of earshot of Chiron, as though his intrusion was feared. Eli had grounds for this deception, yet when Acario had revealed the plan the previous evening, sincerely oblivious of his brother's enforced ignorance, Chiron's sense of desolation and resentment was aggravated, the very thing Eli sought to avoid. He had predicted, in cancelling Silas' lessons until the new year, that his son would lapse into the preoccupied moods to which he was recently prone, but Chiron had proved himself unworthy of the trust granted to Acario. He would not be excused to the barracks to make a mockery of his father's authority. Eli's judgement in this matter was far from unreasonable – he expected Chiron to be suffering nothing more than the pangs of misplaced adolescent affection; had he been able to comprehend the truth of the matter, a fete even Chiron could not accomplish in its entirety, he would have perhaps shown more leniency.

With the barracks denied to him, and the lesser distraction of his tutor excused for the festive season, the only occupation left to Chiron were the visits to the city courts. These had become sporadic, even rare, in the weeks since Leon's birthday, as Eli turned to organising the solstice.

Since assuming the throne the throne Eli had ordained that the date be greeted with a parade. The celebrations of the peasantry would begin at dawn, culminating in a city-wide carnival. The march of the royal caravan would have played a minor part in the proceedings, if not for the addition of three regiments to the convoy, who added a degree of importance to the performance. At the Vorcello theatre a square would be cordoned off for the exclusive use of the nobles, so the princes could browse amongst their kinsmen without fear of undesirables. The negotiations with the commanding officers occupied Eli for a full week: every detail of their route had to be taken into account.

It was the fault of the impending solstice that Chiron was abandoned to the whims of his temper, that he had no subject worthy of thought besides a girl he had once encountered. Yet he had done no more than wonder whether she had asked his sister of him, whether Erin had remarked of his tenacity and daring in tearing her from the hands of fate, and wear all the while the ring plucked from the dirt against his chest. He was unsure of how to act, or whether any action was required of him at all. Perhaps the tedium of his current existence was a test, a torment he must endure before knowing himself equal to Emilia. But Chiron was not as susceptible to such irrationality as Sawney declared, for there remained the possibility that in his darkest moods he disbelieved all of this, and saw his disaffection for what it was.

As he waited for his father to emerge, Chiron imagined his defence if one of the servants were to reveal that he had met with Erin, and repeated to the guards the exchange that had passed between them. He was chuckling at he paced, for the toil of the city was forgotten, and he was left only with the feeling of victory.

Adema had commented on his wan appearance a few days before, but there was nothing truly amiss in his features. He looked the same prince that had suffered Eli's rebuke for interrupting the Advisory Breakfast two months before. Indeed, as he grinned to himself it seemed absurd that some change had stirred his spirit.

From the dejected expressions of the guards, who hastened downstairs five minutes after the exit of the Advisors, as if they hoped racing to resume their duties would compensate for their inability to force even one shred of useful information from the servants, Chiron ascertained that no whisper of the idol had been heard in Horizon. Again he was tempted to share his glory with Acario, though he suspected from his response to the encounter with Emilia that his brother was outgrowing his old unquestioning indulgence.

When Eli stepped out into the corridor he knew at once that his son hovered to petition him about the barracks. Acario had not been sworn to secrecy after all, yet he had assumed the boy would guess there to be a sound reason why Chiron was excluded from their discussions.

"And why do you wait, Chiron?"

"I expect you can guess. I wished to ask whether I can accompany Acario and Leon. You know I have little else to do."

"You wish to go because you are bored?" In Eli's voice this query sounded more a forceful statement of fact.

A lesser man would have submitted to the will of the stony-faced Emperor, admitted himself mistaken and scurried from his presence. His deliverance always expressed a degree of anger at being so disturbed, by counsellor and citizen alike. Chiron understood his fury to be lacking in substance; it was really just a pre-emptive move against pointless digressions.

"Of course not. I meant that there is nothing to prevent me from going," replied Chiron, his patience indicative of the strength of his yearning, "And Leon would welcome my company."

"It is not only Leon you need consider. Acario has surely earned the right to hold these lessons for his own."

"I have no intention of usurping him, father!"

"Your intention may not be so, but doubtless Acario will resent your intrusion."

"Acario -"

"That is my final word. You are to remain here for the time being. Come new year I hope to find you in better spirits."

Eli held his son's gaze for a moment before moving towards the staircase. In brooding, his son had demonstrated that he was undeserving of such trust. Eli was convinced that his refusal had prevented Chiron from again deserting the barracks; the ensuing row was a necessary consequence. In mid-step he turned to answer the prince's following remark: "What would you have me do instead?"

There was an edge to Chiron's voice, sufficient to provoke even Eli to second guess himself. He paused before advising his son, as though he anticipated the reception his prescription would receive. "I suggest you seek out your aunt and cousin. It displeases me to learn that you have sulked in your chamber while their company is available."

"Ava has no interest beyond sulking and you do not challenge her."

"I would hardly have expected her to be your role model," snapped his father, "Find Adema and clear your head of this nonsense."

With a glance Eli silenced Chiron, suppressing his heated retort.

The Emperor set off to meet an ambassador from the trading port, leaving his son to wallow in the sun-bleached corridor. Eli thought the matter would right itself in the course of the ensuing weeks, when Chiron had ample time to procure an understanding of whichever notion first prompted him to try the limits of his freedom. Yet in suspecting Chiron of harbouring an ulterior motive when indeed he held none, he unwittingly drove the prince to those measures he had striven to prevent. The plan of the scrupulous Emperor spectacularly backfired in those minutes when Chiron stood at the head of the stairs and watched his retreat.

Aware that the thoughts which brewed within him as his father stomped out of sight were erratic both in content and in the power they exercised over him, Chiron allowed himself to be overwrought with a burning wish to flee from the palace and succeed where the guards had failed, and unearth the home of Erin. The maid no longer interested him, however: her purpose had been served. It was for Emilia that he would abandon the city.

From the hall he trudged to his chamber, where, for the long hours until he was roused to dine with the family, he dedicated his time to detailing the plan of his escape.

The most considerable obstruction it was necessary to overcome was the increased alert of the guards, although he supposed it unlikely that they had taken to patrolling the gardens, as there was no suggestion that Erin had managed to vaunt the its walls. To the prince this threat was welcome; his very soul ached for such a challenge. Yet he worried more about his route once within the city proper, not for fear of an ambush by a set of vagabonds or for losing his direction in some unknown square, but in anticipation of his own impatience – he wanted no delay. Of the journey which remained once the city's border had been trespassed he bequeathed no thought, perhaps concerned he would lose his nerve. An entire day of meditation brought no more definite plans than these: to leave by the gate in the gardens, to hurtle through Horizon, staying as loyal to the route he had taken Erin as memory permitted, and then to present himself to the girl Emilia.

At dinner his father was unsurprised to find him quiet and contemplative. Adema invited him, along with Acario and Leon, to join Javier and two other guests in the lounge afterwards, but Chiron found an excuse to decline: he had ruled against her company in case she succeeded in calming him. He was committed to Emilia's cause. It occurred as he ate half-heartedly, forgetting that he would not eat again until the next afternoon, that this endeavour, designed for his own pleasure, demanded a great deal in return, but this notion was similarly dismissed.

He attempted to talk to his brother, understanding that Acario had not intended, by revealing that Leon was to instruct him, to further enrage Chiron, and such was the lightness of the young prince's mood that he missed all signs of his sibling's distraction. To Leon, of course, the sight was obvious, but he took his cur from the Emperor, and left Chiron to reach his own resolution. The princess, who slumped in the chair opposite, spent the hour of their meal knotting her hair between her fingers, and paid attention to none of this. She, too, refused her mother's invitation, but in her case Adema insisted she attend.

Chiron was not so lost in his ruminations to ignore the danger of this small gathering; he asked of the chamber it was to be held, as if contemplating stepping in after all, and deduced that he must not linger on the second floor. He had decided to leave rather earlier than on the previous occasion. In this way the moments of excruciating anticipation before he began would be limited, and there was even, if he hurried, the slimmest of chances that he could arrive home without anyone noticing his absence. He had postponed the planning of what he would say to Emilia until he was trekking through Horizon, for in that darkness he would need an occupation.

Already he knew he could not impose his presence on the peasant family's house indefinitely.

He had not been quite as reckless as could be feared, then. No doubt he would reach Emilia only to discover that she was less important than the decision to take action itself, and would return, renewed. Yet Eli drove him to further desperateness. Chiron realised as he watched Ava nibble clumsily on a cut of fish that he could not be called to tomorrow's Advisory Breakfast. He pleaded illness to his father, and requested that he be allowed to sleep until midday. Eli frowned at the indolence of his son and ordered that he appear, fully dressed and attentive, at the usual hour. Acario thought his brother was scheming only to avoid Sawney and clapped him on the back in commiseration.

Although he would be caught, whether by the servant who came to wake him for the Breakfast and then reported the empty bed to his father, or perhaps earlier, if a guard spied him slipping out to the gardens and grew suspicious when he failed to reappear, this news did not spell the end of Chiron's plans. He became instead more determined. The punishment waiting in the future was too far away to be considered a notable obstacle. He would be punished, yes, but first he would flee.

At the close of the meal he again secreted himself in his princely bedchamber. There he donned another shirt beneath his blazer, and gazed from the window, looking through the city rather than at it, for a few moments as he debated whether to leave immediately, while his zeal was still fresh, or to wait another hour, in case someone came to visit him. In pacing his room he managed to waste an hour without any decision being reached at all. At the faint chime of a bell, whose echoes rang softly in the grounds of Delzean, Chiron tore himself from the window, and swept downstairs.

He had no reason to tread with a light step, for the hour was reasonable enough, nor to proceed slowly. Guards wandered within the palace walls but none questioned him when he slipped into the gardens, and fumbled in the lantern-light towards the gate.

Into Arden's garden he battled, and from there he broke into a sprint. Those soldiers stationed at the front of the palace surely heard his thundering footfalls, but if they suspected the sound to be the retreat of a thief with more gall than most they must have believed his capture to be the task of their lesser comrades.

Horizon was quieter now than on his last journey, but the peace of the city was deceptive, a mere lull before the vigour of the solstice day, and the resurgence of nefarious nocturnal doings in the coming year. The closely packed residences of the city's people meant the seasonal chill was kept at bay, particularly in the denser districts, though once in the country this protection would diminish. Whilst passing the estates of the nobles Chiron learned that the city presented a rather picturesque front in the darkness. This impression vanished once he breached the popular stretches of the city, where the streets were tainted with animation.

He traced the path set out for him from memory, deviating only to avoid the gaze of passers-by. There were no close calls that evening, an omen which led him to lower his guard.

It grew later, and he shuddered at a bitter wind, and halted at the sound of men's voices, and he felt the tug of lethargy, and longer for his bed. As a distraction from the panic rising in his breast he thoughts of Emilia:

He would seek out the little dwelling beneath the tree, and beat upon the door. As people of the country they would not resent the early awakening. He would show Emilia the ring on his chest, a fitting show of gratitude. Erin he would tell of the move to arrest her, and to her mother he would promise his protection. Then he remembered the svelte figure of the younger girl, and the smell of her hair when she had walked close, as it too immature to appreciate his lineage. He delighted in her, the emblem of his desires. The Chiron of a few months earlier would have laughed at these thoughts, had not known to whom they belonged.

At last he looked upon the watchtower of the city's boundary. It was most unfortunate that those in the watchtower looked back.

In light of Erin's escape and the approaching festivities, the tower had lately been manned from an earlier hour. It was most unfortunate still that it currently happened to be inhabited by the worst five men Chiron could encounter. The Lieutenant Vikernes and those two soldiers enscripted to the Eyes had requested the duty of overseeing the boundary in order to watch for the appearance of the burglars sent to the mountain settlements. It was predicted that they would return that week, and it was vital that they report to Sawney before snatching more than was their due from the loot. Sawney himself had joined the lieutenant, safe in the knowledge that no other soldier would come so close to the tower to apprehend him. Conn, too, was there, his brow furrowed against the cold as he listened to the discourse of his fellow conspirators.

Vikernes was the once to first recognise the youth skirting through the district towards them as the prince. It seemed Chiron had noticed that the tower was occupied, and was attempting to evade their detection. When he ordered the soldiers to move it was with the utmost stealth. They climbed to the ground before rushing in the prince's direction, splitting up with the aim of cornering him.

Sawney and Conn were forced to leave their perch, as the capture of the prince would prove counterproductive if he reported the unlawful invasion of army property, but remained together, and

Vikernes was instructed to visit the Delarus home at the closure of his shift, where they would be waiting, joined in the early hours by Mathias and Lorian.

The change in Chiron's situation was mercilessly swift. In one moment he was apprehended, at the very edge of the city, and his progress became futile. The soldiers behind him grasped onto his arms but he felt no pain other than that of defeat. Then Vikernes appeared from the shadows and the moon-faced soldier at his side stifled a laugh.

"This is an alarming sight. A prince wandering unprotected through the streets. How did you slip past the guards? The Emperor must know of their inattention. He will be most disheartened to hear you have escaped again?"

The significance of that 'again' was lost on Chiron, as he gritted his teeth in frustration. He was preoccupied with that which had been taken from him. There was a degree of comfort in this, for it diverted his attention from the torment he would suffer presently.

"Why were you heading for the city boundary?"

In response to Chiron's silence his arms were pulled tighter still across his back, and the other soldier stepped closer. They were preparing for him to renew his attempt to flee, for it seemed he had lost his senses.

"March for the palace. Keep hold of him," barked Vikernes.

The grip which crushed Chiron's arm grew only stronger as they moved; he was afraid to struggle lest he was held tighter and his bones snapped. It was humiliating t be escorted in such a fashion even for a few seconds.

Chiron became furious with the Lieutenant and his sneering manner, but thought it wiser to remain mute until he was calm-minded enough to explain his behaviour without revealing that he had journeyed beyond the boundary before. He certainly could not name Erin or Emilia. He breathed heavily to steady himself. An explanation must be to hand when he faced his father – Eli would not settle for a mere admission of wrongdoing. He would be expected to detail his escape from the palace, and his passage through the city.

Whilst the prince was occupied with the scene that awaited him in the palace, unbeknownst to him Vikernes had abandoned his line of questioning to mutter to the other soldier, who then came to walk on Chiron's left side, and whispered something to his captor.

Each time Chiron turned his attention to the progress at hand it was to hear the Lieutenant remark, with a caustic smile, how despicable it was to observe the disobedience of a royal son, how deplorable was his refusal to help those who only wished to help him. He had been overcome with passion, inflicted with madness, continued Vikernes, amidst the agreement of the others, an affliction worthy of a mortal perhaps, but not of a prince.

Their prisoner became agitated as they entered the busier barrows of Horizon (Vikernes was intent on leading him through those reaches where peasants may yet remain to glimpse the prince); it was this heightened anxiety which goaded him to answer his captors.

"I am as sane as you are, Lieutenant. Do not address me like a criminal!!"

His rage was pleasing. It paved the way for further provocation. "Unless you have the permission of the Emperor to have strayed thus far from home, you have committed a crime akin to treason. You are a criminal, your highness."

In disgust Chiron spat upon the ground.

Around them came a hum of distant movement, as the late night procession of tavern crawlers began. For what he claimed was the purpose of Chiron's greater protection, Vikernes enlisted the first patrol squad they encountered on the lonely streets to accompany them to the palace. The procession of these soldiers attracted the interest of a crowd, and when they neared Delzean the guards jumped to attention at the approach of such a horde. The soldiers had deflected all questions from the citizenry, yet Chiron's face was hot with shame as if the whole world knew of his arrest. His entire frame shuddered with embarrassment.

Once within the shelter of his home Chiron suffered a torment which dwarfed that of his previous experience. Vikernes dismissed every soldier save the pair who had borne witness to this arrest, and called for the Emperor to be roused from his chamber.

Eli's alarm at being stirred from slumber by a panic-stricken servant turned quickly to irritation upon entering the Reception Room. There Vikernes bowed to him, and spoke of the watchtower, whilst in the hall's centre Chiron stood, his head slumped, a soldier on each arm. The interrogation lasted in extent of an hour; by its close, Eli's throat was hoarse and Chiron's cheeks burned red.

He was firm in his decision to abstain from mentioning Erin and Emilia, and indeed made no statement to suggest that he possessed any acquaintance beyond the boundary. The story Eli extracted from him by meticulous degrees read simply that he had grown agitated and in a fit of boredom set out to scour the streets. For this foolish notion Eli rewarded him with his deep laughter; it was with an effort that Vikernes restrained his own.

The latter part of the Emperor's questioning concerned the evasion of the guards. Only when he strode forward and seized his son by the shoulder did Chiron admit to the discovery of a gate. Eli was untroubled to learn of its existence: if a lifelong resident of the palace had no knowledge of the entrance it was clear that any criminal to whom the gate would be of use was similarly witless. Instead he decreed that at least the guards had not been plied with bribes. He assured Chiron that the courtyard would be lined with soldiers until he proved himself trustworthy. Indeed, after Vikernes was thanked gratuitously for his cooperation and took his triumphant leave, Eli informed his son that he would be issued with a personal guard, to watch and report upon his movements, who would stand outside his chamber door while he slept in case he was so stupendously idiotic that he contemplated a repeat venture.

There was a bleakness, a bitter resolve, in Chiron's expression when he was finally permitted to retire to his rooms, in the company of a guard. Eli's ferocity stalked his dreams.

The Emperor had thought the gate, a cloaked entrance onto the grounds, to be of little importance. In this he overlooked the fact that Vikernes, a close companion of Sawney, had been privy to the revelation. The lieutenant was not a man to be trusted with such information. True to form he sped to the dank abode of the Delarus three, and imparted to them the events following the arrest. The attention of his listeners peaked when he culminated with the description of the gate. Within the hour Lorian and Mathias had been dispatched to Arden's grounds to prowl for the passageway. The expected return of the burglars was brushed aside as the brothers returned, crowing with victory.

Chapter Fifteen

The shameful capture of the prince soon lapsed into rumour. It was a mere whisper amongst the clamour of the solstice, which had now, at last, dawned upon the city. At daybreak children were unleashed onto the streets whilst their parents capitalized on the day's reprieve from labour and service by squandering the scant bright hours in the taverns. In the busiest of these dank halls, the patrons were crouched in tight arrays across the floor. By midday the sun loomed high above the artisans and performers; it seemed the recent surrender to frostiness had been a simple move of strategy, an attempt to preserve its strength. On this most brief of days, the revellers toiled under a heat as thick as that of mid-summer.

From the farmlands beyond the border came a procession of pilgrims: a body of peasants two hundred strong passed along the road that morning. Tradition dictated that the carnival proper did not begin until the stroke of three, but the citizenry was not one to be happily constrained by such deadened conventions. A troupe of actors, trained in the dances of the country-dwellers, the performance of which was still a spectacle of some novelty, had given rise to a crowd in the Zodiac Gardens. It would be this same crowd, bolstered by the addition of fifty others, which would burst into riot several hours later, and cause the death of two soldiers. The early awakening, for two thirds of the populace awoke before seven; the oppressive heat; and the frenzy which came naturally with excitement; contributed each to a mood at once pronounced and indistinct.

The residents of Delzean were denied a view of these festivities. For the six members of the royal household, the solstice began only after they had dined, and moved to climb into the carriage paused before the palace gates.

Acario and Chiron tramped together down the stairs, the former in a state of anticipation that owed much to ignoring the mood of the latter. Behind them came the guard, whose steps mirrored Chiron's; Eli had been resolute in depriving his son of liberty.

The eldest prince had taken pains over his appearance in order to provide an occupation for a mind that suffered under lack of profitable thought, and had even permitted an attendant to trim his hair. He wore, as ever, Emilia's ring, and above that a shirt and blazer, but despite the apathy which tugged at the corners of his mouth he had adorned, for a change, the smile he had for some while mourned.

Unable to distinguish the tumultuous moods of his brother, Acario was unsure whether the rise in his spirits was to be welcomed. He chose instead to give his own feelings primacy, and there was a definite skip in his step as he headed towards the parade. There seemed little outward change in either brother; indeed, they looked, as they chattered in low voices, wary of the proximity of the guard, much the same princes as before:

"Leon said an acquaintance of Sawney's sons was arrested yesterday," confided the younger, "Will either of them ever succeed Sawney?"

"I hope not," chuckled the elder, picturing the expression of Cyrus and Arden if Lorian were to secrete his loathsome form in the

Breakfast Hall, "But I expect the same question was asked of Sawney himself."

Taking advantage of Chiron's joviality, Acario continued: "Will they be joining the other nobles?"

"Yes, of course, father affords their misdemeanours rather more leniency than mine!"

This aside was only the second time they had spoken of his attempt to leave the city. Acario deduced from his unfaltering smile that the mention caused no upset, but nevertheless hastened to speak of other matters.

The reaction of his relatives had been the source of enduring commiseration to the prince. Although abashed by the sympathetic and yet, perhaps for the fact of her pity, cutting words of his aunt, he was affected more so by the frustration of his cousin, with whom he endured a painful hour in which Leon asked to know of his intended destination, and when it became apparent that no answer would be received, had turned to remarking on the general's idiocy in indulging his secret wanderings before, and culminated in a lecture on upholding the family's honour. It was in light of this lecture that Chiron now tingled with guilt whenever his eyes fell upon the Castilian coat of arms.

Ava's reaction to his disgrace was one of schadenfreude, of smug, undisguised glee. In rejecting her proposal, he had proved himself unstable; here was further confirmation. Yet the princess had been pushed by the entrance of Emilia from his mind, and was no granted no consideration. With Acario, on the other hand, he had dreaded a direct confrontation – he did not believe he was capable of undergoing the disappointment of his sibling. His role was supposed to be that of the dominant, the leader, not the example of folly from which the younger would learn. It proved less excruciating, their meeting, than he predicted: Acario entered his chamber the following afternoon, his admittance granted by the guard stationed beyond the door, whose presence had forced Chiron to seek privacy with renewed zeal, and had asked only whether he had departed for the purpose of meeting the girl Emilia. The prince preferred to view this as a jibe, as if Acario supposed him to be in possession of an ill-fated notion to elope and live as a peasant, rather than an enquiry worthy of an honest reply, and refused him the same intelligence he had denied Leon. To his credit, Acario revealed the truth of Chiron's first foray beyond Horizon's borders to no one; though this could justly be construed as an act of supreme misjudgement – a fair conclusion would be that Acario had come belatedly to appreciate the significance of his own wellbeing, and in such a position was more entitled than anyone to observe without care to intervene, the woes of another.

Emilia had resulted in a gulf between them, a distance which neither were willing to trespass, yet Acario was about to be snatched still further from the confidence of his brother by the actions of that other, Ava.

In ignorance of the evening's end, it was with enthusiasm that Acario clambered into the carriage. The family were snugly seated, three facing three.

Ava had contrived to hide her face from the masses that paved every road from Delzean to the terminating square, by the means of a cardinal-coloured parasol, but as she was placed in the middle of Leon and Adema, it served instead to graze the side of whichever head was unfortunate enough to be on whichever side she directed the device. Eli suggested she throw it to the crowd as a souvenir. By a nudge from her mother, who had taken Eli's suggestion to be rather more kindly than he had perhaps intended it, she was induced to comply, and as the carriage was pulled on from the dislodged parasol's squabbling claimants she folded her voluminously clad arms in a sulk. When she furrowed her brow at every bump in the road both the princes and their father stifled their respective sniggers.

By the time of the parade's closure, a sizeable proportion of the populace lumbered clumsily under the influence of spirits. Many of these saw fit to call out to the carriage, and from the slurred chorus could be deciphered wishes of wellbeing. In response Eli stood every quarter hour to bow to his subjects, but no reciprocal speech was made. He, too, could defy convention: he desired only to slip from the gaze of the crowd into the square cordoned off for those whose favour he had no need to earn, for they denied him no show of affection. By nature the Emperor was a man built to distrust praise when it was offered credulous heaps, but the conduct of his son had pressed him to crave an evening of relentless comfort.

Just as patience deserted the most stoic of the passengers, the carriage came at last to a halt, and the family descended into the darkness.

The square was large enough to accommodate the entire fleet of soldiers. The nearest of the peasants were yet too distant to discern the expression on their sovereign's face; he responded to their applause with another bow, then shook hands with the waiting military officials, before leading his family into the maze of stalls hidden from the crowd's sight. They were prevented from struggling any closer to the nobles by the ring of guards positioned along the circumference of Vorcello.

Those guards not entrusted with the protection of their sovereign disappeared en masse into the theatre. Leon had suggested (he thought it safer, when bargaining, to infer rather than ask outright) that he and Acario be permitted to join them; the younger prince had been witless of the request and its refusal, which was kinder. Had he known of the great hall spread for seven hundred and of the camaraderie his father deprived him, the lurid festivities would have seemed dulled, diminished. A feeling of the sort was shared by the legion of soldiers inflicted with the duty of patrol on the solstice day; these men would react to the cruelty of their superiors by wandering from the busiest plots, turning a blind eye to many conspicuous scenes.

Eli had preferred the princes to remain amongst their kind, the nobles, and to assert their loyalties to the crown. He reckoned their absence from the square to be an insult upon the heads of his patrons. Yet he did not care for his sons to follow him, as they had always done; no pleasure could be derived from sharing his observations with that secretive, sullen pair. He was apt to cast

Acario into the same shade as his brother, and left both to stroll the market at their own pace.

Eli faltered long enough to burden Chiron with a guard, a stocky man for whom he felt a quite unwarranted dislike. As heir to nobles' affection, Chiron was further encumbered with a quadruplet of admirers within moments of his arrival. They were introduced as the nieces and nephews of one Advisor or another. Their company was desired only a touch less than at the ball, but it was for the purpose of aggravating his bodyguard that he shrugged off their approach. He was not in the mood to provide the man with fodders of rumour. Instead he decided to prowl alone, although he would abandon his attempt to prevent any addition to the whispers about his instability being gleaned from the evening if he encountered Leon or his brother.

When the stalls were stripped away the succeeding afternoon it was unimaginable that such a number of people could be contained in that section of the square, yet that evening Chiron could find neither cousin nor brother until the night was nearly at a close. It was not the fault of the darkness entirely, for the odd lantern stood between the stalls, yet the square was undoubtedly darker than the remainder of the city, where a candle had been placed on every doorstep, save for those dwellings on Horizon's very outskirts. The celebrations in Vorcello were the most muted, despite it being privileged with the finest merchants and entertainers.

Beside the royal carriage a band of musicians had began to play. Around them danced only the oldest, most respectable members of aristocratic stock, as the young were discouraged from indulging in such a spectacle. Adema and Javier were the liveliest amongst them. Chiron moved to watch a little later, but for the first hour he watched a juggler, and then a troupe of dancers, the superiors of those who frolicked in the gardens, before pawing at the goods for sale, the sugared fruit and jewellery, held under the light of a candle for his scrutiny. In the scattered stalls of the true city, engravings of his father and handkerchiefs stitched with the Castilian motto would be sold. The stalls of Vorcello were nearly a guise, a means of enabling the nobles to have some cause to meet and prattle.

He found Adema only to be advised that Leon had gone to visit his colleagues in the bowels of the theatre; he wasted no breath asking Eli for the same favour. Acario he glimpsed twice in a circle of those whose company he had appeared to relish at Leon's ball. When he sought him a third time, this time intending to endure the others in order to talk with his brother, the group had dispersed.

His enemy Sawney made only a brief appearance, seemingly just to deposit his sons, who had been celebrating with the rabble since morning. They were sent to stand in place of their father, as business called him elsewhere. The burglary had been successful; it was to the basement den of the Eyes that he headed, after a cordial exchange with the Emperor, to chair another, more exclusive, gathering. The Delarus sons were treated like pariahs in the absence of their father. There was scant need for pretence without Sawney to remind them of the youths' status. Both were intoxicated, though somewhat deflated by the day's activity.

Chiron did not bear witness to the meeting of Mathias and Ava. She responded to his greeting with a mere nod, and would have turned to move towards her mother (Adema had requested that she dance) if he had not afforded her a lengthy, albeit insincere, apology for her neglect. He was correct in guessing the cause of her distemper. He had spoken to her simply because hers was the first face he recognised. Once he embarked on his apology, however, he recalled the other reasons for him to soften the princess. Yet his thirst for information overpowered these purposes:

"I heard of your cousin's *accident*," he began, "How has the Emperor treated him?"

Ava was too pleased of his attention to recognise this as a search for slander, and told him of the guard stationed outside Chiron's bedchamber. This titbit he repeated to Lorian later, to a warm reception.

"We could dance, if you like?"

"No, thank you."

"...You could walk with me through the market, if you want to?"

"I will," answered Ava, as if bestowing him the greatest honour.

They were standing beside the platform erected for the juggler when Lorian pounced. Ava was looking towards the stage, expecting the man to appear from nowhere, while Mathias' eyes were turned towards the larger stage, where the dancers scampered on the tips of their toes. His hand hovered an inch from her shoulder. Lorian had been led to the pair by the remarks of those who perceived them.

The elder of the brothers had pilfered an old coat of Sawney's, and for this seemed sharper, more alert, than the younger, despite having consumed such a share of spirits. His movements were no more ungainly than Mathias; as he lurched towards the princess.

"How *are* you, your highness?" he bellowed, recovering the attention of their neighbours.

"Brother! I thought perhaps you had gone after father."

"But why would I neglect the dear princess here?" To Ava he performed the semblance of a sweeping bow. "Will her highness dance with us?"

"We are waiting for the juggler," replied Ava.

Mathias tittered at her evident unease, and Lorian smirked: "My brother only wants to keep you in sight of the crowd. Let us move along."

Neither cared to disobey him; Lorian had a way of integrating himself as leader. Together they loped along, the fabricated alleys half-empty as the nobles lost interest in all but the musicians by the carriage. Meanwhile, in the far-removed gardens, a fire was started. It would rage for all of ten minutes, yet spread to such a reach of grass that the revellers fell into a frenzy. Within the hour the first of the fatalities was beaten to death by the crowd. In the small hours of the morning Lisandro would relate his experience in the drawing room of the Delarus home.

"Where is your father?"

The princess paused a few feet distant from Lorian, her arms folded. Without her parasol she felt exposed, although had it remained in her possession she would in face have been more noticeable. It was too dark, the brothers were too *strange*; she wanted to return to the light of the centre square. The heat had begun again to dissipate. Her companions were accustomed to this nocturnal ebbing, and she was refrained the offer of Lorian's coat.

"He is occupied with business. But we cannot trouble you with his nefarious dealings. A girl such as yourself should be kept away from secrets."

"He is teasing you, princess. Sawney had a meeting planned for this evening. That's all."

Lorian ignored his brother's warning stare. "We must not sully the princess with our secrets. She is the model of virtue, after all."

The edge to his voice was not too subtle for Ava; he was perhaps too far beyond his senses to convince her of the comment's flattery.

"Then you can trust me with your secrets, can you not?"

Mathias recognised in the girl a longing for power that was quite pitiable. He placed a hand upon her shoulder, and said in a stage-whisper: "We hardly have secrets equal to your interests. Forgive my brother; he forgets himself."

"I do not. I would trust the princess with my very soul, had she only a secret to exchange in return."

Lorian had a similar understanding of her nature: he intended to create a rise in her, to unearth the story of some minor embarrassment to pass on amongst the Eyes. She would, surely, protest against the claim that she had little life of her own. It was a sad fact that the crude, lupine Lorian was shown to be correct.

"I think you are implying I have no secrets. But I do, Mister Delarus!"

"Please, your highness, I beg that you confide in us. We are at your service."

He drew closer to the girl, the better to hear her. The appetite in his countenance was unmistakable. In response Mathias doubled his grip on Ava. The trio remained in these poses whilst Ava made her revelation, the head of Lorian cocked forward, whilst the smaller youth frowned at the ground, resigned.

"I was the one to find Acario after Adrienne fell," she breathed, "and I made him believe that her death was his fault. I told him he was a murderer. I promised to tell no one-"

Here she faltered. She realised the ease with which Lorian had extracted her one claim to power. Yet within a moment she had steadied herself. These two were below accusing her. Even if she had yet to question the benefits of their confidence, she understood it to be a relief. It was more tangible, now, when related to an outsider. The games she played with Acario assumed an adult form.

"-I promised not to tell, and in return he became my slave. I can make him do *anything.*"

Lorian was the first to recover from this most disconcerting revelation. He beamed across at his sibling; Mathias had allowed his arm to fall back to his side, whilst he worked furiously to digest this information, and the smirk he exchanged resembled a grimace.

"What have you had him do, my dear princess?"

A blush had spread across her chest, as though the chill had been vanquished. "I ordered him to cut open his palm, once."

"What do you seek to gain from this?" It was Mathias who spoke, in a tone that suggested he was caught somewhere between awe and disgust.

"..I want to be...*revered*."

Her cheeks now were flushed. The word was one she had borrowed from a tirade of Eli's. He had spoken of the duty they each owed to the family name. She had forgotten that this was the speech made on Chiron's sixteenth birthday, years after the event – was she able to distinguish between this and her original motive?

"The two of us will assist you in any way we can," vowed Lorian.

"Yes," agreed his brother, his decision made, "We must agree to meet again. We have occupied Ava for too long already."

"Her mother will not yet have sent a scout," scoffed the other, fully aware of what Mathias intended to suppress and in no mood to comply. He was extravagant in his reckless turns; while Chiron had jeopardised only his own sanity, the eldest Delarus was prepared to risk the security of his family and associates, of his father's enterprise, on a whim. "Let us repay her honesty."

He extended Ava his arm, which she refused. Nonplussed, he lurched forward with her at his side. Mathias tailed behind as they made hesitant progress towards the main square. He was resolved to suppress the revulsion he felt for Ava – deplorable as her actions were, it meant that a prince could be brought under her control. She had handed to them a means of undermining the Emperor, if that was how they choose to deploy it. It was for Sawney to decide how her confidence could best be abused.

By the time of their arrival at the periphery of the crowd, Chiron had at last stumbled across Acario. A nephew of Arden's had learned of his military ambitions, and insisted that he attend the feast in the theatre. Before he was forced into the grasp of Sawney, then, he at least enjoyed this one, untarnished night.

By this time Ava had been educated in all matters relating to the Eyes: the fact of their existence, the names of its leader and members, and of the role played by her two companions. She would lie awake that night, the disorder of her chamber subdued in the darkness, thinking of Vikernes, and of the doctor Fernandez, who preyed on the vulnerability of those in his care.

In the moments before Adema swept across the square to rescue her daughter, it was agreed that these three would convene again the following evening in the gardens of Delzean, with the notable addition of Acario. Ava was eager to prove the truth of her admission, and assured them he would be as pliable and meek as they could want. In her excitement she declined to ask how the brothers planned to breach the palace gardens.

Chapter Sixteen

The morning light hastened to mock the revelry of the day before. The revellers themselves were sheltered behind shutters and doors, and the sun could only glance between the panes. The Delarus home was flushed with its success, yet even Sawney had succumbed to the city-wide stupor. A dispatch had been sent to forewarn Eli of his absence at the Breakfast and the Advisor slumbered long after his sons awoke. His sleep was always a shallow, dreamless one. It was a mark of his faith in the brothers that he did not call for them before they departed.

Lorian had begun to laugh as he dressed – it had been simple, far too simple, to win the princess' secret. His clothes were in a worse state of disarray than ever and reeked of ale as though it oozed from pores beneath, but these presented no obstacle to his plans. It was not to seduce Ava that they reported to the palace, but rather to secure Acario. A prince they could make use of. Neither were the brothers immune to the after effects of the solstice, however enlivening a prospect their mission posed. Had their quest been of less import both would have remained steadfast in their cushion-beds. They chuckled to each other in gruff voices, and crowed at the mention of Ava's name. Without Sawney's offerings from the royal table their stomachs growled. They felt a mutual regret for the years spent in eager torment of the servants that would have otherwise greeted them with breakfast. Mathias stared at the ceiling while Lorian combed and cemented his hair, pondering the demise of their old feud to gain the princess' favour. It seemed almost innocent in comparison.

The hour was early yet when they vacated the squat little house. After the initial effort to shake life into his legs Lorian began to positively bound forward, brimming with pride at the fruit of their efforts so far. He was determined to parade a princely prize in front of his father's comrades. This energy was catching. By the stroke the five Delzean's unheralded guests had arrived.

They were counting on Arden's estate being infected, too, with the indolence that feasted on the peasants. Fate had spun in their favour, for the Advisor had fallen ill and no servants had been spared to stand outdoors. The shrouded gate was found without a conscious thought from their heads, as though their limbs had their dark intent for a compass.

The guards briefed by Eli to defend the gardens patrolled only the lawns nearest to the palace. Witless of the passage through which Horizon's criminal sons were soon to pour, on this subdued day they patrolled not even these short stretches but lay slumped in the shade instead. Lorian dwelled again on the simplicity of it all as they waited, open-eared, for the sound of an approach.

Acario had been dozing carelessly in his room when Ava entered; the book he used to scribble notes to his mother had, mercifully, fallen from his hand onto the floor, out of Ava's sight. It would have been too cruel a torture for the privacy of that book to be stolen from him, too. For years afterwards the memory of that awakening would bring a chill to his breast.

Ava was swathed in a gown of her mother's, her chest heaving with hectic breaths. She dispelled the comfort of his chamber whilst he lay there inert, at first, and then clambered to his feet when she revealed the connection of the Delarus trio to the Eyes. Such was the magnitude of this revelation and the nightmarish quality of Ava's flushed face that he half believed he was dreaming. She gave him no chance to interrupt.

He was to accompany her to the gardens: his secret had been offered in exchange for theirs. In an instant he understood his situation to be dire, although not yet lost. Ava turned her back for a moment to allow him to struggle into a pair of robes. She could have beamed at his resolute expression had she not been riddled with nerves at the thought of the approaching encounter – here was her chance to surpass the limits of her birth. It empowered her to crush the protests of her cousin; she would have suffered a bitter disappointment if he had meekly accepted the betrayal.

Acario gathered his wits to placate the tumultuous princess as he followed her into the corridor. The place lay bare around them but he hastened nevertheless to raise his voice in the hope of alerting some lurking guard.

"Ava, you must understand what you've done! You have led two traitors onto the palace grounds. We must find my father. How easily we could capture them, and you would be rewarded!"

"Are you not worried for your own safety? They know of your secret; would you have Eli learn it from them?"

The staircase occupied them for a moment, as Ava hurtled downstairs at a speed quite unsafe for one clad in such a cumbersome dress.

The significance of their knowledge had not yet dawned on him, although his early premonitions were hardly encouraging. To be tormented by others with minds sharper than Ava's…It was his fervent wish to obstruct her plans, the consequences for himself notwithstanding, but as soon as she had spoken he was convinced it would be far worse to enter into the brothers' confidence. Better that his father punished him than those rogues.

"Eli would be loath to believe the words of traitors," he replied as she turned to meet his eyes.

"Dare call me a traitor? I would tell him the truth. You deserve to be punished no less than they do."

Her voice lacked the emotion evident in her expression, for she scowled at her young cousin, and he almost trembled at the loathing etched on her pale face. He represented all the qualities that she despised in herself, and as he stood there, close to tears, weak and ineffectual, she cursed him with a hatred she had not known herself capable of.

"Fine! Fine!" he cried. Had her touch repulsed him less he would have seized her. "Tell my father, if you want. But go to him now, not the gardens. Lorian and Mathias cannot be trusted."

"They can help me," answered Ava with a smile, "I am on their side."

She resumed her rapid pace but Acario lingered there, praying that their display would disturb the preparations for dinner. He resolved to appeal to the side of her that he had always suspected, the side that craved a kind of otherworldly power. "Eli is the one you should appeal to. His reward will dwarf theirs. No one will forget that their capture is down to you. Please, Ava!"

He had been right to appeal to her ego. For a moment she regarded him, and it seemed clear, for all of a second, that Eli was the one whose approval she should covet. But then, had he not brushed her aside for years? She would only lose by turning to the Emperor. Her recognition had to be gained through the use of others. When she uttered *"They should have been born princes, not you,"* he knew he was defeated.

There was always the option to run, of course. He could have fled to his chamber, barred the door and thwarted her for an evening. The coming torment could have been avoided for a day, perhaps, but there was no doubt she would find him again. Four walls would not hide him forever.

As they passed at length into the courtyard she instructed him to take her arm. There was nothing suspicious in taking a stroll before dinner, but it seemed less so if Acario was not dragging his feet behind her. The red stones crunched beneath their feet as they disturbed the relative silence of the grounds. The sky was already darkening around them; it seemed intent to add further haste to their progress. Arm in reluctant arm, they slipped into the gardens.

***

As Ava and Acario wound their way deeper into the more furtive reaches of the gardens, the former tearing at an anxious hangnail, Chiron lay sprawled across his bed. When his brother had lain in such a pose across his own bed it had been in expression of the lethargy that naturally followed a long evening of activity, but Chiron's was an expression of deeper fatigue.

Over the course of the past weeks he had exhausted his mental faculties. Emilia had become such a puzzle to him that he had plucked the ring from his chest. It rested now upon his pillow. He failed to recognise the turbulent thoughts that slunk through his head as his own. He had called for a servant to brush the dust from his blazer and donned it again as if to reclaim the self he seemed to have misplaced. Other than this servant he had seen no-one that day. He almost longed for the inane chatter of the dinner table.

The knock on the door came as a welcome diversion – he had begun to think again of his brother's visit to the barracks and the aftertaste of jealously unsettled him. With a shake he righted himself and was confronted by Leon. The elder prince had come equipped with a chessboard to appease his cousin. "I thought it best to seek you out directly," explained the general, "If you would grant me a game?"

Chiron had to grin at this display of diplomacy. "Of course. Anything for my favourite cousin."

Together they crouched onto the floor, and Leon congratulated himself on finding the prince in high spirits. The general had no intention of leaving the chamber until the cause of Chiron's depression was unearthed. Together they could vanquish it in the light of day. He had very little idea of what horrors Chiron's mind was capable of conjuring. Resolved as he was to devote the evening to the case, he saw no reason to rush the matter. Leon hummed behind his teeth as they kneeled around the board, and racked his brains.

The set Leon had fetched was carved of ivory. Every piece was considered one of Delzean's greatest treasures. Chiron's pawn glimmered in the sun as he pushed it across the board. He was as competitive as his military opponent. Despite anticipating Leon's aim in coming to his chamber, the outcome of the game presented a worthy distraction. He gave no thought to how he would answer Leon's qualms.

The two princes formed an incongruous picture as they sat hunched over the minute board.

"Your father told me that not even one of the Advisors arrived for the Breakfast this morning. Do you reckon they were behind the riots?"

"Perhaps. The city will surely fall to ruins now, without the council of those old beggars."

These early signs were heartening. The game engrossed them for a few moments, before Chiron surprised him by asking after the barracks. Although Chiron rebuffed any question about his dark mood, they were able to talk amicably for a while.

"You may know of Javier's brother, Jonas?"

Leon's knight hovered above the board as he contemplated his next move. Although a ruse, the game had succoured the lion's share of their attention.

"He's related to the lawyer Jonas?" Chiron arched an eyebrow.

The name registered only as the subject of many of Eli's complaints. He was of shady repute; it was for lack of evidence against him that his cases were nearly always attended by the Advisors.

"Yes, his brother. They were estranged, you see, but last night Javier complained of his attention. It seemed Jonas was trying to ingratiate himself with my mother to delay his inevitable persecution. He's been suspected of involvement with the Eyes for years. Javier wants some form of protection from his advances. Eli asked me to see whether a soldier could be spared from the patrols to shadow him."

He set down his knight and knocked a pawn from the board. Chiron was ignorant of this setback, however, for at the mention of the Eyes the image of a scrawled note began to pound behind his temples. It must be Jonas Rana that Sawney had addressed. But why would a trusted Advisor make a point of informing someone of such low standing as Jonas of the outcome of a case? It would have been senseless, had he not believed Sawney to be equally unworthy of the palace's faith. Perhaps the Advisor had considered the criminal involved to be useful to Jonas in some way, but what use could he have for a convict, unless Jonas planned to harness his labours in service of the Eyes? And what reason would Sawney have to play a role in this recruitment, unless he too had something to gain?

Chiron had been staring through Leon for near a minute, his mind working furiously, before the general roused him. "Not all is lost, Chiron, take your turn!" He made scant effort to mask his bemusement.

"Jonas…" muttered his competitor in response.

Chiron leapt from the floorboards and dragged out a trunk from beneath his bed. It was within this container that he had confined the notebook abandoned by Sawney in the courthouse. This was the most animated he had appeared in weeks yet the sight filled Leon with trepidation.

"Are you alright?"

"Where is it? Here! Look, Leon…" the prince crouched again before his cousin and offered across the book. "It belonged to Sawney, before. I found it in the courthouse. Look, there, at the edge of the page. A note for Jonas."

"Why would they be in contact?"

Leon found the note most beguiling. As unbelievable as his first deduction seemed, there was no alternative. "If Jonas has avoided arrest because he has been protected by Sawney…"

"More so than that, Leon. You mentioned that Jonas is suspected to belong to the Eyes. How can we be certain that Sawney does not rank amongst their number?"

Chiron's slanderous remark could not be dismissed as the ravings of one with a grudge. Leon held proof of Sawney's ill judgement in his own hands. It was only the extent of his corruption that remained to be determined. "Are there any other notes?"

Relieved that the notebook fascinated Leon as much as it had entranced him, Chiron hurried to answer. "Not any more addressed to Jonas, but several cases attracted his interest. Names have been circled."

"Let me see if I can recognise any."

A whole world of criminal connections now seemed apparent to Leon. He had been in complete ignorance of Jonas' relationship with Sawney. It followed that many others were perhaps connected in this way. Chiron could have had the key to purging Horizon of its criminals festering in his chamber for years. The chess game lay forgotten as Leon skimmed every page of the volume. Chiron paced across to the window and regarded the city.

"Several cases are familiar to me…" said Leon, closing the book, "It would be easy work to research the persons involved. I believe we could find a link between these men and all sorts of underhand behaviour."

"Will you come speak to my father? He may grant your word more weight than mine," spoke Chiron with a wry smile.

"Certainly. I could take this book with me now and search the records in the Scroll Room. It would be unwise to call out an Advisor as a traitor without substantial proof. With your permission, of course."

The general stood, his limbs grateful of the reprieve.

"We must alert him soon…." Chiron was wary of this waning interest. Was Leon merely playing along with his suspicions?

"The barracks can spare me for a morning. We can waylaid him after tomorrow's Breakfast."

They bowed in agreement and, feeling no phrase capable of capturing the moment's magnitude, Leon left in silence. Chiron crouched to gather the pieces of the game. He bore an exultant grin as he arranged the figures on the windowsill. He moved them only to have something to occupy his body. Otherwise he would have stomped his feet and roared in triumph.

Meanwhile, Sawney's sons prowled in the garden, witless that a plan for their father's downfall had been devised in the palace beyond.

Lorian galloped forward at the first sound of footsteps. Mathias arrived to join the circle a moment later and found Lorian stooped over Ava's hand, onto which he planted a lingering, open-mouthed kiss. Acario's arm had struggled free but he was terrified into immobility. Every gesture the older brother made suggested that an ordeal awaited him. They were bolder in approaching the royal children than they had been before. It shamed him to see his cousin fondled by such a pair. The younger brother bowed to both prince and princess – neither gesture conveyed much respect. Acario absorbed their appearances in a glance: they were unwashed, weary and the set of each mouth more resembled a snarl than a welcoming smile.

"Sweetness," beamed Lorian, by way of introduction, for no one else felt inclined to dispel the tension, "You beggar all description."

Ava blushed and gestured towards her cousin. "I brought Acario," she stated, somewhat pointlessly.

"I see that, your highness." Lorian turned his gaze upon the prince. "How much has the princess told you?"

"She has told me much."

Mathias was surprised that the prince managed even this response. How could he not tremble under the knowledge that he was now the property of Sawney? For it was Sawney that had schooled them in how to conduct the meeting; it was their father's wish that they sought to fulfil. He had made it clear, tangibly clear, that this was no time to play with their quarry. It was time to seize the prince and drive him towards action. They would stay to prowl the reaches of

Delzean until this objective had been secured. Lorian seemed nonetheless determined to derive a certain amount of amusement from the encounter. This much Mathias derived from his introductory remark: Lorian had uttered to Ava the phrase they used in turn to charm their female acquaintances.

The prince's singular contribution to the conversation met with a grimace from his tormentor. "Yet I expect there is still more to tell."

Ava allowed him to link his arm through hers, and she fell into step with his bustling strides. "What more do you care to know?"

A defensive tone had crept into her voice. She must be on guard; it was to help herself that she had dragged the prince outside, not to assist them.

"Only as much as you wish to divulge. We are here to help you, your highness," said Mathias calmly, as an antidote to the twitching manner of his fellow.

He walked on the other side of Ava, a step behind. He glanced at Acario every odd moment to satisfy the same sense that plagued

Lorian, the sense that he had been delivered onto them too easily. The boy provoked no pity in the breast of his observer, although this could be credited to the dejected way in which he slunk behind the party. Mathias could better emphasise with defiance.

His interjection was barely heeded by Lorian, who was by now drunk on immorality.

Ava cared not that the subject of her forthcoming speech was present. He was hardly in any position to object to her revelations, in any sense. With another prompting from Lorian she began to divulge every exchange that had passed between her and Acario. They learned, in a walk of half hour's duration, of how he had suffered to clean her chamber on the days she could not stand the company of the servants; how she had ordered the boy to fetch the dress of his deceased mother and had paraded it in front of him; how she had stolen him from every friend in the academy; how she pleaded him to remain in his chamber as often as possible, so that he could be found whenever she needed.

When they learned of how she made him slice open his palm, Acario consented to Mathias lifting his wrist and examining the wound. He sought the gaze of his brother. It came as a relief to see that Lorian's sickened expression mirrored his own.

Already this insight could have crippled the Castilian dynasty. But Acario understood that hearing the history of his torment would not satisfy the brothers. He had listened shamefacedly to the lisping tirade of the princess. Chiron would hang his head to hear of his brother's obedience to this diminutive girl. He was aware of Mathias' flickering gaze but did not trouble himself to acknowledge the brute. Beneath his small, shuddering frame he seethed with the righteous anger of his title, seethed that a member of his family had contrived to lead traitors into the palace grounds.

Lorian responded in turn to Ava's admission. He outlined to her the more outrageous of his and Mathias' exploits, and purloined stories from Lisandro to ensure she was suitably impressed. He invited Ava to admire the scar on his arm, in a cruel parody of Acario's wound, which he had attained in a brawl as a twelve year old. Sawney had never revealed the fate of the youth who had dared to glance his son's skin with a knife.

His audience willing, Lorian moved to charm her further: he complimented every component of her appearance in terms that any right-thinking female would have rejected as nauseating. Yet Ava seemed to swallow every appraisal as sincere. She even thought Lorian naïve to have become so quickly taken with her.

Their spectators reacted similarly to this display. Acario felt disgusted by this feigned affection, for he was certain that Lorian's behaviour was little more than a tease, and pitied Ava's inability to distinguish his manipulation. Mathias stretched his arms in a wide yawn as he listened. Any lingering respect for Ava's character, any shred of desire to prove himself worthy of her notice, dispersed now as the princess clutched onto Lorian's arm. Her faint, sniggering laugh he found incredibly irritating.

It was while Ava giggled in response to Lorian's relation of the tricks that they used to play on the servants (this anecdote earned Mathias an approving smile, which he missed in scrutiny of the trees ahead) that Acario's patience deserted him. Not another moment could be endured in their noxious company. He refused to stand in audience to the evils of the princess and her suitors. All that waited for him was to her, finally, of their plans for him. Ava could tell him after dinner, he decided, when Lorian was through with her. Mathias had retired from supervising his progress and he had the headstart of a few valuable seconds when he burst into a run. He knew that once he reached the palace he would be free. His pursuers recognised this, too.

Despite his bulk Lorian outran the svelte Mathias, and shouted back for him to wait. He saw no good in abandoning Ava, who had, in an attempt to prove herself equal to the challenges of their lifestyle, joined in the chase before falling back, stumbling on the hem of her gown.

Mathias returned to her side and reassured the princess of Lorian's success. There was a coldness in his manner towards her, but to Ava the natures of him and his brother were inseparable. She believed him to labour under the same affection and took no offence. She asked after their father, and he revealed their intention in visiting the gardens: Acario was to be present at the meeting with the Eyes the following morning. Responding to the twitch of her underlip, he assured her that although she was to be excluded from the meeting, Sawney would reward her greatly for the prince's presence. She was to see to it that Acario reached the place where they had first conveyed. Ava realised that they had withheld from her their means of entering the garden but Mathias responded to her query by tapping the side of his nose. In answer to her protests he grinned. Better that she thought they had appeared in the gardens by magic.

He called for his brother to fall back, but a moment later the prince was seized and stumbled to the ground under the weight of the heaving Lorian.

"Get off me!" shrieked Acario, struggling on the grass. His captor scrambled to his feet and began to circle the boy.

"You *are* going to help us, your highness," snarled Lorian, "Do you know what will happen if you refuse?"

"You…brute…" answered Acario, clambering to his feet. The front of his robes was streaked with dirt. He was struck with a blow to the head and stumbled forward. Lorian's fist had taken him by surprise. He anticipated a another attack but none came, Lorian preferring instead to pace around him.

"Run back to the palace, little prince. Hide in your chamber. Ava will tell you what lies in wait tomorrow. Go on," he hissed, and helped him with a shove.

Acario gritted his teeth in fierce resistance and began to walk towards Delzean. He would not give Lorian the satisfaction of forcing him to run.

The guards had not yet troubled to light the tree-hanging lanterns and Acario was soon lost to the darkness. The loss of her cousin panicked Ava – had he gone to confess to Eli? Lorian staggered back to them, savouring the attention.

"He will join us tomorrow. I have seen to it!" He felt his announcement warranted a bow and credited it with one.

"My congratulations," replied Mathias. He turned to Ava and murmured, "We will wait where you found us, from the stroke of seven onwards. The prince will be returned before evening."

"But where will I say he is?"

This was not the moment for empty reassurances. Their hopes could not be pinned on the girl's ability to deceive the Emperor. "If he should be at the academy, then pretend he has gone there. Bribe any servant that questions you. If not, he is simply spending the morning with his cousin. They will see no harm in that."

Ava had many more questions for the youths. Indeed, she would have been content to walk in Lorian's arm in silence but it was clear that the limits of Delzean's security had been tested. Even Lorian understood it senseless for them to delay their exit further. It was all rather anticlimactic for Ava, who could not fathom why Acario was more important to their cause than she. The princess scowled as Lorian raised her hand to his lips for the second time, although she voiced no disquiet. Mathias sensed her disapproval and proceeded to mimic the gesture. She moved away, appeased. In the dark shadows of the garden the brothers grinned. The rest of the night was theirs.

Chapter Seventeen

When Acario was met by Lorian and Mathias he found them to be every inch as exultant as on their last encounter. The heaviness of their motions, however, suggested they bore no affinity for such an hour. They ordered the prince to kneel on the dew-soaked grass. A cloak was fastened around his neck, the knotted chord straining against his skin. His hair and features were masked by the hood. He trembled at the touch of Mathias but accepted the process to be as inevitable as the waiting torment.

Already he predicted his use in performing some mischief to the Emperor. The uncharacteristic watchfulness of the brothers indicated that whichever act of mischief called for his capture was one of no small import. His arm was seized by Lorian whilst Mathias assumed the role of leader. The grip on his limb was maintained until their arrival; the skin was mottled purple with bruises by the hour of his return. The trespass through Arden's estate brought hope to the prince, who could not conceive of such a party passing unnoticed. Faith deserted him when he recalled that the same villains had roamed the very gardens of the palace without detection. Yet his momentary hope was not without foundation: had their intrusion been delayed by just five minutes they would have wandered into full sight of the gardener.

Acario's mind was occupied still with the ordeal of the evening before and was deaf to the whispered threats of his captors. In place of the sluggish morning streets he saw Ava, her etiolated face smug across the table. After dinner a servant had brought word of Chiron's summons but he was kept prisoner in Ava's chamber until nightfall, then woken before he had enjoyed an hour's true rest.

The appearance of the infamous Advisor Delarus's offspring in Horizon's wealthier districts was greeted with trepidation from most, and hisses from some. The likeness of the brothers was well-known. The deeds they boasted of in dank taverns had circulated far beyond the reach of the Eyes' influence. In the quadrants surrounding Delzean they were heralded as rogues. Rather than hasten their progress into friendlier arenas the pair gloried in this reception. Every sidelong glance brought laughter to their throats. Nevertheless they recognised the danger in lingering – the immediacy of Sawney's designs had been well-stressed. In contrast to this instruction, the route they were obliged to follow was a haphazard, circuitous one. It was crucial that, in case of cowardice, or treachery, their quarry was unable to retrace his steps and bring the Emperor's guard to the lair of the conspirators. This caution was excessive: after ten minutes on foot Acario was lost amidst foreign buildings.

The conversation of Lorian and Mathias was limited during this time to childish remarks about the figure cut by the prince, and when this provoked no response, a bawdy critique of the princess' merits. The scant wisdom shared by the pair was sufficient to deter them from any direct mention of the Eyes' members, though they could not help but speculate on the identities of those deemed trustworthy enough to participate in this most ambitious project. No member had volunteered their own apartments for the meeting. Even the celebrated doctor Fernandez, who had suffered less than a second's suspicion in forty years, thought the venture too risky. The Delarus home was, of course, infinitely more dangerous than the innocent abode of Fernandez. It was to the odious realm beneath the basement that they were to report.

In the labouring districts only the young and the vagrant walked free after the stroke of eight, yet Lorian insisted on bustling Acario into an alley to blindfold him, leaving Mathias as lookout. All of their precautions were fruitless if Acario was left able to describe the building to which he had been stolen. As if to punish him for this hypothetical threat, the Advisor's son was merciless in his treatment of the boy. When the prince was hurried forward to rejoin Mathias he was endowed with a crushed hand and a low, sickening ache inside his belly.

The banter of the brothers ceased once the door of the basement was bolted behind them. Blindfolded, Acario stumbled forward. Mathias removed the bind but saw that the prince was covered still by the hood. Their quarry watched Lorian descend the ladder first, eager for his father's praise, and was horrified by the near-perceptible anticipation of those waiting beneath. As the usual swathe of candles had been left unlit, the stink of the sewers suggested a den fit for the Eyes' purposes.

At the foot of the ladder Acario's cloak was torn from his shoulders as Lorian unveiled him to the gathering. The four seated men greeted them with applause. The prince was exposed before Vikernes, Jonas, Fernandez and Sawney.

The first insisted on attending the meeting despite the personal risk, as he was the only guest, Sawney excepted, liable to be recognised by the prince. He found the very notion of absenting himself from the greatest triumph of his cohorts offensive. Whilst the Lieutenant demonstrated an unbounded enthusiasm to rival Lorian's, Sawney sat on his left serene, as though the passive audience of a scene in the courthouse. The doctor, too, seemed unchanged by the occasion, although this could be credited to his role in the proceedings being already fulfilled – a vial of clear liquid was concealed in his pocket. The lawyer Jonas was unsettled by his failure to reconcile relations with his brother. He countered his claim to believe fervently in the success of Sawney's campaign by contorting his form within a heavy, hooded robe. He leaned back heavily in his chair to avoid the flickering light of the lone candle.

"Acario: how were you able to excuse yourself from Delzean?" called Sawney, upon the heels of the applause. What pleasure it was, to be free of the title 'prince'.

At the boy's silence, Vikernes added: "The boy wants respect! Be courteous, then, Lorian, and offer him a chair."

A seat was drawn for him, and the strength of the elder brother forced him to sit. Mathias understood from the shake of Sawney's head to pull another chair close beside the prince. As a further cautionary measure he placed the boy's hands upon the table. Against this gesture Acario made scant protest; he yelped only when each wrist was seized by a brother.

"His excuse?" repeated Sawney, addressing Lorian. The brevity of the utterance was a mark of the matter's significance.

"Be assured, father – answer him, prince," commanded the elder brother.

Of the speaker's clammy hand around his wrist Acario was acutely aware. He mumbled, "The Princess will report that I am with her."

"Have no fear for the exposure of your deceit; we will not keep you long."

In no sense did Acario derive comfort from this remark.

Contrary to this promise, there was little sense of urgency amongst the gathering. Perhaps the boisterous enthusiasm of the Lieutenant and Lorian was too strong to be constrained when met with such a circumstance. Or perhaps the occurrence was of such a rare breed that it merited full exploitation, even by these most professional of thieves. Rather than turn to the matter at hand, the quest for which they had smuggled the prince from safety, the tension which fled with Acario's speech permitted Vikernes to indulge his brutality. His taunts were abetted with Sawney's own, while his sons listened with apprentice ears.

They derided him first of his easy capture, and of the fall he had taken into their midst, but more cutting was their retelling of

Adrienne's death. To be painted as a bumbling, ineffectual boy who was yet guilty of a greater sin than his tormentors...That Sawney, of all the world's men, had the power to damn a prince! Acario felt his true self revealed, and lost, within that ill-lit room. Had the torment been his brother's (though Chiron harboured no such sin), the repugnant men would have been jeered in return, their own faults echoed back at them. Yet the younger prince recognised every word of his tormentors as true: he had killed, lied and shamed his kingdom. He was worthy of exile, of hunger, of quick and brutish death.

In spite of this knowledge, Acario had not surrendered his will entirely. A harsher pain was required before he succumbed to the deepest pity, that of sorrow for his very existence. As he sat immobilised by his sharp-eyed watchers he began to observe each member of the group in turn. In every face he searched for the tiniest measure of compassion, and every face he found wanting. Then he prayed, biting his lip with nerves, for someone, anyone with a kinder heart than his companions, to stumble freely into the basement and cause the meeting to scatter in fear. It could not be impossible that Leon would lead a patrol to inspect such a dilapidated dwelling, ran his consoling thought.

But no footsteps were heard to halt the speaker – "Ava's girlish imagination must have been exhausted in devising your tortures" – and so Acario resorted to plotting an escape through his own energies. He was placed immediately before the ladder. If the grip of the brothers could somehow be placated he would surely be able to clear the ladder before they had calmed enough to make chase. It was left only to struggle against their hold in test of this theory. Mathias turned a moment later to glare at him, whilst Lorian appeared to have felt nothing of the struggle. Acario slumped backward in his chair, defeated.

"Let me see the scar," demanded Vikernes. He shared in the general consensus that Acario was not truly a murderer but his condemnation of the prince was vitriolic to the uttermost degree. Sawney had taken great pleasure in explaining the necessity of convincing Acario of their belief in his guilt. The threat of public denunciation was thus made equal to the threat of physical harm.

"Only a scratch," drawled Lorian, "compared to what *we* could do."

"Yes," breathed Fernandez, "The scars of street brawls are far worse..."

The underlying menace in this lament was sufficient to make Acario tremble. His horror was soon replaced with a more palpable dread as Sawney raised his hand, signalling the circle to fall silent.

"That's enough for now. Time is short. We must apologise for holding the prince for so long without an explanation," smirked Sawney beseechingly. "Let me inform you of our plan, princeling. Your brother, should he take the throne, would have me removed from the palace's service. As you understand, this would be most detrimental to the livelihood of my acquaintances here. It is clear to me that this obstacle must be removed."

"You will not kill him!" cried the prince. His protest was subdued by the guffaws of his neighbours.

"Acario has gotten himself carried away," laughed Vikernes.

"Your brother is only a threat once your father is deceased. Even with Chiron disposed of, neither our aunt nor your cousin would look kindly upon my enterprise. It would suit my ends for you all to be dispensed with. Your entire family is abhorrent to me. And why should I delay in granting liberty to my followers? You will return home soon, Acario, and tonight I will ask you to poison your father. When, in his grief, Chiron wanders from Delzean, he will meet with one of my men."

"…And then you will come for me?"

No consensus had been reached on the best answer to this question: Vikernes and Jonas held that the promise of violent reprisals was sufficient to terrify Acario into doing their bidding, regardless of the fact that this would hurry forward the date of his own demise, whilst Fernandez intimated that to reveal the whole of their plan would undo them – the boy would rather suffer death at the hands of Lorian than leave to commit murder. Sawney was only half-convinced by the latter argument: Acario appeared resigned to the will of others, and too timid to resist their encouragement. Yet the Advisor knew he was not so bent to their will as to condemn his entire family to destruction.

"No. You will take the title of Emperor. My sons will take the positions of your Advisors, and your rule will be advantageous to the designs of my fellows."

"It will not!"

"Has it not already been made clear that you have no other option?" Sawney's voice was terse now, his expression sour. "Or should I leave you alone with Vikernes for a moment?"

"Eli would not believe a word of yours," interjected the seemingly passive doctor, "The poison alone will fail to incriminate us. What evidence could you offer, if you are ignorant of your present location?"

"Ava will hardly rush to support you," added Lorian, "She would happily have you framed as mad."

"I am to dine with your father tonight. In light of Chiron's misdemeanours I have impressed upon the Emperor the importance of your instruction. He believes you are still malleable enough to be redeemed. No servants will attend on us – Eli suspects the palace harbours a traitor. The wine will be waiting on the table when you enter an hour early, whilst the Emperor entertains me in the reception room. The smallest dosage of the poison will be fatal, but you will pour the entire contents into the bottle. Worry not of slaying me – Fernandez has supplied me with the antidote, and I will refuse any drink. If you fail to poison the wine before we enter, take charge of filling your father's glass- "

"I'll drop the vial on the street. You cannot force my hand…"

"Listen, prince, and hear why I have no need to force you," Sawney paused to lift a small vial, no taller than a child's finger, which he placed on the table beneath himself and his rapt audience. The liquid inside was colourless, odourless and allegedly, of course, tasteless, yet its appearance altered the atmosphere in that decrepit chamber, and caused even Lorian to stiffen.

"If your father lives he will one day learn the truth of your mother's death, no matter how desperately you bargain with the princess. Even *she* will tire of your games eventually. But kill your father and he will die believing that his youngest son will maintain the family honour. His fall will be swift, and the servants won't doubt our story. His death will be a tragedy for the empire, but only until you are ready to take the mantle. Eli will likely pass too quickly to realise his pain's cause, absolving you of both parents' deaths. Pay close attention, Acario," drawled the Advisor, "there is more to gain than that.

"Once we have you upon the throne, your dear cousin will be powerless. Ava will be cast back into obscurity, where she belongs. Her treatment will not scar you again. As for your brother, you have nothing to fear from him. He will be as witless as the rest of your involvement. His death will be another tragedy for the kingdom to withstand, but it certainly will survive. For one unhappy in life, death must surely be a release. Your people will be grateful to be spared the rule of your brother and gain instead the sovereignity of a calm-headed king. In power, Leon's respect would be yours, too."

For the duration of his speech Acario had stared downwards at his captured wrists; when Sawney finished and looked to the prince for an answer, the boy consented to meet his gaze. His eyes were held there, until Vikernes stood.

Sawney's rhetoric had assured Vikernes of their success in securing the prince's compliance. The lieutenant had no fear that the boy would fail them. Exultant, he hastened to add to the Advisor's promises.: "Prince Leon would have advanced faster in the army had he sought my patronage. Should you decide on a military career, I will grant you my support."

His addition was approved by Sawney's smirk.

Acario gave no sign that their words had changed his position in any way, but this sudden silence after his protestations was encouraging, and perhaps all the assent they could expect from the introverted prince. Every other member of the party was convinced that they had him hoodwinked. Sawney cared most that he himself was convinced. As his approval had been sealed by his own words, he gave the command for the prince to rise.

The poison was snatched up by Vikernes, who clasped it gently in his callused hands before tucking it into a pocket. The lieutenant and Jonas replaced Lorian and Mathias as Acario's keepers. At Sawney's word he was concealed again in the cloak, and rushed up the ladder. Jonas had protested strongly that he be excused this duty, fearing that this brother would spy him if he strayed near the palace, but the fury of his co-conspirators at his reluctance to assist them in their grandest fete had twisted his will.

Acario allowed himself to be led, dreading, even in the company of two such monstrous men as these, the long, friendless afternoon that lay ahead.

Alone with their father, Lorian and Mathias awaited his verdict. But instead of commenting on the morning's mission, he asked instead to make a request of them. Believing it to be related to their role in the evening's proceedings, Lorian repeated their vow to undertake any command, with a dark laugh.

"I am not worried about you failing to fulfil your duty tonight," answered Sawney, "and unless our plan goes entirely astray there is nothing further I can demand from the pair of you. My request is concerned with the coming hours, when we wait to storm the palace. You must not meet with the princess beforehand: she is too temperamental to be permitted to come close to us. And we must not let a silly little girl undo our plans, must we?"

"*Certainly* not, father!" assented Lorian, whilst Mathias struggled to conceal a yawn.

"Come, both of you. Vikernes will return to us at home. You have hours yet to rest."

Chapter Eighteen

Whilst Acario sat secluded in his bedchamber, wringing his hands and staring at the vial Vikernes had forced upon him, Leon led a similarly agitated Chiron towards the Breakfast Hall. It was too late for the meeting inside to still be underway, but Leon hoped to waylaid the Emperor on his exit, before he was lost to the city courts.

Chiron followed his cousin obligingly, knowing that Eli would place more stock on the evidence of the general. To this end Leon would present the journal and testify that it could be traced to Sawney. Had Chiron come alone, even with the added evidence unearthed in the Scroll Room, the case would likely have been dismissed: the prince was unwashed, and in need of a servant's fussing attention.

Despite spending most of the intervening hours awake, Chiron could have skipped to his father, had he not desired to appear calm before his cousin. At last, he would be revenged on Sawney! Unwittingly, the crook had conspired towards his own destruction and would soon be cast from the palace. Freeing his father from

Sawney's advances would, he hoped, reinstate himself in his father's favour.

The maids that kowtowed to the princes as they passed were brushed aside; the hallways and chambers that offered no help in furthering their course were similarly ignored. It was a chill, midnight day, yet the brightness reflected in the stone walls was almost blinding.

They arrived outside the Hall to meet the Advisors on their way out. Such was their relief at catching the Emperor the princes indulged the old men in their pleasantries. Leon was perturbed to find that Sawney did not rank amongst their number: he had heard, somehow, of their discovery? In his excitement Chiron failed to notice the Advisor's absence.

Inside the chamber they found Eli, sitting still at the head of the table. The Emperor was slicing open a piece of fruit when the princes entered. If their appearance surprised him he gave no sign of it. He waved them over to join him, and pulled out the chair on his right for Leon. Sullenly, Chiron sank into the chair opposite.

"Can we detain you for a while, uncle?" asked the general, placing the journal upon the table.

"Other than my breakfast I have no pressing obligations," replied the Emperor, before offering a plate to his son and inviting him to eat. Keen to please his father, Chiron accepted the offer. He winked across at his cousin, who took this as his cue to share their findings.

"Chiron came to me with a journal he found in the courthouse. It is the property of Advisor Delarus. There seems to be an association between him and several men believed to be involved with the Eyes. Before you ask," he raised a placating hand, "I would not accuse an Advisor without due proof. He made a note to inform Jonas Rana of a man's details: this man later disappeared after being implicated in a robbery, only to be sighted by the city guards on the occasion of numerous other crimes. His case is not unique – I matched up Sawney's records with the official court edicts and found many more connections. Sire, I believe most assuredly that Delzean has been hoodwinked by an agent of the Eyes."

In closure of his case, Leon handed the journal into Eli's possession.

The Emperor's initial response was one of deepest astonishment: he knew Leon to be clever, of course, but he had never expected the general to turn his wits against the Advisor. The grudge Chiron bore the Advisor was, he thought, uncontaminated by any sound reason or evidence. Presented with the journal, Eli understood that he owed the princes an honest explanation. Until he faced his son across the table and prepared to admit his pact with Sawney, Eli had been witless of how shaming such a confession would be. He feared far less the wrath of the Advisor when he found his liberty to be at an end. In Sawney's absence from the Breakfast (no messenger had been dispatched bearing his apologies) Eli detected the first stirrings of rebellion. The other Advisors, now recovered from the festivities, were all aghast at his nerve.

Confronted with the princes, it was a mark in Eli's favour that he decided on the instant of Leon's speech to admit his knowledge of Sawney's misdemeanours. Indeed, only a fool would have otherwise permitted Sawney to remain in his employment – his infamy had infiltrated through even to the Advisors.

"I haven't been hoodwinked," answered the Emperor, at last, "Sawney openly confessed to his involvement, nay, his leadership of the Eyes. By trusting me he gained a certain degree of liberty, while I, in return, received an extensive knowledge of the city's criminals. Only with my permission could his plans proceed, whilst all other rogues were more easily caught, as the Eyes have no interest in safeguarding the security of other crooks."

"Permit me to interrupt: you condoned the existence of the Eyes?"

Leon spoke hastily; he wanted to berate the Emperor before Chiron could, as while the younger prince's anger would be well-founded, Eli would be less willing to explain his behaviour if confronted with one of Chiron's infamous outbursts. The general understood the natures of both father and son better than they themselves.

"I did, Leon. Before you judge me too harshly," an almost pleading note had entered his voice, "Understand that as Emperor of a fledging empire decisions have to be made of which I am not always proud. Over Sawney I assert some level of control; otherwise my life would be spent in audience at the courthouse."

"But what reason did he ever give for you to trust him? What proof that you ever had any control?" barked Chiron, his eyes flashing. "How long have you known? Is this why the palace has been forced to tolerate his noxious family?"

"He risked everything by confiding in me," answered Eli, "His confession is the only proof I need. Sawney has much more to lose than I – it is laughably easy for me to dispose of an Advisor and far more difficult for him to conspire against the throne. As for his 'noxious family', as you term them, they have largely been raised away from other nobles. I hardly think you've been *forced* to tolerate them."

"But uncle, why did you ever accept Sawney's terms? Had you scorned his advances his confession would be sufficient to remove him as Advisor. If you believe that cooperating with Sawney protected the empire from other rogues, then you clearly have little faith in your guards!"

Both princes had risen to their feet, and exchanged furious glances. Chiron respected the man before him now only as Emperor, no longer as a father. He felt miserably disappointed; this scene was utterly unlike the one he had envisaged.

Eli sighed, and fell silent for a moment, his head bowed. "Regardless of the downsides of entering into a pact with a creature like Sawney, I took what I believed to be the best course of action. Now, of course, everything has changed. If he is to be so careless that he inadvertently informs the princes of his conspiracy, I will not risk my neck to protect him. The whole of Horizon suspects him: the city wants only proof. It is no longer possible for me to tolerate his schemes. Tonight I will report your suspicions to him. He may continue to serve as an Advisor, as long as he consents to operate under greater secrecy. Please excuse me, I must attend to the courts."

The Emperor paused by his chair, looking between the princes. Leon bowed his head as a sign of assent, whilst Chiron bristled at the thought that Sawney would remain in the palace's employment. Eli turned away from the dumbstruck princes. He addressed a parting remark to his son as he opened the door: "Your mother despised Sawney, too."

Within seconds of Eli's departure three maids rushed in to the chamber. They spared only a slight bow for the princes before beginning to demolish the breakfast spread, and amidst the flurry of activity the princes had no choice but to slink away into the corridor.

*

The Advisor in question anticipated the evening's meeting with a sallow grin. By the early afternoon he had donned already his finest robes, and for the hour since Vikernes departed after confirming Acario's unnoticed return to the palace he had condescended to lounge in the ramshackle living room with his sons. Both were beginning to tire of their father's clear and uncharacteristic anxiety but each looked forward to the coming hours, although for entirely different reasons. Mathias lay face down on the floor, his slight frame for the most part concealed under a pile of rages. The elder brother was seated, shirtless and paunched, beside his father.

Illuminated by the sharp gaze of the sun beyond, the true squalor of Sawney's home lay exposed. The odour of the kitchen, a room untouched for months, now resembled that of the underground meeting chamber and had risen to taint the air of the rooms above. The spoils from the burglary were here, hidden in plain sight: a sword already claimed by Lorian, sun dials, robes, dye and sacks brimming with coins. These treasures no longer excited the Delarus men, however: a far worthier prize lay in their sights.

With Vikernes present the plan had been revised: if Acario obeyed the meeting's wishes the Emperor would fall dead at the table. Sawney would convince the servants that his death was accidental, and summon the doctor Fernandez to confirm that he had indeed choked. An emergency meeting of the Advisors would be called within the hour to discuss the succession, which would be interrupted by the entrance of the Lieutenant and a handful of men, many of whom would be soon sprung from their prison cells. All the Advisors, save Sawney, would be slaughtered; the palace would then be stormed and everyone inside would be forced to choose between bowing to Sawney and embracing their own destruction. The barracks would be stormed swiftly afterwards, with the aim of eliminating any opposition and inserting Vikernes as Chief

Commander. Whilst Sawney dined Lorian and Mathias would wait in the gardens. If Acario failed, they would slaughter the Emperor and flee, leaving their father to pin the murder on an assassin. Otherwise they would enter the palace with the troops.

The events predicted by Sawney held little in common with the scenario described to the bewildered prince Acario. For one accustomed to working in the relative secrecy of Horizon's back streets, where missions in far flung quarters of the city were imagined first in a chamber secreted below the streets, the coup was a bold step forward. Indeed, the very lives of Sawney, his sons and their compatriots depended on their success. For the reign of the Delarus family to begin, every relative of Eli's must be slain by the morning. Only Lorian was foolish enough to be ignorant of the true magnitude of the night's endeavour. His father had bid him to repeat the plan until he was assured of Lorian's understanding.

"Are you sure of entering the gardens without Arden's notice?" asked Sawney. He found the complacency of his sons irksome.

"Yes, father," laughed Lorian, "Myself and Mathias have been well trained."

"Do you have your blade?"

Mathias remained inert on the floor, his son a bored-sounding grumble. Sawney rolled his eyes; neither son appeared to care much that they would soon be calling Delzean's walls home.

"I do, but it hardly seems fitting for such an occasion."

From a sheath attached to his leg Lorian drew a dark, stubby knife. He ran his thumb along the handle, musing as he did so whether the edge was meant for Chiron or Adema, for Leon or Ava. He wondered who would have the pleasure of cornering Acario in his chamber and exposing Sawney's promises as false. If it was he would had the pleasure to catch him, Lorian would be sure the prince knew the fate of his family before he was struck.

"I'm sure Vikernes would gladly equip us with something more…substantial. I could still make it to the barracks and back before we have to leave."

This sudden animation came as a surprise to Sawney, but Mathias' desire for movement was pleasing. His soon needed to stay sharp for hours yet; they were accustomed to wandering the city at night, however, and would soon be eager for action.

"You must be quick. If you return to find the house empty hasten to the gardens. Take a bribe with you," Sawney waved over to the sacks by the staircase, "in case you're met by guards not yet allied to us."

"Be sure to fetch me a proper sword! Don't harbour the heaviest weapons for yourself."

"That's quite enough, Lorian," snapped Sawney. "Get up, Mathias. You cannot afford to be languorous now."

The brothers shared a look of exasperation at Sawney's flare, yet Mathias was nevertheless quick to rise. He, too, already carried a knife concealed on his person. In order to add this armoury he filled his pockets speedily with coins and with a short, graceless bow he bid his family adieu.

Before he had stepped foot outside the building, before even reaching the stairs, Mathias knew he would never walk within the place again. The coins taken to be offered as bribes and the aged knife were the only tools he possessed with which to carve a new life for himself.

Outside he found the mid-afternoon streets crowded. He enjoyed being barged around in the tide of the mob, and chose not to cut away through the alleys but to remain in the open air, exulting in the idiosyncrasies of the city. It was on a flooded market street like this that he had attempted as a child to pick the pockets of Vikernes, a false move which had led to him gaining a brother, a home and a father of sorts.

He had yet to question his sudden and overwhelming desire to flee from the life gifted to him by Sawney. It was sufficient to know simply that he *must* leave. Mathias was no innocent boy led astray, of course; it was just that his whole youth had been spent playing, and in this game of thuggery he had followed Sawney's instructions willingly. But the stakes had become too high. He was not meant to rule over an empire, and he would not commit a massacre for it. By running he would not impede Sawney's plans or save the lives of those in the palace. But in every abandonment there is an escape. Mathias fled to save himself. To be truly free he had to sever all ties with the city – he had heard of the trading ports beyond the mountains; he was a strong youth, for all his slightness, and capable of hard graft. He would miss the camaraderie amongst the acquaintances that had peopled the taverns of his adolescence, but Lorian was becoming a creature he feared.

As he at last abandoned the market streets to move towards the slums, Mathias felt nothing, no guilt, no fear, only the urge to run until he reached the road. For the remainder of his passage through the city, the last moments in which he would ever call the city home, he thought of his brother. He expected Lorian to demonstrate an initial concern swiftly followed by fury, and here he was not far wrong. He was certain that their paths would never cross again.

Sawney allowed two hours to pass before branding Mathias a deserter. On the stroke of four he ordered Lorian to dress then swept upstairs, refusing to indulge the speculation of his son. He allowed himself a moment to digest the development, which was a significant setback to mar the uprising. Then he dismissed his faux son of twelve years entirely. He felt no love for the man's memory. To save Lorian's mind from wandering he soon retreated downstairs to reiterate his instructions. Within half an hour's time Lorian was dispatched on foot to the palace gardens, whilst Sawney sat alone, anticipating the arrival of Eli's carriage.

Chapter Nineteen

An hour later the Advisor was seated across from the Emperor, the full length of the dining hall between them. The sun had begun to set behind the palace; it filled the hall with a pale, orange light that only loosely illuminated the features of both men. The spread was bounteous enough to feed a full table twice-over yet despite the servants' careful preparation these dishes would be left to moulder on the table, steam from the plates billowing upwards until they were at last shown mercy and destroyed.

The conversation between the Emperor and his guest had been slow and stilted. Eli had not troubled to explain the absence of his youngest son. He himself was clueless that Acario was currently upstairs, confessing all to Chiron. Sawney interpreted his silence on the matter as a warning, a sign perhaps that Acario had surpassed all their expectations and revealed the truth to his father.

This second setback entirely dwarfed the first. Sawney had concocted a plan whilst sitting and idly chewing. He would turn their dialogue towards their sons somehow, and if Eli let escape any hint of subterfuge he would feign a desire for fresh air. Once outside Eli would be swiftly dealt with. All Sawney had to do, meanwhile, was grit his teeth and bide his time.

"I apologise for my absence at this morning's breakfast. I trust I missed nothing important?"

Eli frowned into his wine glass. "Why were you absent? I did not receive your messenger."

"My son Mathias has disappeared," replied Sawney coolly, "You are a father, you understand…"

The Emperor grunted in response, looking towards the empty seats on his left.

Sawney allowed the silence to settle, in the hope that Eli would soon follow his train of thought. He began to twitch his leg irritably whilst Eli glanced around the hall. A master of duplicity himself, Sawney resented the quality in others. He would welcome an open confrontation with the Emperor.

"I believe our arrangement regarding the Eyes needs to be reconsidered," said Eli, shortly, "Lending you my support is no longer…prudent."

"And why is that?" snapped Sawney, his voice sharp. He lay down his cutlery as if squaring for a fight.

"Your name is already infamous within the city, Sawney. How much longer until my name is dragged in? It was in the interests of the empire to have an insight into your operations before, but that time has reached its end."

"Are you saying merely that you do not wish to be informed or is this an order to dismiss the Eyes?"

"What I am *saying*, Sawney," bellowed the Emperor, his temper now shorter than ever, "is that as far as I am concerned the Eyes do not exist. You may act however you see fit, permitted that greater secrecy is exercised. The post of Advisor remains yours."

"Have you learned something which disturbs you? Is our arrangement suspected?" Sawney's questions were shrewd. If he had been met with anger he would take his host's fury to mean that his attempt to blackmail the prince had been discovered. This careful attempt to distance himself suggested another motive. Perhaps all was not lost, after all.

"I have heard rumours," confirmed Eli. "I will not allow my regime to be undermined. Eat, Sawney: I assure you nothing has been poisoned."

Sawney started at the remark but Eli continued to sip from his goblet as though he had uttered a mere platitude. The Advisor reached up to run a hand through his curled hair and speared a fish head upon his fork.

The youngest prince had watched the Advisor arrive from the floor above the hall. As Sawney descended from the royal carriage Acario gulped, and began to pace before the window. He twisted a strand of hair between his fingers as he moved in a frantic circle. He had never known such terror. The vial was stashed in the pocket of his robes. With a decisive cry he grabbed the poison and threw it wildly at the wall. To his dismay it only bounced; his throw was too weak to destroy it.

The servant sent to call him down to greet the guest would soon be knocking tentatively on his door. He could not hide in a lonely chamber until Sawney left, which was his uttermost desire, because his inaction would led to his father's death as surely as following Sawney's orders would. Some other course of action was needed. Yet the question he struggled with as he paced back and forth, faster now, was not *what* to do but whether he could summon the courage to do it. He had to confess. Only by letting someone else in to his confidence could Sawney's gross plan be halted; it was precisely on Acario's fear of confession that the Advisor had pinned his hopes. Acario paused to lean against the wall. Pressing the cool surface against his forehead seemed to calm him, for with a new air of resolve he righted himself and began to race towards his brother's chambers.

Following the abrupt meeting with his father Chiron had retired to his room. He swore to Leon that he would not disturb the dinner as long as the general agreed to meet with him afterwards. They would then go together to quiz the emperor. Accordingly, Leon had excused himself from the barracks and kept a vigil from the window directly above the spot vacated moments ago by Acario.

Chiron had not spent a profitable afternoon. Alternately agonized by his father's secrecy and enraged that Sawney would not be dismissed, his sole relief from these tormented thoughts was to peruse the pages of the journal. Eli had left it upon the table without so much as skimming through the pages to verify their account of its contents. His father's indifference towards an item he had come to treasure pained Chiron.

When his brother appeared, anxious and pale in the doorway, Chiron was again lying on the bed, copying Sawney's notes onto a piece of parchment. In his fervour he carelessly blotted the sheets with ink and stained his fingers blue. He jumped at his brother's entrance before rushing forward, eager to share his discovery.

"Chiron," ventured the younger brother timidly, as the other opened his mouth to speak, "There is something I must tell you."

"Ah, that's curious: I have something to tell you, too."

Resolved to his plan, Acario steadied himself and raised a hand to silence his brother. "Please let me speak first. Father may be in grave danger because of me-"

"What do you mean?" barked Chiron, his smile fading.

"Sawney tried to force me to poison father…I was supposed to do it tonight. He is the leader of the Eyes, Chiron, and I was taken to meet with them. Ava told Mathias and Lorian a secret about me and they used it, they used her, to force me to go along with them. But I can't, Chiron, I can't! You won't call me your brother any more once you know the secret Ava kept but I would rather be banished than see father dead!"

The elder prince stared at his weeping brother. He found Acario's outburst overwhelming: he had learned enough about his family today. As yet he was unable to appreciate the effort it had cost Acario to seek him out.

"Why did Sawney choose you? What was it that Ava told him?"

Acario clenched shut his eyes, and, as if to ward off his brother's fury, he hid his face behind his hands. "She was there when mother died…She promised not to tell father that it was all my fault, as long as I followed her orders."

"What was all your fault?" asked Chiron. He felt he already knew the answer.

"It was my fault she died!" he wailed, "She walked to please me, and then she fell. It was my fault! I killed her! Ava agreed to protect me but now Sawney knows…"

"Ava convinced you that mother's death was your fault. But she *did* fall, didn't she?"

"Yes, she fell…" squeaked Acario, before noticing that the chance he had predicated in his brother's manner had failed to manifest itself. He allowed his hands to fall shaking to his sides and warily opened his eyes.

"What do you mean, that she *convinced* me? Mother was only there to fall because of me…"

Such was his desire to seize upon Chiron's leniency that he could not prevent a hopeful edge creeping in to his voice.

"Yes, but you didn't mean for her to fall! You were only a child; it was not your fault!"

To see Chiron indignant on his behalf meant more to Acario than he could express. "But Ava was so sure…"

"I bet she was," spat Chiron, "The witch. But we will have to wait to deal with her. You said Sawney wants father dead?"

"Yes," answered Acario, hastily, "But he was counting on me to do it."

"A man like Sawney would not depend on one person alone. Father is still in danger. Go and find Leon. Tell him what you told me. I will be waiting by the dining hall – if Sawney raises a finger I'll hear it! Go now, Acario!"

The prince lingered, mesmerized by his brother's new sense of purpose. His revelation had galvanized him into action. This was the brother he needed. It was enough to make Acario cringe at the remembrance of years spent fearing his brother's rejection.

"Yes, Chiron!" His eyes were still wet with tears.

"Wait…thank you for coming to me."

With a smile Chiron approached his younger sibling, and enveloped him in a tight hug. They had not embraced like that in years.

Together they retreated into the ill-lit ante-chamber, before parting wordlessly in the corridor. The floor was sharp on the soles of Chiron's feet; he grimaced at the realisation and sprinted back to collect his shoes. Cursing himself, he stumbled on the stairs as he hurried towards the dining hall.

He arrived to find the doors barred shut and four maids lined up on either side. In unison they attempted to usher him away: Eli had given strict orders that the dinner be undisturbed. Chiron glowered. He turned to the most vocal of the group and whispered for her to hold her tongue. He signalled for them to fall silent, and waved them away. After a long moment in which the maids stared resolutely at the ground they fell away, one by one, and Chiron took their place by the door. With his ear pressed against the wood he could hear only murmurs of the conversation within, but faint as these murmurs were it was enough to assure him that his father still lived. If he heard a raised voice, or a cry, he vowed to breach the chamber. Otherwise he would wait for Leon and Acario, and together they would confront Sawney.

He stood perfectly still by the door, a picture of princely composure. Willing himself to listen he at last heard, as clearly as though the speaker stood behind him, their agreement to take a walk within the gardens.

Then he fled, uncaring that his footsteps must echo in the chamber as he sped away. He was heading to Leon's chamber, to interrupt his conference with Acario and compel them both to follow. His head ached with impatience by the time he circumvented the last stair, crossed the final corridor and threw open the door with a shout.

"They are going to the gardens! Hurry, we can confront Sawney yet!"

Chiron lingered long enough to absorb a glimpse of the scene inside the general's chamber: he saw that Acario's face was soaked with tears before he cleaned himself clumsily with his sleeve, whilst Leon appeared dumbfounded. Sawney posed a more immediate threat, in Chiron's mind, than the scheming princess, and so he neglected to comfort her brother. Instead, he began to retrace his steps, calling out over his shoulder for them to follow.

The general had started at Chiron's entrance and made to move after him before he had cleared the door. A faint touch on his shoulder held him back: he turned to find Acario, his expression now determined. The boy gazed up at his cousin with an appealing look in his eye.

"Are you ashamed of me?"

An unhesitant answer came to this entreaty. "It is not you that shames me, dear cousin."

After a pause, they exchanged a smile, and began to run in Chiron's footsteps through the palace.

Chiron hastened through the gardens in search of his father. As swift as he had been in fetching Leon, the diners had already managed to wander deeply into the thickness. He did not care what emerged when Sawney was at last confronted: all that mattered was to catch him. Acario's story had distracted him from the true danger facing his father. Had his concern not been diluted by the fury he felt towards Ava, the extent of whose deceit he was fast beginning to appreciate, he would have surely understood the idiocy of approaching Sawney without first alerting the guards.

He paused beneath a lantern to peer ahead. At the distant murmur of Sawney's voice his whole frame twitched; in a second he had leapt in the direction of the sound. Wrestling through the shrubs, he caught sight of the odious traitor. He emerged in the open to find it was the very same glade which hosted a gate onto Arden's grounds.

When the prince stumbled into their midst the Emperor and Advisor were debating the case of a man affiliated with Sawney, recently charged with five counts of murder. Eli was adamant that no man be excused on the grounds of familiarity with a palace official. He was disarmed by the lack of heat with which the Advisor argued his case to the contrary. Sawney was waiting on his son to emerge from the trees: he kept up his side of the exchange merely to keep the Emperor off his guard. He was most perturbed to see that it was Chiron was broke in upon them in Lorian's stead.

"Chiron, what are you doing?"

His father's tone was questioning, not accusatory, but Chiron's residual anger towards his father caused him to glare in response.

"I am only trying to save you from this…this *demon!*"

The prince waved towards the Advisor, who smirked.

"What on earth do you mean, Chiron? Your personal feelings aside, the Advisor is not deserving of your contempt. He remains a faithful servant of the palace and presents no danger to us."

"Ha!" scoffed Chiron, his chest heaving. "He is a danger to all of us. Has he told you that he stole Acario from the palace to blackmail him into poisoning you? Why do you think Acario was absent from the table tonight? He came to confide in me. This man is no faithful servant of yours: he means to kill you!"

A heavy silence met his announcement. The Advisor remained impassive, in spite of his exposure. What did he care of this befuddled prince's misguided rescue attempt? Lorian lurked nearby, soon to be joined by Vikernes. Father and son both would be dead soon: what did it matter if Eli gained a few moment's warning before the end?

"Acario came to you?"

Eli stepped towards his son, leaving Sawney half-concealed in the twilight behind.

"Yes…Ava made it possible for Sawney to get close to him. And he made swift use of your son!" Chiron bellowed, moving closer to his father. "Why do you trust him? On what grounds do you believe his bile over the words of your son?"

In his rage Chiron overlooked that Eli was making no attempt to defend Sawney: he looked fearful, of a sudden, and wished Chiron had not come alone.

"Sawney is trusted no more or no less than my other Advisors," answered Eli, his voice catching, "But if what you say is true…"

By now he was standing immediately before his son; with another step he took hold of Chiron's shoulder.

"Where is Acario?" he whispered.

Chiron's eyes were fixed on the Advisor, who appeared not to have moved, and mouthed, *"They are coming."*

Relieved, Eli nodded and turned to look upon Sawney, shielding the prince from view.

"How do you answer this?"

Sawney hesitated before replying, in a perfect imitation of concern: "Eli, I implore you: dismiss this as childish folly. Acario has pandered to the prince's dislike of me and in his blindness Chiron takes these stories for truth."

The shadows enabled Sawney to glance into the thicket. His only reason in protesting Chiron's claims was to stall until the arrival of Lorian: his arrest beforehand would come as a severe blow to their manoeuvre. Seeing only what he himself stood to gain from the night's attack, Sawney believed the enterprise would collapse without him. For a moment he fretted that his plea might fool Lorian, too, but no: he glanced again to meet the face of his son a few yards behind. He beckoned him forward into the fold.

"He lies!" roared Chiron at Sawney's closing word. "I know what Ava told you, and at what cost my brother told me!"

"You will understand why I cannot dismiss my son. Return with us to the palace and speak there -"

Eli's command was interrupted by Lorian's bounding entrance. Understanding all pretence to be at an end, the man appeared brandishing a knife. He looked utterly unlike one who had recently found his life-long companion to be lost; here was the creature that roamed the city streets in search of idle play. He laughed at Eli's start, and scorned the indignation that caused Chiron to furiously roar, "Traitor!"

"Are the rest to follow soon?" muttered Sawney, a placating arm on his son's. He was confident that Lorian could dispatch these two, but only hearing of Vikernes' approach would calm the Advisor.

"They were held up, I don't know why," hurried Lorian, "But they will join us. Shall I strike now, father?"

At the same instant, Chiron shrieked for his father to run. He had no thoughts of self-preservation: he wanted to tear the trespasser to shreds.

"No, no one is running!" snarled Lorian, and he leapt forward. To Sawney's dismay he reached not for Eli but for his son. He launched heavily, and they fell to the ground.

In the confusion both men rushed to the same spot but collided instead. Eli was pushed from his son by the Advisor. Caring little for the cause of Sawney's treachery Eli listened largely to the struggle beyond. He saw two figures rise and begin to circle, one darting towards the other.

"Let me see my son!" he bellowed. Still he was held back. Sawney bore the blow Eli dealt him without complaint, gripping tighter as the blood swabbed his nostrils.

The Advisor was certain of hearing Lorian's triumphant cry; certain that he would bound over within seconds to clear his hands of the Emperor –

Perhaps it was the cries of his son as the prince succeeded in pinning him down, the knife clenched in the fist of its intended victim; or perhaps it was the searching calls of the guards as they ran en masse towards the site that first alerted the Advisor to the fragility of his convictions. He had no time in which to act: Eli had begun to shout in answer to the guards even before Sawney released his arms. He turned to find Chiron crouched over the body. At his step the prince fled, leaving Lorian to choke, and struggle, and lash helplessly as his shirt grew dark with blood. Sawney made to drag Lorian into the trees but the guards were already upon them.

*

Fleet-footed messengers bearing Eli's proclamation were dispatched to every corner of the city. Crowds gathered in the darkness to hear a most extraordinary announcement: the Advisor known as Sawney had been arrested as a traitor, whilst his son and heir had been killed during an attack on the prince's life. The news echoed throughout the streets; by morning looters had laid waste to Sawney's house, leaving only the kitchen untouched. A warning was similarly issued to the barracks. Vikernes and a dozen others were apprehended in Arden's grounds. During the hour in which Acario ventured to describe the Eyes' den to Leon's superior officer the prince stood at the Emperor's side and listened with pride to the weak yet unwavering voice. No one had braved an interview with Chiron yet.

Chapter Twenty

Acario sat cross-legged upon his bed, anxiously twisting a thread of hair between his fingers. His heart was racing, his breath still rushing in short ragged bursts. He faced towards the door but made no move to answer the frantic knocking. He knew who it must be. Ava was the only member of the family he had yet to face in light of the previous day's revelations.

The routine of the palace had been turned upside-down, and no-one had called to escort him to breakfast. If he had to guess, he would place Chiron similarly sequestered in his own room, likely still fuming at the traitor Sawney, but he was too tense to think of the rest of his family. Was Eli now towering in rage at Adema for her daughter's actions? Or had Ava managed to turn them both against him? In confiding in Leon and Chiron he had experienced a relief denied him for years, but now, with Ava pounding at his door, it was impossible to recall that cool sense of peace. He glanced at the book of verses sitting beside him; he had spent a restless night thinking of his mother – it felt as though a solid foundation had been whisked out from under his feet, and he stood trembling now on quaking ground. His anxiety had lessened as the first rays of morning light entered his room, and he felt a sudden sense of possibility and hope: perhaps this would be the first day he was able to know freedom from his tormentor.

This brief bubble of hope was shattered an hour ago by the entrance of a maid. Ava sent said maid to issue a summons on her behalf; the maid appeared uninterested in the recent attempt on the Emperor's life and delivered her message in a bored voice. She seemed similarly unfazed when Acario replied "No!" without thinking, and had left the chamber before he sank to the floor, his legs trembling. He had spent the ensuing hour sitting almost still on his bed, waiting for the intrusion that he feared must come.

Outside, Ava stood in her fine pink gown, her hair patiently braided by the same maid whose return, Acario-less, had incited a cry of fury from the panicked princess. Ava had been undistributed all morning by her family. Adema had sent a messenger to inform the princess that she and Leon would come to speak with her in the late afternoon, after they attended urgent meetings with the Emperor and his remaining Advisors. That was all the information Adema had saw fit to share with her daughter. Ava was left to wonder whether her mother and brother truly understood her role in the previous night's events. What did they think of her now? Did they understand why she had made a bargain with the Advisor's bastard sons? The uncertainty was too great for his fragile mind to comprehend, and Ava had spent the morning in a state of even greater agitation than Acario.

Standing outside the door, she glanced from left to right, fretting that a servant would report her movements to the Emperor. The neatness of her dress was at odds with the twisted expression on her narrow face, while the rich colour of her gown contrasted oddly with the extreme pallor of her skin.

"Acario!" Ava beseeched, as she rattled the door again. "I demand that you open this door! How dare you ignore me like this, after all that we've been through!"

Detesting the pleading note in her voice, the princess changed tact. "You must tell me exactly what you've been saying to my uncle, Acario. I hope you haven't been spreading lies about me, dear cousin. You have Lorian's death on your hands now, too, don't you know!"

The unfairness of this statement stung Acario like a slap. Hadn't he managed to save a life the previous night? Did Ava fail to understand that if she were not a royal princess and the Emperor's own neice, she would be hanged before the city as a traitor? The slim prince scrambled to his feet and steeled himself to face this final challenge. Confronting Ava in the bright light of day must surely be preferable to cowering in his room like a dog.

He walked, self-conscious in his stride, to the door and opened it enough to meet the eyes of his cousin. He was taken aback to see his own turbulent emotions mirrored in Ava's face. In the instant before she opened her mouth, he wondered whether she was truly upset to find that Sawney had failed in murdering his father.

"You betrayed me, Acario!" she shrieked, forgetting that her presence outside his chamber would not be welcomed by anyone else in the palace. "What did you do?!"

"What did *I* do?" blinked Acario, his voice a mere tremble.

"You told on me, I know you did! You spoiled everything! And Lorian has been killed because of you!" Ava scowled at her cousin, their faces only inches apart.

"Lorian…he tried to kill my father…"

Seeing her face so close to his own, Acario felt that he was seeing his cousin truly for the first time in years. He felt the strangest sense of pity, so sharp it almost pained him to continue to meet her eyes. What exactly did this pallid creature want? She had to be sick in the head surely, to truly believe that she had grounds to be upset with him. Yet, a second later, as if in a flash, his mind swarmed with memories of her torture, of her mind-games and tricks, and he thought, not for the first time that day, of his mother, and how he missed her smile. The sense of pity did not vanish, but it was dwarfed by this new sense of resolution.

"You are the traitor, not me." His voice was still little more than a whisper.

"Acario!" Ava shrieked, her eyes and nose beginning to dribble. " How dare you-! You ruined *everything*!"

She lunged to push open the door further, but Acario stuck out his arm to bar the way. It was difficult to tell which of them was the more surprised by the prince's quick action.

"I don't want you to visit me anymore."

Acario's legs were shaking. He willed himself not to break contact with Ava's bloodshot eyes. She had already started to splutter in response but he continued over her, growing slightly in confidence. "Leave me alone, Ava. I know that I'm not to blame for any of this. And I won't…" he stammered, "I won't listen to you anymore."

"Acario! Let me in, now!"

Ava struggled against him and tried in vain to push him back into the room.

"G-Goodbye, Ava." he replied shortly.

He did not trust himself to fight against her influence any longer. With a final effort he pushed her back, and as she stumbled red-faced into the hall he slammed the door shut. Inside, blessedly alone again, he sank down with his back against the door. For a while he listened to her desperate attempts to force her way inside, her increasingly shrill and nonsensical accusations, until her rage subsided, and her footsteps at last echoed in the corridor outside. She was gone.

***

Hours passed and the throne room remained a hive of nervous activity. Reports were delivered, demands made, and condolences lavished upon the offended Emperor as he sat in state with his ashen-faced Advisors. Now that the truth of Sawney's duplicity was exposed like a festering wound to the city, it seemed every nobleman in the capital had swarmed to the palace to convince the Emperor that they had suspected Sawney all along and, most importantly, that Eli had no cause to fear any insurrection from them. The two princes were conspicuous only by their absences, but none of the Advisors noted anything untoward about the absence of the princess. They rarely turned their minds towards the temperamental girl, considering she was unlikely to ever ascend the throne.

In her multi-coloured mess of a bedchamber, the princess in question sat submerged in a sullen stupor. She had angered herself even further by smashing a favourite doll in her fury at her cousin's betrayal. Subsequent to their confrontation she had paced back and forth across her room, and whiled away the afternoon by tearing apart the tightly-knotted braids in her hair.

Leon entered the chaotic chamber first, without condescending to knock. He was dressed in his full regimental uniform, and to his deflated sister, had never looked more adult or more distant. Strung across his back he carried his father's sword. His mother followed close behind, a hand on her son's upper arm to steady herself. Adema had dressed as if in mourning, though she did not appear to notice that her daughter had adorned herself in an ignorant pink gown. Adema fretted to see the extreme pallor of her daughter but reminded herself that this frail, lost-looking waif of a girl had in fact potentially played a pivotal role in an assassination attempt. They had talked all day about the best means of broaching the subject with Ava. Leon's usual tact had been thrown off kilter by the full revelation of her treatment of Acario; such was his disappointment, he wanted to rage and scream and see if he could shout any sense into her. Adema felt utterly broken by the news – it would be Leon who did most of the talking.

"You've ignored me all day…" sniffed Ava. Even she was too embarrassed to meet their eyes, and saved her glare for the floor.

"Have a seat, Ava," ordered Leon, and waved her to the chair by the dressing table. "There you go, mother." He steered herself to the bed, while he stood between them, a towering point of authority.

"Yesterday Acario spoke to me and Chiron about you. Sawney Delarus devised a plot to stage a coup and seize the throne." Leon spoke as though each word caused him great pain. "I need to know why you acted this way. Did you understand what Sawney planned to do?"

Ava sat in a sullen silence before bursting into tears. Adema and Leon looked at each other, startled; they hadn't thought Ava would admit any culpability so easily. What she said next dispelled their hopes of redemption.

"Chiron-stabbed-Lorian! And now Mathias will be caught as well-"

"The one you call Mathias seems to have fled the city. If your only concern is for the welfare of those bastards, then I believe we are wasting our time."

"Leon," soothed Adema, as her son glared at her daughter, "She is disturbed…otherwise she wouldn't…"

"I have no idea what she wouldn't do anymore…" Leon sighed, knowing that his anger would only encourage his sister's silence. He moved to crouch beside her, and placed his hand on her bony shoulder. Her tearful eyes met his. "Tell me why you used our cousin."

Despite his calm tone, Ava felt panicked. She struggled away from him and continued sobbing. Whether she cried out of pity for herself or Lorian, or out of some small shred of remorse, was anyone's guess.

"Eli says that you are to leave the palace," Adema spoke over the sobs, "What can I do if you won't admit your guilt?"

Ava raised her head to stare out her mother, loathing every feature on her regal face. Leon, still crouched beside Ava, narrowed his own eyes. "Mother defended you. You will not be thrown in prison or exiled. You only have to leave the palace once Mother joins Javier's residence. What do you say, Ava?"

"I s-suppose you want me to thank you…" sniffed the girl. She was too distraught to understand how lenient her family were being, and what a momentous gift this leniency was. "I don't want to leave!"

"You do not have a choice." Adema rose to her feet. She was too drained to prolong the painful encounter. Leon was surprised by the finality in her voice. He stood, too, but placed a hand under his sister's chin and forced her to meet his gaze.

"No one outside the family knows of your involvement. Consider that a blessing, or you would have to leave the city entirely."

He struggled, still, to reconcile the horrible detail of Acario's accusations with this small, sickly-looking girl. "Mother and I will make sure food is sent up for you. Send a messenger if you need us, sister."

Leon turned his back on her, and took his mother's arm. They looked so serious and detached from their surroundings, as if they had already left her room far behind them. Ava did not want to spend the next few days alone, wasting away by herself; what was the point of having pretty gowns if no-one cared to see them?

"I hate this place!" she shrieked, slamming her small fists onto the dressing table.

Her mother started but did not turn back. Leon turned his head to say "Then you should be glad that you're leaving soon."

The two figures soon disappeared beyond the door, leaving only a pained silence behind them. Ava sank her head into her arms and began to shake as she sobbed.

Chapter Twenty-One

One of the many messengers flitting about the palace had been dispatched that morning to request the presence of Prince Chiron in the throne room. Chiron was being hailed by some as the hero of the evening, but most of the Advisors were too preoccupied with the near loss of the Emperor to applaud the survival of his heir. Chiron had spent a restless night, alternating between a savage pride in his defeat of the treacherous Lorian and an all-consuming fury that Sawney had launched such a brazen attack. The arrest of the Advisor, whose presence had been distracting the young prince for years, was a great source of vindication, yet he still felt too unnerved by the rapidity of the events that had unfolded yesterday to feel the full impact just yet.

A small tray of breakfast lay beside him when he first sat up in bed; evidently he had succumbed to sleep after what felt like an endless night of fitful thoughts. He was just thinking how grateful he was to be spared the company of his family when a rap sounded on the door.

"What do you want?" called the prince, still dressed in his daythings under the bedsheet. The knife had been taken from him by the palace guards when they lifted Lorian's body, but he had only removed his blood-stained blazer once he had retired to his chamber. He had been far too drained to answer any questions last night. It was only due to Eli's firsthand experience of his son's stubborn nature that he had not been asked to submit to examination by the palace physician.

"Your highness, His Majesty the Emperor requests your presence in the throne room."

"Tell him that I'm not quite ready to share my account of last night. I'm sure he will understand." *Or rather, I'm sure he won't, but he can't rush up here to drag me from my chamber.*

"As you wish, sire."

Alone again, Chiron stretched, unable to prevent himself from glancing over at the discarded garment that was glutted with Lorian's blood. *He tried to kill me,* he thought, *but I killed him first.* Despite the sickly sensation in his stomach, and the heavy, tired weight of his eyes, he felt like one of the ancient heroes in the tales he had read with Silas. If he could overthrow Sawney, then what was stopping him seizing the life he wanted? The life he deserved? He had no desire to be fussed over by the Advisors. He wanted to tour the city in a carriage and have his heroism hailed from all corners. He wanted the viper Ava to be thrown from the palace and pelted with dirt from the streets. He wanted to speak with Leon, though not enough to spent the entire day in meetings in the throne room – and Leon's matter-of-fact attitude would likely rile him in his current agitated state. He thought mutinously of Ava again and then remembered a far more favourable girl: Emilia. He still wore the ring and now felt its weight against his chest more keenly than ever. Chiron rose to his feet with a great sense of purpose. He was unwashed, his forehead beady with sweat, but he was a royal prince. And more than that, he was a prince who had proved himself worthy of the name. He would take Emilia for his bride and the whole city would celebrate their union.

He pulled on a fresh shirt, smiling as he thought idly of a small cottage shadowed by a spreading tree. He expected the palace to be bustling with activity but rather than daunting his hopes of escape, this thought filled him with a greater certainty. All the attention will be centered around his father in the throne room. While the gate between Arden's grounds and the palace gardens would be under heavy guard, he could surely find a quiet spot elsewhere in the garden to clamber over the connecting wall. *The news from Delzean will have excited the entire city*, he mused, *and no-one will share a thought to spare for a passing stranger.*

Emilia's bare-footed, rugged existence was so foreign to his world of royal excess that he could not help but be drawn to her. As he peered out into the corridor, he grinned to find it empty. It looked as though fate was on his side today. He began to stride across the corridor. The bright sun matched his sense of a new beginning.

Before even leaving the palace, his mind was already racing ahead to imagine his return. Eli would be taken aback, of course, but how could he not accept Chiron's decision after he had saved his life only yesterday?

Chiron hurried down the stairs. He began to hear voices as he descended into the palace but mercifully the sources remained out of sight. The right to choose his bride was a fitting reward for his heroism. At least no-one would ever suggest he wed his cousin. He would present the red-haired girl with the same ring she had once given him. He hoped he could find her on her own, as he did not think his patience would last if he had to explain himself to Emilia's mother. He amused himself by imagining her reaction to the splendour of the castle. He vowed, however, to keep her from becoming entirely spoiled. He could not imagine the svelte little creature ever growing up.

The prince's daydreams were interrupted brutally when he reached the corridor leading onto the largest courtyard. While it was far quieter on this side of the palace, it was not as deserted as Chiron had predicted. A maid and a manservant stood in front of the closed doors like sentinels. They were staring intently at the floor and made no attempt to clear a path for the prince as he drew towards them. Chiron was an all-powerful prince; how dare they bar his way?

"Are the gardens out of bounds?" he asked, standing offensively close to the maid.

"The Emperor has sealed the grounds for the castle's safety, your highness." stated the manservant.

"I have proved myself perfectly capable of dealing with those who threaten this castle," answered the prince. He wondered how the petulant servant would react if Chiron shoved him bodily out of the way. He heard footsteps behind them and turned, fearing his father's approach. He found instead a slightly familiar-looking soldier.

"Prince Chiron," greeted the man, bowing his head. He wore the same regimental uniform as Leon. "Prince Leon requests your company in the throne room."

Chiron wondered whether Leon had asked this man to spy on him and felt a flush of anger towards his cousin. In fact, Leon had asked every soldier and servant he encountered that morning to pass his message along to Chiron if he presented himself. Leon was concerned that the upheaval of the previous night had unnerved him.

"I'm not going to the throne room," came the prince's curt reply.

He scowled to find himself entrapped between the soldier and the palace servants, and without another word he began his retreat back upstairs.

"I will send the general your apologies, sire." stated the soldier to his retreating back. He was somewhat bemused by the prince's response.

Chiron felt himself cornered and shackled by the fact of his royal birth. He was unable to walk free from Delzean and ask for Emilia's hand. He felt like a caged beast in the zoological garden. Chiron imagined Emilia being claimed by some ignorant peasant and felt himself burn with jealously. Why should a peasant boy have greater freedom than the prince? As he climbed the stairs, he wrenched Emilia's ring from the chain around his neck and cast it away. He wished he could cast away his longing as easily.

*

Delzean played host to many bitter confrontations over the ensuing days. Eli raged in meetings with his Advisors while the city was scourged of any loyal to Sawney. Even the drinking companions of Lorian and Mathias had been forced to flee or face imprisonment. Spies sent across the empire to search for the deserter had so far failed to discover any trace of his whereabouts. Leon was leading the investigation at the barracks, and remained determined to hunt down anyone that remained loyal to the captured Vikernes. The sources of discontent were not all outside of the palace's fortifications. Adema continued to defy Eli's wish that Ava be immediately removed from the palace. Ava, meanwhile, continued to sulk in her chamber, mourning the collapse of her ambitions. She was still barred from attending meals with the rest of her family. Her place beside Adema at the table was filled most evenings by Javier.

The Emperor was to be found several days later seated at the head of the table. His crown had been newly polished; a sign, perhaps, that he was keen to project an image of renewed authority. The cavernous hall was slightly more crowded than usual, as a larger number of manservants had been commanded to wait upon the family at meals. They were also joined, as they stood against the chamber's pale walls, by three soldiers hand-picked by Leon. Chiron, his blazer similarly freshly scrubbed, sat beside Acario. The former was deep in a moody silence, while the latter ate heartily of the banquet piled before them. Leon sat opposite Chiron and the two places beside him were occupied by Adema and Javier. Leon was the most talkative. While his news was addressed to the Emperor, the current intrigue surrounding Sawney held the attention of every guest at the table.

"Sawney has been impeccably behaved, I hear. No complaints have reached the prison guards about the conditions of his cell or paltriness of his meals. Apparently he did not even seem to start when one guard baited him with the news that his house has been wrecked beyond repair."

"I take it he's been kept apart from the other prisoners?" inquired Eli, pausing with a fork to his mouth.

"He has," answered Leon, and after a quick glance to Chiron he judged it prudent to change the subject. Sawney's criminal connections went far deeper than most knew, even now, and the Emperor feared that Sawney's associates would find a means of breaking him from his cell. Recent discussions on the subject had caused Eli and his eldest son to butt heads. The organisation known as the Eyes would not be mentioned during Sawney's trial because Eli feared the exposure of his bargain with the villainous ex-Advisor. Besides, as he had argued to his stony-faced son, it was certainly not the case that they lacked support for Sawney's conviction. Chiron could not fathom why his father had ever permitted Sawney to enjoy such a close relationship with their family.

"I hear that Vikernes is proving himself a less than perfect prisoner," he continued.

Javier smirked. "Oh yes, I don't envy whoever is charged with defending him."

"What has he been doing?" asked Acario. He still felt afraid of these men, even with them sealed up in prison, but knew he could not shy away from the subject forever.

Leon rewarded his courage with a small smile. "He's been calling out vile curses to the guards, screaming his guts out in the hopes that his old friend Sawney will hear him, and rumour has it he succeeded in luring one guard close enough to spit in his face."

Chiron and Acario looked awed by the report of this debauched behaviour. Adema sniffed, and Eli muttered, "Disgraceful. The sooner they stand trial the better."

"When will Sawney stand trial?" asked Chiron, suddenly awakened from his moody stupor by the mention of his enemy's comeuppance. "Will I need to give evidence?" He was excited by the prospect of sharing his long-standing suspicions before the court.

"I'm afraid not, Chiron," answered the Emperor. He was pleased by his son's loathing of the ex-Advisor, which had for so long been an inconvenience. "He will not be graced with our presence ever again.

A statement has been prepared on our behalf and given my official seal. Treachery will not be treated like a common criminal matter. He will be in that court no longer than half an hour before sentence is passed. You have my word that he will hang for this."

Eli smiled at his son to show he understood that this news would please him. Yet Chiron could only weakly return it as he felt anger rise like bile in this throat. He had a terrific case to make against Sawney; it was he, and he alone, who had recognised Sawney for what he truly was. And now he was to be denied his proper revenge. This latest unfairness was larger than his ongoing irritation with the closure of the palace gardens. It seemed he was to be denied everything he wanted.

"Any more arrests in the barracks?" Eli did not seem to notice Chiron's unenthusiastic responses to the news of Sawney's inevitable death.

"We have uncovered a few more men with some allegiance to Vikernes, although they deny having any knowledge of the planned coup."

"Of course they would."

"But even so, my superiors have deemed it unwise to allow any of dubious reputation to be equipped with arms. We find ourselves rather short of soldiers at the moment." Leon offered Acario a knowing grin.

"What's the meaning of this?" Eli glanced between the two. He had been paying particular attention to his youngest son these past few days; with the terror of Ava lifted from his shoulders, he wanted to see what the boy could become.

"Acario and I have been speaking about the army. He is going to join me tomorrow and learn about our training."

Acario gave a nervous smile. Eli cast his son an appraising look. "You told the Advisors all you were able about Sawney's den?"

"Yes, father," answered Acario. He grinned as his reply as acknowledged with a proud nod in return.

Although Eli had been careful to say 'Sawney's den' and not 'the Eyes' den', he had skirted too closely to this source of contention for

Chiron's liking. The elder prince scowled at the grinning Acario. "We've had no success finding it so far, but it appears Sawney stored most of his illicit gains in his own house. As long as we round up the people involved, we have nothing to fear from a meeting place."

Eli turned his gaze to his sister-in-law. Adema had been careful to keep out of the potential volatile discussion but now it appeared she was going to be dragged in regardless. Javier, who thought of himself and Adema as man and wife already. prepared to face the wrath of the Emperor in her defence.

"Speaking of *people involved*," began the Emperor, "Why does Ava still remain resident in my castle?"

Acario looked down at his plate, wishing to go unnoticed while they discussed Ava.

"She will not be here long," replied Adema. "We have been thinking of how best to move forward…"

"How *best*? That devil does not deserve the best!"

Chiron could have applauded his father's fury.

"She has acted horrendously and shows no remorse for anyone but herself. But I can only ask you, Eli, to show her some small degree of mercy. I don't believe she truly understands her own actions."

Before Eli could retort, Javier continued, "I agree. But of course we understand the severity of her crimes. Adema and I believe it may be best for Ava to leave the city altogether."

This news came as a shock to all, save for Leon. He knew his sister would be distraught to leave her home but he saw no other way to please the Emperor. Acario brightened as he enjoyed the thought of wandering through the palace without fear of crossing paths with Ava. There had been no contact between them since had had barred her from his room.

"Where will you send her?" The Emperor appeared slightly placated by this development.

"We will set her up with a small household of her own in the Oslen Mountains," answered Adema. She wondered if Ava would agree to let her and Javier visit. "The question of her marriage will be set aside for now."

"Of course it will. I would warn any man against becoming entangled with her."

"Does this plan meet your approval?" asked Javier. He choose to disregard the Emperor's last remark. They all knew that Ava, exiled to the mountains and in disfavour with the Emperor, would hardly present an enticing prospect to potential suitors. Speaking of her daughter's lonely fate in front of Adema, however, was an unnecessary cruelty.

"Since she cannot be cast off the face of the earth…then the further she is from Delzean the easier I will rest. She must leave as soon as possible."

Javier patted Adema's hand beneath the table.

With a wave of his hand Eli called over the surrounding servants; they began to remove the heaped dishes while others queued behind with further lavish plates. The royals fell silent as they observed this bustle of activity. For Acario, the Oslen Mountains evoked the spectre of his mother more vividly than any other phrase. Yet, seeing as his strange relationship with Ava had started in that far-flung place, it seemed a fitting punishment that she would be consigned to live there, forever stuck in their past. Perhaps she would one day understand what had given spark to her cruelty. The elder prince found this apparent justice far less satisfying. The princess was allowed to leave the confines of Horizon while he remained trapped; how on earth was that fair? No-one would care how she acted out there. He felt he was being punished for thwarting Sawney's plan while she was rewarded for consorting with thieves and murderers. He looked over at his timid brother. Surely Acario's grievances were not assuaged by this meagre punishment?

Chapter Twenty-Two

Ava had dined alone in her bedchamber. The selection of morsels sent up from the kitchen had failed to impress the pale-faced princess, however, and she had only toyed with her plate before abandoning it on the floor. Surrounded by her wealth of trinkets, Ava would have looked the epitome of royalty had it not been for the deep scowl she wore. Her long hair hung limp around the armchair on which she was enthroned. She occupied herself sewing a floral pattern. Every so often her concentration wavered, resulting in her fingers growing red with nicks from the needle.

Her governess had been dismissed on the Emperor's orders. Aside from Adema, who had tried in vain to embrace her daughter the day before, Ava had been bereft of visitors. Servants still arrived to cater to her needs, but she hardly thought they counted. She dressed herself up every day for the sole purpose of indulging in her annoyance that her efforts were wasted. This morning she had commanded the maid bearing her breakfast to dress her in a resplendent ruby-hued gown. She looked paler than ever despite trying to pinch colour into her hollowed cheeks. Her thoughts did not stray further than the next hour or two ahead and she certainly had no plans to move from her chair. She remembered her exchanges with Mathis and Lorian. In some particularly imaginative moods, she had envisaged Mathias materialising out of nowhere to stage a dramatic rescue. She was just beginning to relive this favourite daydream when footsteps in the corridor disturbed her concentration. Frowning, she vented her frustration on her sewing.

A moment later, the sewing fell to the floor as Ava leapt to her feet. Chiron had burst into her room, unapproved and by no means with her permission. Ava struggled to comprehend his sudden appearance. Blazered, tall, black-haired, there was no mistaking his identity. He, at least, knew exactly what he was doing in that sickly-smelling chamber. He coughed slightly as the incense fumes engulfed him before moving with swift steps into the room. The door remained wiped open behind him, though this was the result of careless inattention rather than design.

"What do you want?" screeched the princess. His rapid intrusion incited a genuine feeling of panic in her breast. "Who gave you permission to trespass here?"

She stood, her chest heaving and an authentic blush blooming in her cheeks, and watched as the prince surveyed their surroundings. Every glance he bestowed on her belongings felt like a gross violation; this was *her* realm. Her eyes widened as it dawned on her that he might have been dispatched to start shifting her possessions from the palace.

"A prince requires no one's permission to explore his palace," replied Chiron.

His own eyes were bright and flickered between the eclectic objects in Ava's possession. The bright, airless atmosphere of her chamber only served to heighten the agitation he was experiencing. He had sped from the dining hall to Ava's room like one possessed. There was a great deal he wanted to say to her, yet he was almost too frantic to begin.

"This room belongs to me! You should remember your manners, prince. And don't you dare touch my things!" she spat as he fingered a discarded comb on the dressing table. She did not move from her spot by the chair.

Chiron scrutinised her face as her cast her comb to the floor. "These aren't your things anymore. You no longer live here. Have they not told you?"

Chiron exulted in his power over Ava. Once again he felt that brief exhilaration at getting his own back at the world. As he waited for the full effect of his words to sink in he glanced over at the tapestries. He felt akin to the great heroes their patterns depicted; he was embroiled in his very own struggle against the treacherous snake he called cousin.

"What do you mean?"

As Chiron ignored her in favour of examining his appearance in her mirrors, she continued in a shriller tone, "Who says I'm going anywhere?"

"Your mother did. Not an hour ago." Chiron gloated. He took a step towards her, his eyes still feverishly bright. She was the stuffy Advisors, the droning Silas, the far-away Emilia, the duplicitous Sawney and his wrong-footed father.

"Where exactly does she think I will go?" demanded Ava, stamping a foot beneath her gown. "I don't want you here!"

"You are going into exile. Did you really expect to face no punishment for your crimes?" Chiron's voice rose out of his control. "You blackmailed my brother and turned him into your plaything! You fed our secrets, the secrets of our royal house, to our enemies! You are stupid little girl, besotted with murderers and thieves!"

Ava began to weep. She stamped her foot again and screeched back at the black-haired prince. "You're the thief! You spoiled everything! You're the one who took Lorian away from me!"

"He was never yours to lose! Did you fancy yourself his one true love?"

Chiron threw back his head in laughter. Could she really be confused enough not to understand the true nature of their relationship? She had mistaken Lorian's self-serving approaches for real affection.

"I killed him," he told her, glorying in the bluntness of the expression, "He threatened to invade this palace and slaughter the lot of us like lambs. You may fool your feeble little mind into believing that they would have spared you, but you are wrong. Sawney must have been so pleased when he heard that Lorian had won your confidence. How cheaply is a princess' trust given away!"

Ava's face was bloated and streaked with tears. "You are a murderer! You killed him! Killing must run in the family, since you know as well as I do that Acario caused the death of your mother!"

This lie wiped the gloating smile from his face. "What did you call my brother? You dare speak of those old lies?"

He drew closer again, his blue eyes piercing into Ava's tearful face.

"You spoiled everything! You killed him!" she shrieked, before covering her face with her pale hands.

"Yes, I did!" roared the prince in triumph. He seized Ava's wrists and wrenched her hands away from her face. "Your beloved Lorian was carried from the gardens soaked in his own blood. They have strung up his corpse as a warning to all his fair-weather friends. His father will shortly be going the same way-"

Ava interrupted his tirade by slapping him straight across the face; the shock was far more powerful than the blow itself, but the triumphant grin she wore sent his temper roaring to greater heights.

"You dare lay a hand upon me? You bitch – you common fool! You have no right to live in this palace! You are a disgrace to our name!"

As he spat out his fury in her no-longer-grinning face she tried to raise her hand again. He seized her by the wrist and without thinking slammed his first into her stomach. Seeing her doubled over in front of him, clutching herself and struggling against the grip he maintained on her right hand, he experienced a jolt of satisfaction.

She scrambled up, her fingers extended and made to claw at his face. He flew at her in return and in a blur he attacked her. He felt separate from himself, as if watching the scene unfold from above, but he did feel a distant sense of vindication as she wept and struggled, her bony frame helpless against his superior strength. He came to his senses only when he started to feel beads of perspiration dripping from his brow.

He found himself suddenly on the floor. Ava was crumpled up like a broken doll in front of him,. Chiron was surprised that she had stopped weeping. His anger had not left him, so it was without tenderness that he shook the bedraggled princess. Her head tilted downwards, shielding hr face, but he was able to see a trickle of blood dribbling from her nose. Her face, still wet with tears, was swollen and twisted. She looked smaller than he had ever seen her before. As his senses returned, Chiron rose to his feet. He stood before her, with trembling legs and shaking hands. His whole sense of self had been crushed beneath the weight of his mounting terror.

He had no idea how long he stood there. Adema burst in, after what could have been a minute or an eternity, and her screams were the last sound he heard before he collapsed in a dead faint on the floor.

Chapter Twenty-Three

Only a handful of seats in the grand courthouse were occupied but the stifling heat of the mid-morning sun was sufficient to make even that spacious chamber feel stuffy and oppressive. The air was thick with motes of dust. Prince Chiron sat inside a wooden dock. An armed guard stood on either side. A ray of sunlight beamed directly against the prince's back, illuminating him as the focus of the court's attention. The sun was roasting on the back of his head but every time he stirred in his seat the guards shifted in response; the atmosphere was leaden with mounting anticipation.

Aside from Chiron and his guards, the courthouse's other occupants were the judge, who sat in a throne-like chair at the head of the chamber, his features shadowed by a hooded cloak, and a select group of noblemen, numbering no more than four. They had been chosen to stand as witnesses to the trial. The court scribe busied himself acquiring signatures from the nobles before retiring to the pew behind them. During a popular trial, fifty or sixty could be crammed into the courthouse. The hall was almost ghostly in its barrenness.

Those gathered inside heard the faint cries of the crowd outside; they were thankfully shielded from the full tumultuous uproar by the thick stone walls. Momentarily, however, they were exposed to the thunderous cries and accusations erupting from the crowd gathered by the court's doors and swarming further afield across every narrow close in the court district in the hopes of bearing witness to this latest imperial tragedy. While the public had been banned from entering the trial, they were eager to fashion themselves into the unfolding events. Hawkers shoved through the crowd selling grisly tokens, such as locks of hair allegedly plucked from the princess' own head, and cuts of bloodied material sworn to belong to the prince's blood-stained blazer. Adema had succeeded in burying her daughter without public intrusion: a small, nearly silent ceremony had conducted her coffin into its resting place in the palace gardens. Barring the public from the funeral, however, appeared to have only increased their interest in her death.

Chiron flinched to hear the baying of the mob outwith; he had been too preoccupied with his own destiny to wonder how it affected others. A troupe of guards escorted the royal witnesses into the courthouse. They were escorted in as swiftly as decorum permitted, so that they doors could be sealed again against the peasantry.

Adema led the way to the frontmost pew, her eyes already wet with tears. Javier assumed the place beside her, with Leon following next. Acario took up the rear, and from his place he was only feet apart from his brother. He felt as though they were worlds apart already. The young prince had spent a sleepless night. The sole effort he was able to make the fit the formality of the occasion was to tie back his long hair.

Two lawyers, both elderly, bearded men, emerged from the side-doors. They swept across the stone floor ground thin by the passage of decades of lawmakers and bowed before the judge. Their entrance forced Chiron to accept that his father really wasn't coming. Sorry as he felt for himself, he still had room to be bruised by his father's latest oversight.

Eli had decided that it would be too painful to face the sentencing of his son. He had taken some steps to acknowledge the reality of his loss. On his orders, Delzean stood decked in mourning and black flags waved throughout the city. In his heart these flags hallowed the loss of his son, who even he was powerless to save from justice, while they officially marked the sad end of Ava.

"Rise now and present your case," called the judge. His gravelly voice echoed against the pale stone walls.

The lawyer representing the victim loosened the scroll he bore in his left hand. As his cleared his throat to read, Chiron was glad that he wouldn't live to know such infirmity.

"I read herein the true and honest statement of her highness, Lady Adema. Four days ago, Lady Adema dined with the accused and the rest of our esteemed royal family. The accused, Prince Chiron, sped from the hall while his relatives remained after the meal. Her ladyship planned to visit her daughter the Princess Ava-"

Of all the royal witnesses, Leon was the most conflicted. He had no desire to consign his cousin to such an early death, but he had suffered twice-over: firstly, through his own grief, and then by bearing witness to the agonising grief of his mother. Chiron's eyes were wet but he had no concern for his accusers. He stared across at his family as if desperate to commit every detail of their appearances to memory. Acario stared back at him. The brothers had not been allowed to exchange even a single word since Chiron was apprehended in Ava's chamber. Acario wondered if it was to revenge him that Ava had been killed. He had no idea whether his father would allow the story of her blackmail to be committed to the court's records.

"-Upon entering the bedchamber, Lady Adema discovered the accused standing over the body of her daughter"- a general gasp emerged from the nobles – "On behalf of his majesty, Emperor Eli, I beseech the justice of our city to issue the proper sentence for this treasonous act."

The judge waved forward the other lawyer. This man, as withered and aged as the first, had been Chiron's lone visitor in the cells. At first Chiron had found him sympathetic, until he mentioned the name of Sawney Delarus. The lawyer wanted to hear no mention of Ava's involvement with Lorian or Mathias; he only wished to hear described that had unfolded in Ava's bedchamber. Chiron sensed his father's censorship at play.

"I present herein my true and honest observations from private interviews with the accused, Prince Chiron. His highness the Prince assures me that he sought out the princess only to speak with her and that this crime was not a premeditated act. Her highness the Princess Ava was known to possess a highly strung temperament. Prince Chiron attests that on the evening in question the Princess became angry with him and that a fistfight broke out between them. It was an accident resulting from her slight frame and the prince's greater strength that led to the tragic death of the late princess. The accused does not deny his role in these events."

Chiron stared almost beseechingly at his younger brother. Acario's throat was thick with repressed tears. Javier's hand was growing numb in Adema's vice-like grip but he did not pull away. His brother Jonas had been taken to the cells only the night before to face questioning. It appeared Sawney had at last accepted that the Emperor would not be sending a reprieve and was determined to drag everyone else down with him. Only the doctor Fernandez escaped his wrath, as he had passed away peacefully in his sleep.

"All rise for the verdict," called the hooded judge. The eight spectators and the lawyers stood as one. Almost every eye was turned upon Chiron.

"His highness Prince Chiron stands accused of the treasonous murder of Princess Ava. As the accused freely confesses his guilt, I hereby declare him guilty on the charge of murder. In light of his royal birth, the court will grant the prince a private execution, to be conducted forthwith."

The guards stationed beside Chiron lifted the latch sealing him inside the dock. Acario watched as they led him towards a narrow door in the back wall of the courthouse. The guards pulled Chiron along so swiftly that Acario cried out, longing for another look at his brother's face. With the lawyers following close behind, the accused was led out to the small yard behind the building. The city folk swarming in front of the courthouse would be denied the public spectacle they craved.

Acario sat and stared at the empty dock. His mind was swimming with memories of his brother – Chiron had such vigour and potential. Not so long ago they had shared great laughs together. He wanted more than anything to recapture that joy. He vowed to laugh as often as possible in honour of his brother.

Adema and Javier both had their heads bowed. Leon's sun-worn face was streaked with tears. He met Acario's eye and knew that this latest turmoil would bring them closer, rather than tear them apart. They both had the loss of a sibling in common.

Beams of sunlight poured into the courtroom for the short moment the door fell open. It closed quickly again on the heels of the lawyer who had spoken in Chiron's defence. The elderly man bowed his white head firstly to those waiting in the pews and then to the judge. He addressed the room at large: "Sentence has been carried out."

He retired to the shadows behind the dock as the judge rose to dismiss the court.

The wide front doors were cast open. Acario stood in unison with the remainder of his family. He heard the roar of the waiting crowd, his future subjects. Soldiers lined their passage to the carriage beyond. With a deep, calming breath, Acario took his first step out into the light.

Printed in Great Britain
by Amazon.co.uk, Ltd.,
Marston Gate.